T

ALEX SCARROW

GrrBooks

Copyright © 2023 by Alex Scarrow

All rights reserved

This book is a work of fiction. Names, characters, places and incidents are either the product of the author's imagination or are used fictitiously, and any resemblance to actual persons, living or dead, business establishments, events or locales is entirely coincidental.
No part of this book may be reproduced in any form or by any electronic or mechanical means, including information storage and retrieval systems, without written permission from the author, except for the use of brief quotations in a book review.

Published by GrrBooks

For my perfect wife, Debbie....

*
*
*
*
*
*
*
*

*The author may have left the dedication page unattended before his 'perfect' wife uploaded the manuscript.....

1

Jacob, at just seven years old, was only a few minutes away from an event that was going to change the trajectory of his life.

For the next few moments, however, he was Jacob Driscoll, epic explorer and Finder of Hidden Treasures. And Twatter of Bad Guys. (Although that last title was one he kept quiet about. Mum would go mental if she heard him using a Dad word).

Jacob felt like the hero in that old film *Indian Jones*. An odd name, he thought. The hero didn't look like an Indian. But bum that – he wasn't just *like* him, he WAS Indian Jones. He'd watched the film on Sunday afternoon and for the last few days every obstacle in his path – his cat Parker, a pair of Dad's trainers and his smelly balled-up socks, a dislodged cushion from the sofa – had become a jungle trap for him to navigate around, clamber over or simply... overcome.

This Friday morning, Ms White and Mrs Webb had decided to take their classes out for a nature walk in the woods around East Hill, which suited Jacob down to the ground. The trees, the brambles, the gnarly roots and branches all became Amazonian, the actualisation of the jungle he'd had to conjure up in his mind's eye back home. It was as if Mrs Webb had read his mind and treated him to a proper adventure instead of a boring morning of reading and multiplication at school.

The others in his class had their activity sheets in hand and were busy ticking off the 'Things To Spot!' as they bimbled on ahead of him. Jacob, however, had far more important matters to attend. Off the path, through the undergrowth and down the gentle slope to the creek at the bottom – he was absolutely certain about this – lay the overgrown entrance to an ancient Incan temple where a hoard of treasure and dangerous obstacles awaited him.

Marjorie Webb repeated what she'd done God knows how many times already this morning: 'Keep together, kids!' Then she did a slow three-sixty-degree turn to count the heads. There were eighteen in her group; fifteen in Karen's. A total of thirty-three little terrors to keep track of. The counting process was made far more complicated than it needed to be with Ryan Durrant running round her in dizzying circles, and Jacob Driscoll who was in the habit of lagging behind the group, poking his head under low-hanging trees and humming, '*Dun-dun-da-daaah*' as he did so.

Jacob was one of her favourites, polite and low-maintenance. His mind was often somewhere other than where it was supposed to be, usually swashbuckling with pirates or zapping imperial storm troopers. Marjorie was of the mindset that a vivid imagination and zest for adventure would serve him better through the rest of his life than a set of acceptable SAT test results next year. The crushing weight of education-by-numbers could wait a while longer for Jacob, in her opinion. In the meantime, let the little chap have his barmy adventures.

She completed her count: thirty-two kids. The one she was missing was Jacob. Unsurprisingly. The last time she'd spotted him, he'd been peering intently into the undergrowth just behind the group.

'Karen,' she called out. 'Jacob's gone off-piste again. I'm going back to flush him out.'

Karen White, who was a little ahead, squatting beside a cluster of wild flowers with a group of her girls, nodded. 'I'll keep an eye open for him too.'

The kids were all wearing high-visibility vests from the PE closet. Amid the dark olive greens and dusty browns of the woodland walk, the neon yellow of their vests was relatively easy to spot.

Marjorie backtracked down the trail to the point where she'd last seen the boy, hunkered down and peered into the flora.

'Jacob!' she called out in a sing-song voice. 'Where are youuuu?'

She bent down further to look beneath a low-hanging branch, her knees cracking and complaining as she did so. Karen was twenty years younger and as fit as a flea. She could match the kids for energy and agility. Marjorie, on the other hand, was at the other end of the age scale and could really do without off-roading. Or even bending down, for that matter.

'Jacob!' she called out again. 'Come on! Back on the path please!'

There was no reply. That didn't worry her. Often she had to say his name several times to coax his wandering mind back to the world of reality.

'Jacob!' she called again, a little less sing-song and a little more insistent this time.

Again, no answer.

Oh, marvellous.

She ducked under the bow of the tree and peered into the sloping undergrowth, hoping to catch sight of a flash of neon yellow below. But no. The first prickling of concern ran up the back of her neck and into her scalp.

'Jacob!' she shouted, injecting a clear note of impatience into her voice. 'Come back up here. Right now!'

Still no answer, and still no reassuring flash of neon yellow.

She took a couple of steps down the slope, well aware that she'd have to slog back up the same slope, which was going to be absolutely murderous for her old knees. She called again, before descending another few yards, through nettles and brambles, nearly losing her footing on a loose branch near the bottom.

'Jake!' she snapped angrily. The little boy might be one of her favourites, but right now he was severely pissing her off. 'Come here, *right now!*'

The voices of the other children and her colleague had dwindled to a distant sound, blocked by the slope she'd inelegantly staggered down. Now all she could hear was an echoing chittering of birdsong descending through slanted beams of sunlight, along with the crunch of her own footsteps through a carpet of long-dead leaves.

'Jacob!' Her voice bounced back off knotted and contorted tree trunks. It felt as though she'd entered a different twilight world. Her very own C. S. Lewis moment.

'Jac–' She stopped as she spotted a sliver of bright yellow through the veil of bamboo stalks that had managed to take root here. The neon-yellow strip didn't move or even twitch in response to her voice. Marjorie stepped to her right to make her way round the thicket, fighting a growing sense of dread that Jacob had somehow lost his footing, tumbled down the slope and knocked himself out.

Or worse.

She rounded the bamboo and saw his vest. Not discarded – thank God. Jacob Driscoll was wearing it, but standing perfectly still and staring upwards.

'Jacob!!' she snapped furiously. 'Why didn't you answer me?'

He slowly turned to meet her glare, eyes rounded. He raised a finger to his lips as she crunched impatiently across the forest floor to grab his hand.

'Shhh... I think it might be sleeping?' he whispered.

'What?' She'd had enough of his vivid imagination this morning. 'What are you talking about?'

He raised his finger and pointed upwards into the branches that loomed above them. 'The green man up there.'

Marjorie followed his finger until her eyes settled on what he was pointing at. She let out a short, strangled gasp.

2

Boyd hurried along the motorway's hard shoulder alongside the traffic jam of cars, his own car abandoned, the driver-side door left wide open as he'd spilled out onto his feet. He picked up the pace as flashing blues and several spotlights lit up the night and the spitting rain ahead of him.

He approached a traffic cop who was manning a line of cones and clearing the fast lane of debris, ready to begin the process of easing the build-up of traffic behind the incident. Boyd lifted his lanyard and waggled it.

'DCI Boyd!'

The copper waved him through without a word.

He hurried towards the mangled vehicles: two large trucks, one behind the other with an unrecognisable mess concertinaed between them. The rear vehicle was a freight-container truck. At the front was a builder's flatbed truck, with a stack of aluminium sheeting on palettes, piled high like a pack of playing cards.

As he neared them, he recognised the mashed-up car as a dark-blue Vauxhall Corsa.

Julia's Corsa.

Beside it were two ambulances and a fire engine.

'You Bill Boyd?' someone called out.

'Yes!' Boyd whipped his head round and spotted a paramedic standing beside the open doors of an ambulance.

'They in there?!' Boyd called.

The paramedic waved Boyd over. He went to peer into the back of the ambulance to see if the treatment cot was occupied, but the paramedic grabbed his forearm firmly.

'Bill, listen, they're both in the wreck still.'

Boyd tried to pull himself free.

'Stop! Bill... Please, you need to listen to me first.'

The tone in the paramedic's voice confirmed every worst-case scenario that had been running through his head since he'd got the call at the station. 'Bill, listen... Your little boy's gone. I'm so, so sorry...'

Boyd felt his stomach flip over, his sense of balance deserting him as a wave of dizziness washed up and over. His legs failed him and he sat down heavily on the rear step of the ambulance, the vehicle rocking gently beneath his weight as he doubled over to catch his breath.

'But your wife's still alive.'

Alive. The word dissolved in the air like a breath-cloud on a cold night. 'Your wife' stung him like a papercut. *Why not both of them? What about Noah?*

'She's alive... but, Bill, listen to me... she's not going to make it.'

Boyd lifted his head. That seemed to make absolutely no sense. She was alive. Surely they could get her out, into the ambulance and off to A & E.

'She's trapped in the car. The firemen can't get her out. And she's not going to last much longer.'

The spits of rain descending from the dark sky seemed

to slow down, almost to a stop. The noises – a growling generator, the pneumatic clunk of a metal cutter, the hiss and rumble of traffic passing on the other side of the divider – all seemed to fade to a distant muted hum. Only the paramedic's voice seemed to pierce through and reach him.

'She's lost a lot of blood, Bill. If the firemen try to move what's trapping her in the seat, what's left in her is going to flood out.'

Boyd had a fleeting image in his head of one of those silly casual 'swiping' games you see in Facebook ads – *Pull the pins to save the trapped Princess... but be-e-e-e careful!*

'Bill, look at me.'

He did as he was told.

'You've got a few moments with her. She's conscious still. She's aware. She's lucid. Do you want to –'

'Yes.' Boyd got up unsteadily.

The paramedic led him to the crushed metal that had once been Julia's car. The firemen and paramedics currently clustered around it all took a step back to clear a path for him. Boyd could see the same expression on all their faces: *You poor, poor, fucking bastard.*

Boyd picked out the silhouette of Julia's head inside the car. It was tilted back, resting on an inflatable neck brace that had been placed around her shoulders. He looked behind her at the rear seat. Noah's head and shoulders were covered with a bloody dressing and a hand towel. Not to staunch any blood, but to save Boyd glimpsing the mess of his son. As he ducked into the wreckage to perch beside Julia on the passenger seat, he could see the rest of Noah's little body in the booster seat at the back. Unharmed, unmarked, one small hand still clutching an Avengers action figure.

'Hey, Jules,' he whispered, avoiding looking down at her

lap. There was much too much blood pooling there. Fatal amounts of it. And not just blood. There was solid matter too.

Her eyes flickered and focused on him. 'Noah?' she whispered. 'Where's Noah?'

'He's fine, honey.' He managed a smile that deserved a BAFTA. 'He's going to have a corker of a bruise tomorrow, though.' He grabbed her hand and squeezed it. 'They're going to get you out next.' He tried to be funny. 'Tell me you renewed the insurance?'

She smiled and rolled her eyes.

He looked down. There was so much blood. She hadn't seen how much.

'You're going to be fine.'

Only she wasn't. She was far from fine. She was almost completely cut in half by a jagged shard of the dashboard that had splintered. It had separated on impact and all but bisected her.

Her eyes met his. 'Don't be an idiot.' She managed a smile and grabbed his hand. 'I know... I'm... dying.' She frowned. 'I can't see Noah. How –'

'He's out, love. They got him out. I just saw him in the back of the ambulance.'

'Oh God,' she rasped. 'How bad is he?'

He managed not to glance at the back seat. She'd see that; she'd know there was something ghastly behind her headrest. 'Just scratches and cuts,' he said.

Her face creased with relief, a single tear tumbled down her cheek and nestled in the crook of her mouth.

'He's in shock, Julia. He's not going to remember any of this.'

More tears spilled down. 'He's not going to have his mum. Nor is Emma.'

'They're going to be okay, love,' he replied, his voice reduced to a faint whisper. He wiped tears out of his eyes. He wanted his last moment with Julia to be a clear one, not blurred. 'I'm going to be there for them both.' He smiled. 'You can supervise things from *up there*.'

She snorted a wet laugh, then rolled her eyes. 'Idiot.'

Her eyes began to roll upwards again, but it wasn't forbearance this time. This time it was her body closing down.

He leant forward, 'Jules. I love you,' he whispered in her ear. Then he kissed her. 'I love you.'

He felt her squeeze him back to let him know she'd heard. To let him know she loved him too.

Then she was gone.

~

BOYD WAS JERKED out roughly from the wreckage of the Corsa and that horrific memory from years ago as he surfaced from a restless sleep.

His groggy mind, slowly emerging from slumber in baffled fragments, began to piece together some semblance of where and *when* he was.

The *when* was five years later. The *where*? Hospital.

There was a soft beeping beside his head and he turned to see an IV drip bag of morphine, he guessed, and a plastic tube snaking down into a cannula stuck in his left arm. For a moment he wondered whether he'd been involved in a traffic accident, the crushed car still a very real presence in his mind's eye, but then, gradually, puzzle pieces from the last five years began to slot into place: the move to Hastings, transferring to Sussex Police, the big house on Ashburnham

Road, an abandoned trailer park, the ruin of an old tower on a windswept marsh...

... a woman with auburn hair on a shingle beach...

... Charlotte...

... a burning brewery.

Most recent and most vivid of all: a man in a balaclava, shot dead just a few feet away from him...

The breadcrumb trail of returning memories led him, at last, to the here and now.

The cancer. The surgical procedure.

The *six-weeks delayed* surgical procedure.

The final, most recent memory fragment was of being wheeled into the theatre, the anaesthetist looming over him with a mask ready to place over his nose and mouth, and the surgeon reassuring him.

'*I promise you, Bill, if we can do this without leaving you with a stoma bag, we will...*'

Instinctively, Boyd dug his left hand under the bedsheet to feel his left hip...

3

Okeke took the card off Sully and looked at what he'd written in it.

Get well soon, Boyd. I've already stolen your office chair. Your stationery holder's next.
    – Sully

'Touching,' she replied flatly. 'That's very touching.'

Sully held out her fountain pen. 'When is he under the knife?'

'I think it was first thing this morning.'

Magnusson rolled her chair across the floor from her desk and took the pen from Sully's hand. 'You heard anything yet? Did he end up with a bag?'

'Bag?'

'Stoma,' she said, taking the card from Okeke. 'A poo bag strapped to his side.'

Okeke shook her head. 'I haven't heard anything from Emma or Charlotte yet.'

Magnusson scanned the messages already scrawled inside as she looked for some space to add hers. 'Aww... lovely one from Her Madge: *Hurry back – crime doesn't wait*.' She turned the card over to check the cover.

It was a spoofed Mr Men character: Mr WTF!, complete with head-to-toe bandages and linked by drooping cables to a hospital monitor. She smirked and nodded approval at Okeke's choice.

'He's got form on that front,' explained Okeke, gesturing to the cartoon character. 'My first case with him, he nearly lost an ear.'

'I presume there wasn't a Mr Should-Have-Waited-For-Backup card?' asked Sully.

'Not at Tesco... no.'

'Should have Moonpigged it,' he replied, as Magnusson resumed her hunt for a blank space inside the card.

'Something with a little compassion, maybe?' suggested Okeke. 'It's mostly piss-taking stuff so far.'

Magnusson pulled a face. 'I'll try.' She found a space and began to scrawl something.

'We doing a collection?' asked Sully.

'I emailed you the link a few days ago. Check your inbox,' Okeke told him.

Sully pulled it up on his screen. 'Oh, yes, you're quite right – you did.' He clicked the link. 'What are we getting him?'

'Dunno yet. I'm open to suggestions,' Okeke replied.

Sully clicked on the 'donate' button and began to tap in his details. 'He's going to be a grandad soon, isn't he? How about a SAGA magazine subscription?'

~

OKEKE LEFT the hushed calm of the CSI side of the floor and crossed the hallway. She pushed through the double doors and entered the comparatively noisier CID bullpen. She weaved her way back to her desk with Boyd's get-well-soon card in one hand. To be fair, it was relatively quiet in CID this morning. There were several absences and a silence from beyond the partition where the Rosper team had their desks grouped.

'Any space left in there, love?'

She turned to see DCI Flack standing behind her, pen in hand, looking expectantly at the card.

'Oh, right, yeah...' She handed it to him. 'You might have to write on the back.'

He opened the card and his moustache flexed with a smile as he read the various messages. 'When is he on the butcher's block?'

'This morning, sir,' she replied. 'Should be done by now, I think.'

Flack placed the card on the corner of her desk and managed to find a modest gap. He scrawled a message, signed it and handed it back to her. 'You taking the card in?'

She nodded.

'Tell him we're all rooting for him over on my side.'

'Will do.' She nodded at the far end of the floor, partitioned by a Mexican-border wall of brown hessian panels. 'It's quiet over there.'

'They're all out,' he replied, pocketing his pen. 'Got an op going on.'

She watched him turn and head back towards the partitioned wall that corralled the Operation Rosper team, then squinted down at what he'd written.

Cancer's a bitch. Kick its arse from me, Big Man – Jeff Flack

Warren looked up from his monitor after Flack had disappeared. 'He write something nice?'

'For Flack, yeah, I s'pose.' She sat down, slid the card into its envelope and scrawled 'To The Guv' on the front. She then woke up her monitor with a waggle of the mouse.

'When are you going in to see him?' asked Warren.

'Probably lunch break.' She checked her watch. In about two hours' time.

'Can I come along?'

With Boyd off, Minter taking leave to prepare for his NPPF inspectors' exam next week, DI Fox on a pre-transfer refresher course, and DI Abbott on a training seminar, Sutherland had left her in charge of the young 'uns: O'Neal and Warren.

'I guess if nothing turns up... sure,' replied Okeke with a shrug.

Warren smiled. 'Well, it's been pretty quiet so far this morning.'

'Noooo!' She wagged a finger frantically at him. 'Never, ever say *that word* out loud. You know the rule –'

Several of the phones around the floor began to trill.

Warren laughed at the perfectly timely coincidence, and Okeke shook her head wearily. It wasn't coincidence... it was jinx. Proof right there that the superstition was an Actual. Bloody. Thing.

'There you go you, idiot... see?' She sighed. '*You* did that, Warren. That was *you*.'

4

Okeke shaded her eyes as she peered up through the branches of the horse chestnut tree. Sully had managed to scoot up in his bunny suit with surprising agility, like a squirrel desperate to store away a juicy nut. He was now closely examining the rope and the branch to which it had been secured, taking photos, it seemed, from every possible angle.

'At what point are you considering lowering the body?' she shouted up to him.

'When I'm done, Okeke. When I'm done,' he called. 'It's all about the knots you see... and about how uniquely we tie them.'

She let him prattle on about ropes and knots and methods of tying them until he'd got it out of his system.

'That seems quite high up,' she said when he'd finally fallen silent. 'I mean, for a suicide, right?'

He glanced down at her. 'I don't know if there's a consensual agreement on height when it comes to this kind of thing...'

'I'm just saying. It seems pretty high,' she said, squinting at the sunlight as it dappled onto her upturned face and momentarily dazzled her.

Sully straightened up and rested his back against the trunk of the tree. 'Maybe he was being considerate. Hiding himself away? Perhaps he didn't want to ruin anyone's morning walk? Or scare any kids?'

'Seriously?' she replied.

With Sully, you could never really tell if he was saying anything seriously. His snark-voice and his business-voice were practically identical. He resumed taking photographs of the rope, the branch it was suspended from, and the body dangling beneath it.

Warren joined her, tucking his notepad away as he looked up. 'Looks like it didn't work out so well,' he contributed. 'I mean... it was a kid who spotted him.'

Okeke sighed. 'Yeah, well, at least he made an effort.' She looked over at an older woman standing with one of the uniformed officers. Apparently she was the one who'd called it in.

'I'm going to talk to her. What's her name?' she asked Warren.

'Marjorie,' he replied. 'What do you want me to do?'

She shrugged and nodded up at Sully. 'Keep an eye on Monkey Boy up there and make sure he doesn't dislodge any conkers down onto your head.'

Warren glanced up again and took a few steps away from the tree. 'Fair point.'

Okeke walked over to the woman, pulled a glove off and extended her hand. 'Marjorie, is it?'

The woman nodded.

'I'm DC Samantha Okeke – Sam. How're you doing, my love?' she asked.

The woman sported short grey hair and a face patterned

with lines that suggested a lifetime spent smiling more often than not. 'Still very much in shock, obviously,' she said.

'Yes. I can well imagine. I believe one of the children in your class discovered the body,' Okeke said.

Marjorie nodded. 'Jacob Driscoll. He's a bit of a dreamer. The wandering adventurer kind.'

'He came down that slope?' Okeke asked, pointing to the incline she'd half stepped down, half slid down.

Marjorie nodded. 'Off the path. Exactly as he was told *not* to do.'

Okeke smiled. 'A future Ray Mears, huh?'

Marjorie nodded. 'Exactly.'

'I may need to chat to him later, with his parents,' said Okeke. 'If that's okay?'

'You'll be careful with him, won't you?' Marjorie asked. 'We haven't discussed mortality with the kids yet. And certainly not something as ghastly as suicide.'

'I will,' Okeke assured her. 'I'm going to have to speak to him with one of his parents present. Have they been informed?'

'Yes, I asked Ms White to call them as soon as she got our kids back to school.' Marjorie looked over at the tree. 'When will your forensics man lower that poor soul down?'

Okeke turned to follow her gaze. 'He's being very thorough. As he should be.' She paused, realising that she wasn't actually answering the woman's question. 'Soon. Very soon. Then we'll find out who he is... and why he did this.'

Marjorie shook her head and tutted. 'It's so horribly, horribly sad that for some individuals doing something like *that* seems to be the only way they can see out of a problem.'

Okeke nodded and sighed. 'From what I can tell, he doesn't look that old, either.'

'Oh dear.' Marjorie shook her head again. 'That's even

more tragic. Kids these days seem to have the weight of the world on their shoulders almost from the moment they're born.'

'We'll hopefully identify him quickly... and then we can talk to his family,' Okeke said.

Marjorie looked at her. 'Good grief, that must be the worst part of your job.'

'It is,' Okeke said, nodding. 'By far. Which school have you come from?'

'Dudley Infants,' Marjorie said.

It wasn't far. 'Can I offer you a lift back?' Okeke asked.

~

OKEKE STARED at the little boy. 'Jacob, you know... it's okay to feel sad, to be upset about... this.'

'He's a very sensitive boy,' said his mother. 'And he struggles to vocalise his feelings.'

Mrs Webb nodded in agreement. She was sitting on the other side of Jacob Driscoll. The school's head – Mrs Harper – was on the sofa opposite them, beside Okeke. 'Jacob has been diagnosed as being on the autism spectrum.'

Okeke noticed Jacob's mum bristling slightly. 'I think they say that *everyone* is somewhere on the spectrum,' she added.

Mrs Harper nodded vigorously. 'Quite. Yes.' She smiled uncomfortably. 'Everyone's a little different one way or another, aren't they?'

'That man in the tree was a dead man,' said Jacob. It was hard to tell if he was asking the question or helpfully informing them all.

'Yes,' replied Okeke. 'Yes, he was, I'm afraid.'

'Was he a bad man?' he asked. 'Because that's what used

to happen back in the olden times to men who did crimes. They used to hang them.'

His mum put a hand on his knee to quieten him. 'Jacob's very keen on history. He's read all the Horrible History books at school.'

'In the olden, *olden* times... they used to chop their heads off and cut them in quarters,' added Jacob. 'But then they invented hanging, which was much kinder.'

Mrs Webb and Mrs Harper exchanged an uncomfortable glance that suggested they might review what books were currently available in the school library.

'We don't think he was a bad man,' said Okeke. She looked around at the three other women in the room and decided that explaining the concept of suicide to Jacob was probably best left to one of them. 'It could have been a terrible accident,' she said finally. 'He might have been climbing, slipped and the rope just caught around his... around him.'

The other women nodded vigorously.

'Which is why tree-climbing is so very dangerous,' proclaimed Mrs Harper.

'Right,' said Jacob's mother. 'There are so many dangerous things outside, Jake. Cars, roads, cliffs, trees, the sea....'

Christ, Okeke mused, *no wonder kids are all neurotic these days.*

'Trees?' cut in Mrs Webb softly. 'It's good for the little ones to get out every now and then and appreciate nature.'

Mrs Harper cut her off with a stern look. 'While *carefully* supervised,' she emphasised.

'Yes, of course,' Mrs Webb agreed quickly.

Okeke leant forward. 'Jake?'

'Hmm?'

The Archive

'What made you go wandering off down that slope? Was there anything you heard down there? Anything you saw?'

He shrugged. 'I was exploring the jungle. Just like Indy.'

'Indy?'

'He's been watching those Indiana Jones films,' explained his mother. She glanced quickly at Mrs Harper. 'Not that I approve.'

Okeke's phone buzzed in her pocket. She pulled it out and looked at the screen. It was Sully. 'I'm sorry,' she said to Jake and his mother. 'I have to take this.'

She got up and left the head's office to take the call.

'What've you got?' she asked.

'The body has been taken down. It's on its way over to Ellessey as we speak,' Sully informed her.

'I didn't manage to get a decent look at it,' Okeke said. 'What's –'

'IC-one, male,' Sully cut in. 'I'd say he was in his early to mid twenties.'

'Are we still going with suicide?' she asked.

A pause. 'Nothing I could see there this morning is screaming anything else to be honest with you,' he replied.

'You don't sound utterly convinced by the idea.'

'It does seem like rather an ambitious climb to make in order to go hang yourself,' he mused.

'You managed it pretty easily,' she pointed out.

'That's because I'm superbly fit and agile for my age, Okeke.' She heard him signalling to turn in his van. 'I can't help wonder, though... if you've reached the point in life where you'd want to end it all, whether you'd be particularly motivated to climb so high up a tree?'

'Maybe he *really* didn't want to be found?' said Okeke.

'Public spirited? Even in death.' She heard him sucking his teeth. 'It's possible, I suppose.'

'Is there anything on the body that'll help us ID him?' she asked.

'Nothing. Not a single bean. No keys, no wallet, no note. Just the clothes he was wearing,' Sully replied.

'So that's consistent, then,' she said, 'with not wanting to be ID'd too easily.'

'Indeed,' said Sully. 'But again, why care so much about that?'

'You got me some prints? Some swabs?' she asked.

'No, I spent the last hour collecting prize-duelling conkers with Warren.'

She blanked his sarcasm. 'Is he still with you?'

'Speaker's on,' replied Warren. 'I'm blagging a lift. Seeing as how you just left me without a ride back.'

'Great. When you get back to the station, could you run those prints on LEDS for me?' Okeke asked him.

'I *could*...' Warren replied. 'If you asked nicely.'

She sighed. 'If it's not too much bloody trouble.'

One sergeants' exam and a few months' worth of assessment to go and she was going to sit one rank above the twat. Then she'd insist on a 'sir' from him every now and then, just for the shits and giggles.

5

Boyd shuffled slowly back to his bed, wheeling the morphine drip beside him. Charlotte plumped up his pillows as he eased first one leg onto the hospital bed, then the other, *oofing* like an old man as he did so.

'Is it painful?' she asked.

'Just a bloody bit,' he grunted. He pressed the morphine delivery button on the drip-stand several times.

'You might want to go easy on that, Bill,' she told him.

'You can't overdose. It times out,' he replied. 'More's the pity.'

He pressed the delivery button again and it beeped to inform him he was being a nuisance and that he could have another hit in ten minutes' time if he behaved himself and stopped jabbing.

'See? Spoilsport,' he muttered thickly.

'Well done for getting up for the toilet,' she said, tucking him back in. 'You did good.'

Boyd vaguely recalled the surgeon and several fresh-faced junior doctors peering down at him earlier today as though he was a newly discovered species of microbiological life sitting in a Petri dish. The surgeon – he couldn't remember the man's name – had told him the sooner he got up on his feet and walked about the ward, the quicker his recovery would be. He also remembered the surgeon proudly pointing out that there'd been no need for a stoma bag; the operation had gone better and more tidily than he'd expected.

The jagged pain in Boyd's side quickly eased as the morphine did its thing and all of a sudden he felt strangely blearily, content with his lot in life, lying on the bed and listening to the man in the next bed, groaning loudly.

'How long have you got, love?' he asked woozily.

She smiled. 'As long as you want me here,' she replied.

That confused him. 'Uh? What about work?'

'It's over for the day,' she replied, nodding at a clock on the wall opposite. He looked. It was quarter to six. He could have sworn it said one o'clock five minutes ago.

'Are the kids back from school? Is someone minding them, Julia, love?'

Her brow furrowed for a few moments, but then she said, 'Everyone's fine, Bill. You just take it easy, lovely.'

He wanted to tell her about the doctor's visit earlier, about not having to have a bloody bag strapped to his side, but his eyelids felt heavy, his mouth sluggish. That bit of good news could probably wait until later...

~

'How's he doing?'

Charlotte looked up from her Kindle to see Okeke

standing at the end of her Boyd's bed with a carrier bag in one hand. 'Oh, hello there, Sam!'

Okeke shuffled round the side and gave Charlotte a hug. 'I've got a card from the guys at the station,' she said digging into the carrier bag, 'and some grapes, some chocolates.'

Charlotte took the grapes and a box of Ferrero Rochers from her and set them on Boyd's bedside table. She didn't have the heart to point to the 'no solids' notice on the small whiteboard behind his bed. 'Oh, that's really very kind. Thank you.'

'The boys and girls in CID also had a whip-round for him,' continued Okeke, 'and we got him this.' She pulled out a small box.

'What is it?' asked Charlotte.

'A Nintendo handheld thingy. With some puzzle games as well.'

Charlotte took it from her and stared at the colourful cartoon characters on the front of the box, baffled by the childish designs. 'Uh... right...'

'There's a detective game,' Okeke added. 'Solve puzzles, clues... that kind of thing, to make sure he doesn't miss work too much.'

Charlotte nodded a little too eagerly. 'Oh, yes. I see... lovely. He'll really like that.' She placed it on the table beside the confectionary that Bill wasn't going to be able to eat for a while.

Okeke took a seat on the other side of the bed. 'So, how's he doing?'

'He's sore. But the op went well, according to the surgeon.' She explained about the worry he had had about waking up with a bag strapped to the side of him, and his utter relief on waking to find that hadn't been necessary.

'Right now he's thoroughly enjoying the morphine,' she concluded.

Okeke chuckled. 'Oh, I bet he is.'

'How're things at the station? Are you all coping without him?' Charlotte asked.

Okeke gave her a thumbs-up. 'There's nothing big going on at the moment, to be fair.'

'It's quiet, then?'

'Uh...' Okeke shook her head and smiled. 'We never use that word. Like *ever*.'

Charlotte smiled back. 'Oh, I get it.'

'How's Emma doing?' Okeke asked.

'Fine. She's doing really well, actually. She's in her last trimester now,' said Charlotte.

'Any idea what kind of bread she's baking?'

It took Charlotte a moment to get what she meant. 'Oh!' She laughed. 'No, she doesn't want to know until it happens.'

'I bet Boyd does,' replied Okeke.

Oh, boy, does he, mused Charlotte. She'd lost count over the last six months the number of times he'd gently pestered Emma to ask next time she went in for an ultrasound. And of course Emma had politely pushed back and informed him that it was, in fact, *her* baby, not his... and was gender really such a big deal these days anyway?

'Has he got to do any follow-on treatment after this?' asked Okeke, looking at Boyd.

Charlotte nodded. 'There will be chemotherapy. Six months of it.'

Okeke frowned. 'That sounds like a lot.'

'The consultant said they wanted to saturate him with the treatment to make sure any...' She paused... *What phrase* had he used? Oh yes. 'To nuke any rogue cancer cells hanging around, looking for a new place to set up shop.'

'Right. Does that mean he's going to be off work for six months?' Okeke asked.

Charlotte shrugged. 'I suppose it'll depend on how bad the side effects are.'

Boyd stirred just then. His eyes cracked open and he woozily grinned at Charlotte, then noticed Okeke sitting on the other side.

'Hey,' he croaked.

'Hey, guv... how're you doing?'

'Pleasantly stoned.'

'Enjoy the drugs while they're on the NHS,' she replied with a wry smile.

He laughed softly. 'Anything interesting going on at work?'

Okeke wrinkled her nose. 'Nothing major.'

'Minter being a good boy and doing his revision?'

She nodded. 'He took some leave this week. His exam's next week.'

Boyd nodded, remembering. 'Right. And yours is...'

'Next month.'

'Good.' He reached out for the glass of water on his bedside table and took a swig, before settling his head back on the pillow. 'Make sure you do the same.'

His eyes closed and a few moments later he resumed softly snoring.

'I suspect that's your lot from him this evening,' said Charlotte. She glanced at Okeke and noticed her looking a little pensive. 'You all right, Sam?'

Okeke threw a quick smile onto her face. 'Yeah, just a little knackered. It's been a long day.' She pushed her chair back. 'I'd better get home. Jay's cooking his special tonight.'

Is there anything I can get you before I go, Charlotte? Tea? Coffee?'

Charlotte shook her head.

'Do you need a lift back home?'

'That's very kind of you, Sam. But I'm going to hang on here for a bit.'

6

'Hanging from a tree, you say?' Okeke nodded. 'Suicide is what we're looking at, obviously.'

'Most likely.'

She waivered. 'Most likely.'

Jay turned from the cooker and looked over his shoulder at her. 'Poor bloke.'

'He was so young as well,' she said with a sigh. 'I mean, he *looks* really young.'

Jay picked up a jar of chilli relish and spooned a generous dollop into the pan along with the onions, chopped tomatoes and cubed chicken. 'Teenage young?'

'No.' She sipped her wine at the kitchen table. 'Early to mid twenties. Still way too young to end up like that, though. He was right up in the tree, you know? Not dangling from the lowest bough but really high up.' She let out a dry humourless huff. 'Sully's explanation was that he was doing the decent thing and tucking himself away out of sight. Didn't want to spoil anyone's woodland walk.'

Jay gave the pan a stir, then turned the hob down a

notch. He joined her at the kitchen table and topped up their wine glasses. 'This one's got under your skin a bit, hasn't it, babes?'

She looked up at him. 'A bit, yeah.'

He sat down. 'You don't want to get into the habit of bringing it home, Sam. That's –'

'I don't....' She took another sip of her wine. 'Well, mostly I don't.'

She shook her head, unsure as to why she had on this particular occasion. Maybe it was because Sully was right, that he'd gone to so much trouble to hide himself away. An act of... *consideration* in the middle of whatever personal shit-storm he was going through. Thinking of others while his own troubles whirled around him.

'Hopefully somebody'll report him missing over the weekend and we can ID him,' she said.

'You run his prints yet?' Jay asked.

That made her smile. Since his recent Big Life Switcheroo, suddenly deciding that he wanted to become a private investigator, Jay had consumed everything he could get his hands on regarding police procedure and crime investigation. Not always the accurate stuff, mind. The internet was awash with 'experts' who gained their wisdom exclusively from Wikipedia. Or worse... Sky's true-crime channels. The end result was Jay trying to sound more like a copper than her.

'Yeah, we did,' she replied. 'Nothing, though. No previous form. Sully took swabs and we might get something on the NDNAD over the weekend, but that's pretty unlikely.'

'Hmm... yeah, the National DNA Database,' he voiced aloud. 'Good shout.'

Okeke shook her head, suppressing another smile.

'So...' Jay took a deep breath, then flexed his shoulders and cracked his knuckles. 'How's the guv doing?'
'Doped up on morphine, but otherwise fine,' she said.
'Did he end up with the strap-on poo bag?'
Okeke lowered her chin to stare disapprovingly at him.
'Otherwise known as a *stoma*. No, he didn't. Which Charlotte said he was well chuffed about.'
'I can imagine,' said Jay. He got up to stir the pan. 'His op went okay, then?'
She nodded and explained that his next big hurdle would be the next six months of chemotherapy.
'Ah, shit,' he replied. 'Poor bastard's hair's all gonna fall out, isn't it?'
'Not necessarily. Depends on which drug they use. Sometimes it's only body hair; sometimes only facial hair...'
Jay turned to her. 'Shit. Boyd *without* a beard?'
She nodded. *Weird*. She'd only seen him without one for the first week or two after he'd started at Hastings, and even then he'd still had a face fuzzy with stubble. She tried to imagine the guv with no hair at all. A bald head she could imagine. In fact, it would probably suit him, like it did Jay. But the lack of any bristles below his nose and the absence of those thick, expressive, caterpillar-like brows of his that bobbed, dipped and sometimes locked together and broadcast his inner thoughts like news ticker tape... that would be very strange.
It was her turn to change the subject. 'You ready for your big jolly up in London, then?'
He looked over his shoulder. 'The "advanced surveillance training course", I think you mean...'
She strongly suspected that each day would consist of a few PowerPoint presentations and practical exercises followed by a piss-up down the nearest pub. Still, at least

the course was being paid for by Jay's new boss, Mr McGuire.

'Yeah.' He shuffled the pan back and forth. 'I'm really buzzed about it. It's going to be fun.'

'Hey, don't have too much fun,' she replied jokingly. Maybe *half* jokingly. 'You're there to learn, not party it up.'

He handed her his mock-offended face. 'Like I'd do that without my babycakes.' He grinned. 'You getting all territorial?'

She huffed.

'If you want to mark your turf –' he made to slide the pan off the hob – 'dinner can wait.'

She rolled her eyes. 'Later. I'm hungry.'

'You know, you don't ever need to be jealous,' he said, serious all of a sudden. 'You're my girl.'

Was she jealous? Nah. Well.... maybe. Just a bit. He was going away for a few nights. Not that she didn't trust him, but... there was no denying that he looked pretty hot in his tan work boots, faded jeans, tight T-shirt and three-quarter-length cream woollen mandigan. Jay pretty much hit the sweet spot when it came to the 'hunky gardener' look. And if he was going out afterwards, getting pissed up? Well, there was always the possibility of a chance encounter.

Question was... was he going to think with his big head or his little one?

He came over to the table with the sizzling saucepan and a wooden spoon. 'How do you want Jay's Special this evening, ma'am? Hot?' He grinned. 'Or *sizzling* hot?'

7

Just as Okeke had been hoping, a welfare check request had been logged over the weekend. A patrol car had been sent over to a flat in Ore to check on one Adam Cocker. His mother had made the call after his line manager had contacted her saying that he'd failed to turn up for two successive shifts.

The officers who'd attended the welfare check had failed to get an answer but had stopped short of forcing an entry.

Okeke had seven open cases sitting in her in-tray, all requiring either legwork or a phone call, but she deemed all of them trivial enough to bump for the morning. Top of her list coming into work this morning (and playing on her mind since she'd logged off on Friday afternoon) was identifying the young man found dangling from a rope in the woods. She put in a request for a forced entry for the Ore flat as soon as she'd logged onto her terminal, and by the time she'd come back down with a coffee and pastry from the top-floor canteen, a reply had pinged into her inbox with a warrant attached.

By quarter past eleven she was standing on the second-floor landing outside Adam Cocker's apartment with a couple of uniforms beside her.

'Adam?' She rapped her knuckles on the door for a third time. 'It's the police. You need to open up or we're going to have to force your door open!'

She waited, ear close to the plywood door and listening for any sounds coming from the other side. Three times was enough as far as she was concerned. A growing instinct was telling her that this was the right place, that no one was going to be answering this door.

She nodded at the nearest police sergeant to get on with it.

He gave the door a hefty whack with the battering ram just below the handle and the flimsy door splintered and juddered inwards.

'Adam!' called the sergeant. 'We're coming in!'

Okeke let him and the probationary PC he had under his wing step inside first, then followed them into the narrow hallway. It appeared that Adam Cocker lived in a small studio flat: one room to loaf, cook, eat and sleep in on one side of the hallway, and, opposite, one tiny bathroom to shower and shit in. The sergeant opened the bathroom door and peered inside.

'Empty.' Then the main room. 'Empty,' he said again.

Okeke nodded. 'All right. Seems like we've got the right place.'

She stepped into the main room and looked around. It was surprisingly tidy. She'd forced entry into enough grotty little flats occupied by a single male in her time and had grown used to the sight of crushed beer cans and pizza boxes, balled-up socks and grubby pants littering the floor, and encrusted dishes and plates piled high in slimy sink water.

The Archive

But Adam Cocker's humble studio flat was well kept. A slatted blind was pulled down over the room's one window. Slashes of sunlight leaked through and painted the grey carpet with a ladder of stripes.

The sergeant looked at her. 'This to do with the suicide on Friday?'

She pressed her lips together, then nodded. Out of unconscious habit, she pulled a pair of nitrile gloves from her jacket pocket and snapped them on, then wandered over towards the blind and the windowsill. She pulled the blind up and the room suddenly filled with daylight and a cloud of swirling dust motes.

There was a bonsai tree as well as several framed photographs and a number of opened brown envelopes on the windowsill. She studied them for a moment, then picked up a payslip. The name at the top was the same as the employer who'd called Adam's mum, concerned he'd not turned up for work again on Sunday: Campion House Residential Home.

Okeke nodded sadly. 'Yeah, I'm afraid this looks like it's our lad.'

8

Jay held his cup and saucer beneath the tap of the Thermos hot-water dispenser. It was set on the refreshments table like a decorative centrepiece. He tried pressing what looked like a button on the top again. Nothing happened.

'What the bloody...'

He pressed the button even harder, holding it for longer. Still nothing. 'Oh for...'

Clearly the button didn't do anything. He started prodding and pressing various other potential knobs and buttons at the top of the large steel cylinder with mounting frustration.

'You ever seen the start o' that movie, *2001: A Space Odyssey*?'

The question came with a flat American drawl that Jay took a moment to translate into English. He turned to look at the person behind him in the queue, for some reason expecting someone taller. Instead he found himself staring down at a short, slim woman with boyishly short dark hair and a nose piercing.

'Huh?'

She nodded at his fumbling fingers. 'You're just pressing the lid, you dumbass.' She reached forward and pressed a release button on the tap itself, and hot steaming water quickly filled his cup.

'Ah, right. Yeah,' said Jay.

'Modern technology, eh?'

He shuffled along to the left to let her fill her cup as he grabbed a sachet of coffee, tore it open and poured it into his water.

'It'd be handy if there was a "press here" sign on the stupid thing,' he grumbled.

'True, but then you'd need to be able to read.'

Jay grabbed a mini pot of UHT milk and a couple of sweetener sachets from a plate and backed away from the refreshments table, looking around for a seat. But there were none left. So he remained standing, holding the cup and saucer in one hand, the other clasping the wad of printouts and pamphlets he'd been handed during this morning's introductory session.

After a few moments of awkward standing, he went to the end of the refreshments table, found a space to place his cup and saucer and began fumbling with the milk and sugar. The milk jetted out and mostly overshot his cup onto the tablecloth. The sweetener was one of those bloody little pills that was almost impossible to find in the too-big sachet.

'You seem to be struggling a bit there.'

He looked up to see that the American woman had had the same idea. She'd popped her papers next to his while she faffed with her coffee. She took the sweetener sachet from him, upended it over his cup and tapped the side. The pill plopped effortlessly into his coffee.

'First time making a brew?'

'Very funny,' he muttered, stirring it

She sipped hers, then set it down. 'Well, this is busier than I thought it was going to be.'

He nodded. The course was taking place in a function room at the Leonardo Hotel in Croydon. To Jay's eyes, it looked as if it had pulled in fifty, maybe sixty paying customers. He'd overheard someone say the course fee was fifteen hundred for the full four days. He crunched the numbers. Roughly £90K worth of attendees.

A nice little four-day earner for their three course instructors.

'You pay for this yourself? Or is someone else paying the tab?'

'Someone else,' he replied. 'There's no way I could afford this. Jesus. What about you?'

'I'm paying.' She hunched her shoulders. 'It's tax deductible, according to my IRS guy. Provided I earn enough this year to be taxed in the first place.'

He grabbed a Hobnob and took a bite. 'You working for yourself, then?'

'Yeah, just me. R. Kirk and Partners.' She squeezed out a wry smile at the look of confusion on his face. 'The partners bit is to make the business sound more established, like.'

'Right. And you...'

'I'm the R. Kirk bit.' She stuck a hand out. 'Veronica Kirk. Ronni, if you want to save yourself some letters.'

He shook her hand. 'Jay Turner.'

She swigged her coffee. 'How're you finding it so far?'

'The course?' He nodded. 'Yeah, great. Really interesting.'

Their instructors had wasted little time this morning in establishing their credibility. Sitting in a row at the front of the room and facing their audience, the three wiry old men had spent the first hour sharing a bunch of blood-chilling anecdotes from their undercover days.

'I don't *believe* that Mossad bloke's story about using the piano wire,' said Ronni.

Jay grimaced. 'I just don't *want* to believe it.'

She grinned. 'Nah. Just some scary war stories to wake us up on a Monday morning is all that was about.'

Jay grimaced again. 'Decapitation? Hmmm... that woke me up, for sure.'

Ronni shrugged. 'A bit of creative licence, maybe?'

The sound of hands clapping together, slowly and loudly, cut through the murmur of conversation and quickly quietened the room.

'All right, people,' announced the bloke from Mossad. 'Session Two is beginning in five!'

Jay eyed the old man's small calloused hands as he stopped clapping and they dropped to his side. Actually, Jay could well imagine those fists had done some troubling things during his long career.

Ronni placed her cup on the table and picked up her pack of handouts. 'You wanna head in now? Get a seat right at the front?'

Jay pulled a face. 'How about one row back?'

9

Okeke flashed her ID at the receptionist. 'I'm here to see the manager, Kathleen Bracy?'

The receptionist's eyes rounded at the sight of the CID badge. 'Oh God,' she whispered under her breath, before quickly recovering herself. 'This is about Adam, isn't it?'

Okeke had rung ahead to let the manager know she was on her way. Word must have spread. She nodded.

'I'll take you to her.'

The young lady came out from behind her desk, led Okeke to the foyer's inner door and tapped in a code to open it. She looked at Okeke. 'That's to stop the residents wandering out when the front desk isn't manned.'

Okeke was led down a corridor, windows along the left looking out onto a courtyard garden where several of the home's elderly residents were sitting in deck chairs with blankets over their knees, staring wistfully at the colourful flower beds.

The receptionist stopped before a door and rapped on it lightly. 'Kath? It's the police.'

The Archive

She pushed the door open to reveal a small windowless office, the walls peppered with Post-it note reminders and shift rotas. The floor space was almost completely taken up by a desk, chair, several filing cabinets and a visitor's chair. Behind the cluttered desk sat a middle-aged woman with short blonde-turning-grey hair, wearing half-moon spectacles attached to a strap that dangled down around her neck.

As the receptionist returned to the front desk, Okeke stepped into the tiny space and held out her ID again. 'I'm DC Samantha Okeke. I called you earlier, Ms –'

'Oh, ah, it's just Kath. Everyone here calls me that.' She looked *and* sounded a little flustered. 'Sorry, where are my manners? Please ,take a seat.'

Okeke edged carefully around the chair and sat down.

'I just can't believe...' Kath began, her voice faltering slightly. 'I can't believe what's happened to our Adam. Does his family know yet?'

Okeke nodded sympathetically. 'Yes, there's someone with them now. I'm really very sorry. It's a tragedy. He was *very* young, wasn't he?' She had a vague recollection that she'd used that exact same phrase on the phone earlier.

Kath's bottom lip quivered. 'He was just twenty-six.'

Older than he'd looked, then. But still, Okeke reflected, depressingly young.

'Was it... *suicide*?' asked Kath.

Okeke nodded. 'It does look that way at the moment.'

'Good God...' Kath sighed, then shook her head. 'I wish I'd recognised how... how *low* Adam had got. Perhaps there might have been something I could have said to him...'

'You shouldn't blame yourself, Kath.' Okeke paused a beat before asking, 'So, he *was* showing signs of depression?'

Kath nodded. 'He was normally really bright and chirpy. A proper ray of light around the home. The residents all love... *loved* him.' She smiled sadly. 'I should get used to the past tense, shouldn't I?' She sighed again.

'So...' Okeke pressed the matter. 'His behaviour? You're saying it was different recently?'

'Yes. I mean, he was still lovely and cheerful and kind... but just a bit quieter than usual,' Kath replied.

'Can you think of anything that might have happened to him, or anything he might have said that would suggest he was having problems at work or at home?' Okeke asked her.

Kath shook her head. 'He seemed to really enjoy the job. He was always volunteering to do extra shifts. He was genuinely a sweetheart with the residents. Very caring and very close to a number of them.'

'What about his personal life?' Okeke asked.

Kath shrugged. 'I don't really know much about that. He certainly didn't mention having any problems at home.'

'What about partners? A girlfriend? A boyfriend?'

Kath shook her head. 'He was single as far as I know. To be honest, I didn't get the impression he had much else going on relationship-wise in his life.' She paused. 'But...'

'But... what?'

'There was a resident who passed away recently. A really old chap who Adam was particularly fond of.'

Okeke nodded, waiting for the detail.

'I would say he was Adam's favourite.' Kath shrugged guiltily. 'Actually, we all have our favourites. Some residents drive you round the bend, but others... you just wish you could take home with you at the end of the day, you know?'

Okeke nodded as she flipped open her notepad. 'What was his name?'

'Jim. James Crowhurst. He passed away a few weeks ago.'

Okeke jotted the name down. 'And would you say that his death could have had an impact on Adam?'

Kath gave it a moment's thought. 'Yes. Yes, I think it probably did. Adam used to spend a lot of time sitting with Jim in his room.'

'Doing what?'

'Chatting to him. Reading to him. Sometimes the newspapers. Sometimes from his books. He spent a *lot* of time with Jim, now that I come to think of it.'

'And what did Jim die of?' Okeke asked.

'Old age... I think the medical jargon they used was respiratory failure. But basically he'd just reached the end of the road. He was in his nineties. He had advanced dementia. He was always the perfect gentleman, though. Never rude to anyone.'

'And was he close to Adam?'

Kath nodded. 'Yes, I'd say he liked Adam the most out of the staff here. I think Adam had managed to establish a real bond, a proper connection with him. He even went to Jim's funeral. He volunteered to say a little piece about him, actually.'

'Does that happen often?'

'No,' said Kath, shaking her head. 'I mean, generally, not at all. That's a line we don't cross because you have to remember, they're clients. We're professional carers. A funeral is really meant to be for the family. The loved ones.'

'But Adam attended Jim's funeral?'

Kath nodded. 'He was quite insistent about it. He wanted to say his goodbyes.'

'So, *very* attached, then? To Jim?'

Kath nodded again. 'Yes... But I can't imagine that would have been enough to –'

'It could have been a contributory factor,' said Okeke. 'Sometimes it's not one thing, but a whole basket of events that can tip a person over the edge. Maybe Crowhurst's death was a final straw for Adam.'

'Maybe,' Kath echoed absently. 'We still have his room to clear out. Do you want to look it over?'

Okeke almost shook her head, but then thought there might be something to help explain Adam Cocker's attachment to the old man. 'Sure,' she replied.

Kathleen Bracy gestured at the door and got up from behind her desk. Okeke manoeuvred her way out of the small office first, with Kath following close behind.

Outside, Kath flagged down a girl – she looked like she was still a teenager – wearing a mint-green uniform and a nametag.

'Megan love, would you show Detective…'

'Just Sam will do,' offered Okeke.

'Sam… to Jim's old room.'

'Sure,' said Megan.

'If there's anything else you need…' Kath said to Okeke, 'just knock on my door. I'm usually trapped in here.'

Okeke nodded. 'Thanks for your help.'

'It's this way,' said Megan, gesturing for Okeke to follow her. 'It won't take too long. I'm afraid this old place is a bit of a rabbit warren.'

They passed several residents' bedrooms, the wide-open doors revealing small rooms, some cluttered with personal belongings, others practically spartan, but all of them occupied by bed-ridden residents staring listlessly into space.

'These are the most incapacitated residents,' explained Megan.

'Do they get up?' asked Okeke. 'Out of their rooms, I mean?'

Megan shook her head. 'Rarely.'

She tapped in a security code in a keypad at the next set

of double glass doors. On the other side was an old woman in slippers and a dressing gown. She clutched a handbag as she stared through the glass at them, waiting for a door to be opened.

Megan pulled one of the doors open and stepped through with Okeke.

'All right there, Joan?' she asked cheerfully.

Joan beamed brightly. 'Oh yes! Yes! I'm just off out to play bridge at the ambassador's club, dear.'

'I'm sorry,' said Megan gently. 'The club's closed today, my lovely.'

'Is it those bloody Nazi bombers again?' Joan asked, as Megan discreetly closed the door.

Megan nodded. 'Hmm, yes... It's safer to stay indoors today, I think.'

Joan nodded. 'Yes, perhaps you're right.' She turned away and shuffled slowly down the corridor.

Megan looked at Okeke apologetically. 'Sometimes it's easier... and kinder to go along with whatever they're saying.'

Okeke nodded. 'Makes sense.'

They turned a corner, overtaking Joan.

'So this is about Adam?' asked Megan.

'Yes, it is,' Okeke replied.

'It's true, then? He's actually... *dead*?'

Okeke nodded. 'I'm afraid so.'

'Oh, God.' Megan stopped in her tracks, her narrow shoulders starting to shudder.

Okeke placed a hand on one. 'I'm very sorry, Megan. You guys were close?'

Megan nodded.

'Romantic close?' Okeke asked.

The girl shook her head and laughed snottily. 'Oh, God,

no. Adam's gay. We're just really good mates.' She stopped herself, suddenly realising that she was referring to him in the present tense. She shook her head. 'I can't believe it. He was just, I mean, I was just working alongside him on Thursday. He was... so...'

'So?' Okeke prompted.

Megan shook her head again. 'So... cheerful. So friendly.' She sighed. 'So much fun. He really made working here...' Her voice faltered.

Okeke rubbed her shoulder. 'It's okay.'

'It just doesn't seem...' Megan dabbed at her eyes. 'It doesn't seem real. Ms Bracy told us this morning that it was suicide.'

Okeke remained silent, waiting.

Megan took a deep breath and resumed walking. 'I can't believe that, though. He was so full of life and... I mean, yes, he was upset when Jim died; we all were. He was a lovely old boy, but, like –'

'You don't think it would have hit him *that* badly?' Okeke asked.

'To take his life?' Megan shook her head. 'I mean, I know he was down about it, but –"Did you ever socialise with Adam outside work?' Okeke asked. 'Did you go for a drink with him after –'

'No. He never drinks... well, drank. Adam was teetotal. Vegetarian. Very, very healthy.' Megan stopped beside a closed door. 'This is it. This was Jim's room.' She pushed the handle down and pushed the door inwards.

'Normally the family are asked to come in and collect all the personal belongings... Someone – his grandson, I think – did pop in to have a look, but I don't' think he took much, if anything, away with him. Jim didn't have any other family, so we're going to have to clear it out ourselves. And soon.

There's another resident due to take over this room next month.'

Okeke peered around the room, which was cluttered with personal belongings. The walls were lined with book-laden shelves. The windowsill was crammed with dusty miniatures and model aeroplanes.

Megan saw her looking at them. 'Jim liked making those old Airfix kits. Adam used to bring one in for him every few weeks or so.'

'Out of his own money?' Okeke had no idea what the staff were paid here. Probably not a lot.

Megan nodded. 'Adam was always so thoughtful.'

Okeke wandered over to the model aeroplanes. She thought she recognised a Spitfire, but the rest were just planes from 'the war', as far as she was concerned.

'How old was Jim?'

'Jim?' Megan's brow flexed for a moment. 'He was late ninety-something. Maybe nearly a hundred?'

'And he was able enough to assemble these models on his own? That's pretty impressive,' Okeke said, picking one up for a closer look.

Megan shrugged. 'He had pretty advanced dementia. I mean... like Joan you just met, perfectly able to have a brief conversation with you, just... you know... very muddled about things. But yeah... he could use his hands pretty well. He made those himself.'

Okeke stepped towards the shelves. 'He was a big reader?'

'I guess he *used* to be.' Megan absently straightened some of the books on one of the shelves. 'But I've not seen him read since I've been working here.'

'How long have you been here, Megan?'

'Three years. Adam was already here when I started.'

'Right. And Mr Crowhurst?'

She shrugged. 'God knows. Years and years. I think he's one of the longest stayers we've ever had here.'

Okeke briefly studied the books – there were works by Rudyard Kipling, Nevil Shute and H. G. Wells among others.

'Adam used to read those to him. *The Jungle Book* was Jim's favourite.' Megan smiled. 'I didn't know it was a book first. I thought it was just a cartoon.'

Okeke looked at the dog-eared and sun-faded cover, and then noticed there were a number of leather-bound journals, piled up at the end of a shelf. She picked one up and opened it. The pages were thick with faint spidery handwriting.

'So, Jim kept diaries?' she said.

Megan peered down at the open pages. 'Yeah. Kath found them hidden away in the communal library. We think he left them there hoping that someone would find them an interesting read.' She smiled sadly. 'If no one comes back to pick them up soon, I guess they'll be thrown away too.'

Okeke spotted some dates. 'These are from quite a while back. Some of these are decades old.' She pulled another from the shelf. 'Look at that – 1963. Wow.'

'Yeah, ancient times,' said Megan. 'I suppose that's actual history in there really, isn't it?'

Okeke nodded. 'You're right.'

10

Boyd eased himself down onto the sofa. 'There you go,' said Charlotte, looking out of the lounge's tall bay window. 'You've got a view.'

Boyd had a fine view of Ashburnham Road and the side of the DHL van parked right outside his house. 'Great, I can watch Amazon parcels come and go,' he grumbled.

Charlotte plumped up the cushions behind his back. 'Oh, now, Bill, you're not one of those people who turns out to be a terribly grumpy patient, are you?'

'I've got cancer. I'm allowed to be grumpy.'

'*Had* cancer,' she corrected him. 'It's out now.'

'There could still be bits floating around,' he reminded her.

'And they'll be very sorry if they are,' she said firmly, 'once your treatment starts.'

Emma waddled into the lounge with a plate of Marmite on toast cradled in the crook of her arm against her bump, a mug of coffee in one hand and her phone in the other.

'Oh, let me help you with that, dear,' Charlotte said, hurrying over to help Emma before the plate toppled to the floor. She shooed Ozzie and Mia out of the way as she set the plate on the side table and Emma eased herself down into the armchair.

Ozzie took the nose-level plate as an invitation to curl his pink tongue out and sample the generous helping of melting butter and Marmite, scooping out a scallop-shaped swirl from the toast.

'Ozzie! No!' snapped Emma, shooing him away.

Charlotte looked at the toast, then at Emma. 'You want the same again?'

Emma nodded. 'Oh, please.' She smiled gratefully. 'You've got your hands full looking after us Boyds, eh?'

Charlotte smiled back cheerfully. 'It's going to be a bonding experience for us all, I reckon!'

'Charlotte, if you're going back to the kitchen, could you be a lamb...' began Boyd.

She turned to look at him. 'What now, Bill?'

'My phone,' he said. 'It's on the dining table. Could you just...'

Charlotte smiled. 'Yes, of course.'

'Oh crap,' said Emma. 'My laptop...'

'Where is it?' Charlotte asked.

'Also on the dining room table,' Emma said sheepishly.

Charlotte kept her smile going. 'Do you want me to...'

'Be a lamb?' Emma still sounded rather sheepish, as she rubbed her bump absently. 'Please?'

Charlotte nodded and headed out of the lounge and down the hallway, the two dogs following her hopefully.

'Oh, and could I have some paracetamol?' Boyd called out after her. 'And a glass of water. Please!'

They both heard her reply with a harried 'Yes, coming!'

'And a bit of toast, like Emma's got!' he added. 'To wash it down...'

Emma glanced at her father and grimaced guiltily. 'Poor Charlotte. We're going to be a nightmare, aren't we?'

∼

OKEKE RETURNED to the station feeling strangely down. She couldn't put her finger precisely on why, but she figured it was probably her visit to the residential home. Despite the best care of the staff there, who frankly seemed wonderfully patient and professional, there was an air of melancholy about the place. She presumed *any* old people's home would have the same ambience, no matter how many brightly coloured flowers were stencilled on the walls, or inspirational mottos were taped to the doors. There was no escaping the fact that such places were nothing more than cheerfully decorated departure lounges.

Her thoughts kept flitting back to the old man who'd died. Jim Crowhurst.

And Adam...

Thanks to Megan and the manager, Kath, she had the mental image of Adam dutifully spending whatever time he had spare sitting with the old man and reading classics to him. In her mind's eye was a sentimental, sun-dappled scene of Jim as some charming, wizened old man with an Anthony Hopkins voice, and Adam, a doting and earnest young man beside him, listening to Jim's croaky wisdom, forging a bond across the decades.

She needed to get a grip.

The old man may have been recently cremated, but, looking around his room, she'd sensed his presence in the books lined along the shelves, his old journals and the few framed photos dotted about. There was one of him as a young man in a British Army uniform surrounded by a platoon of grinning Gurkhas. In another he was a little older, wearing an academic robe and standing behind two rows of freshly scrubbed schoolboys wearing blazers, shorts, neatly pulled-up socks and *Just William*-like school caps.

Megan had said that Jim had no family beyond his grandson. Apart from a short-lived marriage, he'd been a bachelor for practically all his life and had most likely outlived any siblings, if indeed he'd had any.

Her thoughts flipped over to Adam as she sat down at her desk. The more she thought about it, the more possible it seemed that Adam might have become too close, almost dependent on the old man. Weren't there carers out there, whether paid to do the job or doing it out of familial duty, who lost their sense of purpose in life when they lost the person for whom they'd been responsible? It was a thing, she was sure. Some sort of syndrome.

The mental image she had of Adam was of a sensitive and kind young man, but one with little going on in his life outside work. In his apartment there'd been none of the markers of a young person with an active social life: no scribbled reminders or scrawled Post-its on the fridge, or goofing-around-with-mates photos on a pinboard. She'd rationalised that these days kids kept all that stuff on their smartphones or tablets, but, then again, she'd seen no evidence that he'd had either of those things either.

And that was particularly odd. What person in their twenties *didn't* have a smartphone? A tablet? A laptop? A gaming console or even a handheld gaming device?

Her work phone buzzed as if to emphasise the point. It was an unknown ID. She answered it. 'DC Okeke.'

'Hi Sam, it's Laura Palmer.' The first name threw her for a moment, but then she remembered. It was Dr Palmer from Ellessey Forensics.

'Ah, hi,' she replied.

'I'm sorry. I must have just come up on your phone as an unknown. I broke my phone over the weekend,' Palmer explained, 'so I'm on a new one with a new SIM card. I called your boss to get your number.'

'You called Boyd?' Okeke asked.

'Yes. I didn't know he... uh...' She sounded awkward. 'He has cancer.'

'He's been trying to keep it quiet,' said Okeke. 'But you can probably guess how successful he's been with that down at Hastings station.'

Dr Palmer laughed politely. 'He sounds like he's doing okay, though?'

'Yeah, they didn't mess around. Got him straight in and snip-snip. He's out of the hospital now,' Okeke told her.

'Yes. He is,' said Dr Palmer. 'I could hear dogs barking in the background.' She paused to indicate she'd used up her small talk. 'I'm calling about Adam Cocker – the body that came in on Friday. I looked him over this morning. The cause of death was asphyxiation by strangulation. The ligature marks around his neck were consistent with hanging. That's how he was found, right?'

'From a tree, yes,' Okeke confirmed.

'There were no broken neck bones or torn ligaments.' Dr Palmer made a sucking sound with her lips. 'Which would have meant a short drop, if any. That's not good.'

Okeke really didn't know what constituted a short or long drop. All she knew was that if there was too much rope and too much drop, there was the risk of decapitation.

'Suicides tend to underestimate the drop needed for a clean break,' added Dr Palmer. 'So it can be... unfortunately, a slow process sometimes.'

Okeke sighed. 'Shit. Poor boy,'

Palmer tutted sadly. 'Yes, he did appear to be rather young.'

'He was twenty-six, actually. Looks younger. But, yeah, that's still way too young.'

'I did a toxicology. I was not surprised to find a fair bit of alcohol in his system,' Dr Palmer said.

Okeke raised her brows. 'I was told by his colleague at work he was teetotal. How much had he had?'

'Seven or eight units. Given his slight build, I'd say that would have left him pretty inebriated,' Dr Palmer said.

Dutch courage, pondered Okeke. 'He was quite high up,' she said. 'Twenty-five, thirty feet maybe.'

Dr Palmer sucked in whistling air again. 'Eight units and climbing a tree? I suppose that's possible. But he would have been pretty incapacitated at the time. I'm no expert on climbing trees. Never having done it myself. Anyway... that's for you to puzzle.'

'Thanks,' said Okeke.

'I'll email the report over to you. You're SIO on this one, right?'

'Yep,' confirmed Okeke. 'We're all out of senior officers at the moment.'

'Ah, so it's your time to shine, then?'

Okeke grinned. 'That's right.'

'I'm afraid I have to go. Looks like Conquest's pathologist has got too much on his plate, because we had another one come in last night. A house fire.' Dr Palmer sighed. 'They're like London buses. You wait half an hour and then they all come along at once!'

Okeke hung up. *Adam Cocker drunk?* Megan's words circled back to her: *He never drinks.*

Maybe she needed to take a more careful look around

Adam's apartment. Just to settle her mind. Presumably there'd be some empty bottles or cans in his kitchen bin.

'AWWW-RAAAAAAARRRRRR-EEEEAAWW!'

Okeke was jerked from her thoughts by a loud outburst. She spun round to find Sutherland standing right behind her, stretching his arms out above him, his mouth wide open, revealing a row of gold fillings.

'Jesus!' she snapped. 'You made me jump out of my skin!'

Sutherland closed his gaping mouth and smacked his lips, as if he'd just been wine-tasting. 'Sorry about that, Okeke. The missus moans that I'm a bloody noisy yawner. I'm a bloody noisy sneezer too, apparently.'

He looked around the virtually empty floor. Warren had headphones on and was slumped low in his chair as he tapped away at his keyboard. 'Where's O'Neal?'

'Rang in sick,' she replied. 'Again.'

'He's a bloody slacker that one,' grumbled Sutherland. 'What's the matter with him?'

She shrugged. O'Neal had been pretty surly recently, she'd noticed. Arsier than his normal arsy self.

'Blimey, it really is like the *Mary Celeste* out here,' sighed Sutherland.

Not for the first time, Okeke wondered if there weren't too many bums stuffed into chairs on DCI Flack's closed-off side of the partition and not enough over this side, dealing with the steady flow of non-drugs-related cases.

'Right then... coffee,' announced Sutherland sleepily as he headed towards the kitchenette. He was nearly there when he stopped dead and muttered to himself. 'Bloody idiot. Almost forgot the reason I stepped out.' He returned to Okeke's desk. 'Fire. Last night. In Ore.'

She looked up at him.

Sutherland scowled. 'You haven't read last night's activity log yet?'

'I've been busy, sir, with the suicide case this morning. But, yeah, I heard about a fire.'

'Yes, well... there was a fatality. Someone needs to hop over and liaise with the fire inspection team.'

She nodded silently over at Warren.

Sutherland smiled. 'Aye, well, not that you've got many to choose from.'

11

Okeke slowly picked her way more thoroughly around Adam's flat the second time around. Having visited the residential home, she had a much better idea about the type of person Adam had been. A bit of a loner outside work. His job had seemed to be his whole life.

He'd had a cat, as evidenced by the bowl on the floor and a bag of kitty litter in the cupboard beneath his sink. The bonsai tree on the windowsill was tidily trimmed and obviously well cared for. On the arm of the small sofa was a ball of pale-blue wool, some knitting needles and a foot-long scarf, or whatever it was intended to be one day.

He knitted? She was taken aback by the sudden prickling of sadness she felt as she looked at it.

She spotted the box for an Airfix model of a Lancaster bomber, unopened, on a bookshelf, still in its cellophane wrapper. Adam must have bought that for Jim but never got a chance to give it to him, never got a chance to watch the old man carefully assemble it. Adam, clearly, had kept it. For sentimental reasons.

She snapped on the lamp on his bedside table and opened the drawer. She found a wallet, a bus pass and his ID lanyard for the residential home. But, still, no phone.

'Come on, Adam... what did you do with it?' she muttered under her breath.

Nobody – literally *nobody* – these days went without a mobile. His apartment didn't appear to have a landline that she could find – therefore he *had* to have had a mobile tucked away somewhere. Surely?

Okeke was about to call it a day when she spotted a pad of yellow Post-its on the floor in the narrow space between the bedside table and the bed. It must have been knocked off the top. She reached down to pick it up, pausing only briefly as she realised she wasn't wearing gloves.

She pulled out a pair from her jacket and snapped them on, then carefully picked up the pad. She was half expecting to see a very short goodbye note. A simple sign-off from Adam.

But the top Post-it was blank.

She could, however, detect the faintest indentation of something that had been written on the removed note above. She picked up the bedside lamp and angled it across the pad's surface to highlight the indentations into a harder, more legible relief.

With her other hand, she pulled out her phone and, playing around with the angle of lighting from the lamp, took several snapshots. She could make out some letters and could hazard a guess at the few words that had been scribbled down, but if she had a spare moment back at the station, she could upload them onto her computer and play around with the image-processing software's contrast settings on a much bigger screen.

The Archive

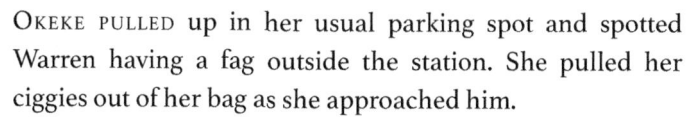

OKEKE PULLED up in her usual parking spot and spotted Warren having a fag outside the station. She pulled her ciggies out of her bag as she approached him.

'You back already?' she said, eyebrows raised.

'Apparently,' he replied sarcastically, pulling out his lighter for her. 'To be fair, there wasn't much for me to do, really. The firemen were starting to pack up. The fire inspection guy said it looked like it was probably accidental. The old person who was living there was, like, a bit of a hoarder.'

Okeke blew out a cloud of smoke. 'Dead?'

'Uh-huh. An old lady. They found her still in her bed. She died of smoke inhalation, he thinks. Which is for the best, considering.'

'Considering?'

'There was a wheelchair beside her bed. If she'd woken up, she wouldn't have stood a chance of getting out.' He blew out a cloud of smoke. 'Poor Eleanora.'

Okeke's brows bounced. 'Eleanora?'

'Eleanora Baxendale. The old lady. Died in a fire? Wake up, Okeke,' Warren said, laughing.

She rolled her eyes. 'I was just thinking it's a nice name. Eleanora Baxendale...' She said it slowly. 'Like something out of an Austen novel.' She took another pull of her cigarette. 'What kind of stuff was she hoarding?'

He shrugged. 'A bit of everything as far as I could see. Shoes, books, hats, dolls... You know, the usual crazy lady stuff.'

'Was anyone else injured?' she asked.

He shook his head. 'She lived alone. The inspection guy said hoarders are a constant headache for the fire service.

An accident waiting to happen... especially if the person's a smoker too.'

'And Eleanora was?'

Warren nodded. 'She had a ton of empty ciggy cartons in her wheelie bin. She was quite a heavy smoker by the look of it.' He stubbed out his cigarette and dropped the extinguished butt into the bin that had recently been installed there. Someone at the station had complained about the constant scattering of squished butts barely feet away from the main entrance. It apparently 'sent out the wrong message', although what that message was remained a mystery to Warren.

'How's the suicide case going?' he asked.

Okeke nodded. 'Still going. It's early days.' She stubbed her cigarette out too and tossed the butt into the fag bin. She tipped her head towards the entrance. 'Come on then, Boy Wonder – time to do all that lovely paperwork.'

'That's exactly what I was trying to do before you sent me out...' he grumbled.

'And now you have some more. Yay for you,' she said cheerily.

~

DESPITE HER INTENTION TO wrap up her report on Adam Cocker's death, she found herself distracted by another task that had been in her in-tray since last week. The police sergeant who'd pulled over a TWOC – a frequent car-stealing offender – and brought the 'little rascal' in had come down from the second floor to enquire whether she'd managed to build the case file up to a point where the CPS would be happy to consider investing their time. Her brusque answer was that she hadn't even started on it yet.

The thunderous and florid expression on his face had convinced her to put the suicide case to one side for the remaining hours of her shift and get cracking on the TWOC before Sergeant Impatient had an aneurism. So it wasn't until much later, after she'd ended her shift and was standing in a basket-only queue at Tesco (which seemed to be progressing glacially), that she suddenly remembered the snaps she'd taken of the Post-it note.

She pulled her phone out and brought up the photos she'd taken. She decided to have a quick play with the photo app's limited range of editing tools, using the image that looked the most promising. She zoomed in on the indentations and studied a section of the image that showed what could well have been the arch and ascender of a 'h'. Okeke ramped up the contrast slider, and the 'h' emerged more clearly. She scrolled to the right. The letters following it had been bleached out, so she dialled down the contrast a little and pulled the general brightness of the image down. A few more faint letters began to emerge: 'a', 'r', 'd'. She scrolled back to the 'h', still visible, then went to look at the letters before it.

O-r-c-h-a-r-d.

Orchard.

'Okay,' she muttered, then slid the zoomed-in picture upwards to take a look at the indentations below. These letters were clear and waiting patiently for her.

Marble.

Beneath that was a third word. It looked like 'apple'.

'It's your turn, love.' She looked up to see an awkwardly large void between her and the waiting cashier.

'Oh, yeah. Sorry,' she said, pocketing her phone and swiftly dumping the contents of her basket on to the conveyor belt. She packed her shopping quickly, trying to keep pace as the cashier scanned her items. She paid with her phone and then nodded apologetically to the shoppers who'd been waiting behind her patiently.

She headed across the car park to her Datsun, dumped the shopping on the passenger seat and slumped down inside. Rather than start the car and join the peak-time logjam of cars trying to exit the car park, she got her phone out again and returned to the photo app; the image she'd being playing with was still zoomed in and waiting for her.

There was a letter – no, *two* more – in front of 'apple'. She played around again with the app's contrast and brightness sliders until finally the faint curves coalesced into discernible letters: 'G' and 'r'.

'Grapple?' she said aloud.

She put the three words together: *Orchard. Marble. Grapple.* Then a thought occurred to her. She switched apps to What3words.

'Surely not?' she muttered hopefully.

Okeke typed the three words and sighed disappointedly as they took her to a blank square of ocean off the coast of Indonesia. 'Okay, so it's not that, then.'

She wondered whether she was in danger of making too big a deal of this. It was only an imprint of three random words on a Post-it note.

The phone buzzed in her hand and she almost dropped it. It was Jay. She swiped to answer it. 'Hey there, love.'

'Hey, babycakes!' he shouted back at her. Okeke could hear a lot of background noise that sounded very much like a busy pub.

'Shocker,' she replied. 'It sounds like you're on the piss, babes.'

'Just the one pint, my love. I'm keeping it professional, you know. Like I said I would.'

'What's the accommodation like?' she asked.

Jay's boss at the agency, Mr McGuire, had said that Jay could use his London apartment during the three-day seminar. He'd given him an address near Clapham Common and a PIN number to let himself in.

'Very posh, Sam. But very small.' He chuckled. 'I mean, bleedin' tiny.'

'Well, that's London for you,' she replied. 'You don't pay by the square foot; you pay by the square inch.'

He laughed.

'So, how was your first day? Did you make any friends?'

He laughed again. 'Yes, I made friends with Ron,' he replied.

'Ron, eh? Say hi to him from me. What about today's seminar? Was it any good?'

'Uh... this morning we had a load of handouts and some very boring PowerPoint stuff, but this afternoon –' she could hear the grin in his voice – 'we did some hands-on stuff.'

'Hands-on? I thought this course was about discreetly surveilling people, not beating the shit out of them,' she said.

'No... we had practical demonstrations of how to frisk a person without it being too obvious.'

'Seriously? How the hell do you do that?'

'With distraction techniques. You look for telltale profile bulges, then create an opportunity to cop a quick feel,' he explained.

'Right. Well, that doesn't sound at all pervy,' she said.

Jay chuckled. 'It's using similar skills to pickpocketing, actually. It's an art, Sam.'

Okeke rolled her eyes. He sounded as if he'd had more than one pint. 'Look, I'm doing a bit of take-home work right now, so...'

'All right, babes... I'll love yer and leave y–'

'Don't get too rat-arsed, Jay. Seriously. You don't want to let McGuire down.'

'Yeah. Fair point. Love you, babes.'

'You too.'

Clunk. He was gone.

She sighed. Maybe she was over-mummying him. Since Jay had decided he wanted to be a PI, he'd actually been pretty disciplined and dedicated when it came to putting the hours in. All the same, let loose in the Big Bad City, she couldn't help but imagine him being led astray by a bunch of burly men with shaved heads and tattoos, war stories and names like Ron and Steve. She just hoped he didn't succumb to peer pressure and end up blowing all his pocket money in a ridiculously expensive titty bar.

12

Ronni Kirk got up from her seat in the pub booth and dug into her jeans to pull out some more money. 'Another one, big man?'

Jay looked at the dregs of beer in his glass. He'd already had three pints this evening, which, despite his bulk and the eight hours' sleep he planned to get back at McGuire's place, probably wouldn't entirely metabolize overnight and leave him fresh as a daisy for Seminar Day Two.

He was currently at the point of what he liked to call 'peak merry' – tipsy enough to be happy, and yet still very much able to make some Big Boy, sensible decisions. Another pint and he'd start slurring his words, drunk-dialling and talking dirty to Sam.

'Nah. I think I've probably had enough, thanks, Ronni.'

The woman, half his size and whippet thin, had consumed the same amount this evening and seemed sober enough to land an F18 on a carrier. 'Aw, lightweight... Go on have yourself one more...'

'No, seriously. I should probably head back to my place.'

Ronni grinned. 'Oh, yeah... The big boss's fancy pad!'

'Well, it's not *that* fancy, to be honest.'

'Got to be nicer than my Travelodge cell,' she replied.

'And that was dumb fuckin' expensive, mind. Jeez... London hotel prices.'

The evening had been fun. Several dozen of the course's attendees had flocked into the pub opposite the Leonardo Hotel. They were a fascinating mix of people, all ages, from all walks of life: ex-solicitors, ex-coppers, ex-army... There was a woman who used to be a head teacher, and an older Irish bloke whose current – waning – income came from working as a film extra and who had once been a barbarian warrior in *Gladiator*.

After the first couple of hours, the crowd had thinned out to those who didn't need to hurry off and catch a bus or a train home for the night. Now, Jay looked around and realised it was pretty much himself and Ronni. He let out a big *'Well, that's me'* sigh and drained the last of his ridiculously expensive London-priced lager.

'You off, then?' said Ronni.

He nodded. 'Yeah, think so. Might go back and review some of the notes I made and then –'

'How about taking me back with you?'

'Huh?'

She said it again, then grinned. 'You know, show me what *fancy* looks like?'

Jay wasn't sure, but he could have sworn she'd just winked at him as well.

'Take you...'

She rolled her eyes at him. 'Jesus H. Christ I'm actually pretty sure I'm speaking English. I'll try again.' She leant forward across the table and raised her voice loud enough to turn a head on the next table. 'Nice an' simple. Do. You. Fancy. A. Shag?'

Jay's mouth dropped open.

Not that it was the first ever time in his life that a woman had approached him – as a matter of fact, it was the second. The *first* time had been Okeke. She'd picked him up with a slurred and corny one-liner.

But... this time, it was the sheer brazenness of it that caught his attention.

The loudness, too.

'A little bit of fun, numbnuts,' she added. 'Nothing more... and none of that awkward shit in the morning. Just have some fun.'

Jay looked around and scowled at the person staring their way. He turned back to Ronni. 'I... That's... a really nice offer, Ronni...' *Shit did I just say that?* 'But, I'm, uh... married.'

She grabbed his left hand and turned it one way, then the other. 'Don't see a ring on there, nor a worn mark.'

'Right. Okay, not married, but I'm steady. You know... steady, steady.'

She hunched her angled shoulders (he had to admit) very attractively. If he'd been on the market, so to speak, she'd probably be the type he'd be drawn to: athletic, lean, threateningly gothic with that dark eyeliner, her one-eye-hidden fringe, nose piercing and leather jacket.

'I uh... I should p-probably head off,' he finally stammered.

Ronni shrugged, like it was no big deal. 'Oh, well, your loss.' She tapped the folder of handouts and notes he was in danger of leaving behind on the table. 'Don't forget your homework!'

'Ah, right.' Jay scooped up the folder and backed out of the booth. 'See you tomorrow?'

'Yeah.' She pointed a finger-gun at him and fired it. 'Tomorrow, big man.'

Jay emerged out of the noise and fug of the pub onto the orange-hued street. A Croydon night bus rolled by as he sucked a deep breath.

Then exhaled.

∼

OKEKE HUNKERED down on the sofa with her laptop and the bottle of San Miguel she'd pulled out of the fridge. She reached for the remote control and muted Graeme Hall standing in some woman's kitchen in his tight jeans and plaid waistcoat, towering over a pair of badly behaved Dachshunds.

She flipped her laptop open and placed her phone on the armrest. 'Right then...'

Orchard. Marble. Grapple. Three entirely random words that clearly, and disappointingly, *weren't* a location marker.

She tapped the first two words into Google because 'Marble Orchard' sounded like it could well be a place. In return, she got a few results: a grunge band from Oregon; a novel by someone for sale on Amazon. It, was also, apparently a US slang term for a cemetery. The rest of the page was filled with useless hits that used one or other of the search terms.

'Okaaaay... let's have all three of you, then.'

She took a slug of her beer, tapped them in and hit return, expecting nothing but an 'ooops' message from Google with a helpful suggestion of a similar search string to try out.

Instead she had a hit.

One. Just one.

A link with no metadata description. A URL that was a meaningless string of characters and numbers. Curious, she clicked on it and a moment later found herself staring at an almost completely blank web page. A dark blue, featureless background with a single grainy black-and-white image in the middle.

She moved the cursor over it to see if it was mouse-sensitive and would open up another page, but there was no functionality to the image at all. It was just there. One grainy picture alone on an otherwise blank page.

She studied the image, which was little more than a thumbnail image. She hit the keys on the keyboard to grab a screenshot and zoomed in on that.

The image was poor: low-resolution and pixilated. However, it resembled a single tree. Stripped bare. Possibly fire damaged. A silhouette of a figure stood beside it, looking up at the sparse branches. There was nothing else apart from a barren landscape of rock and dirt. The figure seemed to be wearing a gas mask and hood, but that could just have been the angle or a result of data compression: the cylinder of the gas mask could just as easily be a beard or a rogue pixel.

She returned to the meaningless, functionless web page on her screen.

'What the actual fuck?'

13

Boyd stared at the lunch that Charlotte had prepared for him: Cheddar cheese sandwiched between white bread. 'No pickle?'

She shook her head. 'I'm afraid we've got to keep it as plain and simple as possible for the first few weeks,' she reminded him.

'It's the all-white diet,' said Emma.

Charlotte nodded. 'Your consultant called it that. White bread, white rice, cheese, butter, milk, cream, pasta, chips, pastry...'

'It's basically all the nasty, fattening, refined carbs, Dad. All the stuff you usually love...'

He pulled a face. 'I like a cheese sandwich. But this is going to get old... fast.'

'I'm afraid it has to be bland,' said Charlotte. 'Now, stop being a pain in the arse and eat your lunch.'

He looked at the unappetising stack of triangles arranged on the plate in front of him. Charlotte had even removed the crusts. 'Right then.' He took a bite out of the nearest triangle, smiled for Charlotte and made some perfunctory *yummy* noises.

Before he could take another bite, the doorbell rang. Ozzie launched into a barrage of ear-splitting barks. He bounded out of the dining room and down the hall to tell whoever it was to Foxtrot Oscar. Mia followed in his wake with a volley of high-pitched yips that might as well have been translated as '*Yeah, what he said.*'

Boyd looked at Emma. 'Danny?'

She shook her head as she checked her phone. 'DHL, I expect.'

The spare bedroom next to Emma's had been repurposed into the nursery for her as-yet-ungendered bump. Over the last few weeks, she and Charlotte had embraced the task of turning it from a dusty old guest bedroom, with its thick, dour dark-brown curtains and cobwebs running along the coving, into a vibrant and cheerful gender-neutral space. Emma had decided to paint the room – for some inexplicable reason – to resemble an underwater cartoon kingdom of seahorses, merpeople and clown fish. It was still a work in progress: the bottom of the walls were a deep navy-blue that she'd been attempting to blend with patchy success to graduate into an eye-watering bright turquoise at the top.

'What've you got coming?' Boyd asked Emma, as Charlotte went to get the door.

'Some mermaid stencils,' she replied.

Emma's attempt at hand-painting one had produced a ghastly-looking chimera that wouldn't have looked out of place in Guillermo Del Toro movie. Boyd wasn't sure whether murderous maniacs came into the world with their psychopathy preloaded, or whether their twisted drive was the product of a disturbing childhood environment. Taking one look at Emma's gnarly nightmare creation... Well, he didn't fancy finding out the hard way.

'Ahh.' He nodded. 'Probably a good idea.'

A few moments later, they heard the squeak of sneakers on the wooden floor in the hallway.

'Morning, guv.'

Boyd twisted in his seat to find Okeke walking towards him. He checked his watch. It was quarter to twelve. 'Bit early for your lunch break, isn't it?'

'Sort of lunch break, sort of not,' she replied as she stepped into the dining room. 'Hey, Ems.'

'Hey,' Emma replied.

Okeke's eyes rounded at the sight of her. 'You're lookin' *big*, girl!'

'Feels like I'm brewing a sperm whale,' Emma huffed.

Charlotte walked in behind Okeke. 'Tea, coffee, Sam?'

'Coffee, please.' Okeke glanced at Boyd. 'How's the patient?'

Charlotte hesitated a moment. 'This isn't a police work visit, is it?'

Okeke clamped her mouth and puffed her cheeks. A guilty 'sort of'.

'He's meant to be taking it easy,' said Charlotte, to which Boyd rolled his eyes.

'I know, I know... I just wondered if I could get his advice on something. Just a quick thing,' Okeke said.

Charlotte narrowed her eyes sceptically. 'A quick thing? Promise?'

'Promise.'

∼

BOYD STARED at the web page on his monitor. 'That's it?'

'That's it,' Okeke replied.

He sat forward in his study chair and looked more closely at the photograph in the middle of the screen – a grainy black-and-white image of a skeletal tree in a barren and empty landscape and a solitary figure looking up at it.

'Well, I'll admit it's a bit creepy,' he mused aloud.

'That's what I thought.'

'Okay.' He settled back in his seat. 'So, are you going to talk me through why you're showing me this?'

'There was a suicide last week,' she explained. 'A young man found hanging from a tree...' She told him about her visit to the residential home, the friendship that Adam had forged with the now-deceased resident Jim Crowhurst, and him attending the old man's funeral.

'And where does this web page fit into your story?' Boyd asked.

'I took a second look around Adam's flat. There were no suicide notes, no scribbled farewells...'

'Maybe he emailed or texted one?' Boyd suggested.

'There was no tech.'

Boyd frowned. 'How old did you say this lad was?'

'Twenty-six.'

'So what do you mean by "no tech"?' he asked.

'As in there was nothing.' Okeke shook her head. 'No phone, no tablet, no laptop, not even a games console.'

Boyd's suspicion was suddenly tweaked. 'No signs of adaptors? Spare leads, cases?'

She shook her head. 'Either he was completely old school or...'

He looked at her and pulled a face. 'You're thinking someone cleaned up?'

She shrugged.

'That's a reach, Sam. Maybe he was just very old school. Some people can be quirky like that.'

'Nobody, in the whole world, under forty... is *that* old school,' she replied testily. 'Come on. I mean, what if he needed to call in sick at work or contact his mum? There wasn't even a landline!'

'Takes all sorts,' he replied.

'Yeah, well, I found a pad of Post-its on the floor and could make out an imprint of what he'd written down last. Three words that took me to this web page.' She shrugged. 'So, clearly he knows about the internet.'

Boyd shook his head. 'That's a bit of a stretch. Are you sure you read those words correctly? I mean... you said it was an imprint, right? Maybe –'

'Yes. It was those three words,' she said firmly. 'And typed into Google, they yield one hit. This page.'

He looked at the words she'd written down on his desk pad: *Grapple. Orchard. Marble.*

'Did you try What3words?'

'Yeah, of course I did!' she replied. 'Unless the lad had plans to go swimming in the middle of the Indonesian sea, I think that's a dead end.' She pointed at the screen. 'However, as a search term, this page is the only direct hit.'

'Only? Or –'

'*Only*,' she cut in. 'On the entire internet, guv. The *whole* internet.'

Boyd looked again at the strange image, his curiosity now somewhat piqued. 'Do you think this picture meant something to the lad? Do you think it might have contributed to pushing him over the edge?'

She shrugged. 'Maybe... if it meant something to him. If he knew what it was about.'

'Could it be a picture he was familiar with?' he asked. 'Something from his past? Could that figure be him?'

'It's old. It's grainy.'

'Yup, but you can make a picture look old and grainy in Photoshop.'

She nodded. 'True. But if that's him... who took the picture? Right?'

Boyd nodded. 'And why's he wearing a gas mask and a hooded suit.'

'Some kind of prank maybe?'

'And the tree,' said Boyd. 'Is that even significant?'

Okeke shrugged again. 'Fuck knows. It's just a creepy picture that makes no sense.'

'What about the web page itself,' asked Boyd.

She nodded. 'Well, that's kind of why I came round. Your IT mate Sunny. Could he take a look at the HTML code? See if he can work out who put this web page up?'

Boyd shook his head. 'I've put more than enough asks his way lately. What about Jay's brother?'

'I messaged Karl last night,' she replied. 'He hasn't come back to me yet. I guess he's too busy making loads of money.'

She pulled her phone out to check if he had actually responded. 'My bad. I just missed call from him.' She hit the call icon and put it on speakerphone.

He answered almost immediately. 'Sam?'

'Hey there,' she replied. 'You got my WhatsApp, then?'

'Yeah,' Karl replied. 'And hit the link. Weird picture.'

'Yeah, me and Boyd were just thinking the same thing.'

'Listen, I've already had a look at the web code. Sam, this is dodgy stuff.'

'Yeah, right? Listen, I'm on speakerphone and Boyd's right here.'

'Hey there,' said Karl.

'Hi, Karl. You okay?' said Boyd.

'Yuh. Fine.' Karl sounded as though he wanted to dump the small talk and get on with what he had to say. 'Look, Sam, that webpage is a search trap.'

'What's that?' she asked.

'It's a page specifically designed to be the top hit for a particular series of key words. You hit the link, you arrive at the page. The page can be anything – a fake ad or blog, whatever – but the point is, as soon as you arrive, the page quietly harvests your IP address.'

'You think it does that?' asked Boyd.

'I *know* it does that,' replied Karl. 'I looked at the code and identified the two lines that do exactly that job.'

'Shit.' Boyd reached for his mouse and clicked to close his browser.

'Was that you shutting your browser down, Sam?' Karl asked.

Boyd cleared his throat. 'Uh-hum. Yup, that was me. She's on *my* computer.'

'Well, it's too late,' replied Karl. 'Somebody, somewhere, now knows you're interested in whatever that page is all about.' He paused. 'Unless you've got an IP blocker,' he added hopefully.

Boyd remembered Sunny had installed one of those on his PC a while back. 'Yeah, I think I do, actually.'

'Good. Then it won't have grabbed your number. What about you, Sam?'

'No,' she replied. 'No, I used my laptop at home.'

They heard Karl draw in a long breath. 'Look, I don't want to sound all creepy and weird, but this is kind of stalker-like. Whoever's behind the web page – and I'm guessing they're more savvy than your average hacker –

they'll also now know your IP details, Sam. And if they know that, it'll be a piece of piss for them to extract a location, even an address.' He paused. 'Someone knows who you are and where you live, sis.'

'Great. Thanks, Karl.'

'Just saying what I'm seeing, Sam. Look, it might just be some kind of a scamming thing. But, either way, you're on someone's list now.'

14

Jeremy Warner was very much looking forward to retirement. He was sixty-five years old and he was damned if he was going to push through to the government's new, mandated sixty-seven in order to be eligible for a state pension. He had savings. He had a private pension. Maybe sometime this year or next, he could hand the keys to the kingdom over to Moira to run the department, until it was either downscaled again or, more likely, mothballed completely.

He just needed, for his own peace of mind, to hang on until the oldest file in his in-tray had been closed and shredded. A metaphorical in-tray, of course; it wasn't as if the cases that remained outstanding were literally papers in a dusty manila folder sitting in a plastic tray any more.

These cases were far too sensitive for that.

Back in the day, it had been a different matter. But today all the eyes-only stuff had been digitised and held in the digital equivalent of a locked filing cabinet.

And in his mind.

There were a couple that went back so far that they'd

been old, *old* news even when he'd joined the 'Boutique', tucked away down here in the basement floor of Downham Manor. And of course there had been several new ones since. The Kelly incident, for example. Nasty one that... but sorted quickly, thank goodness, and 'shredded'.

It was the oldest one that bothered him the most. The one that kept him up at night. The one he wanted to sort and shred before he could peacefully retire. The one that had loitered in this small department's watch list since before he'd been recruited.

It had a name. As they all did: nonsensical names that bore no relationship or inferred meaning to their content.

Marble Orchard.

That was the one that he wanted to see wiped off their books before he cleared his desk and shuffled out of the Boutique's dingy offices to spend his twilight years fly fishing, trimming rose bushes or trying his hand at watercolours.

Marble fucking *Orchard.*

A truly nasty one. From a very different time, over sixty years ago now, when matters of this magnitude were handled more ruthlessly. And it was his role to make damn sure that no one ever, <u>ever</u> got to learn about it. At least not while it remained on *his* watch list.

To that end, and to his immense relief, it looked as though this point, when it could be closed and purged, had finally been reached. The old chap Crowhurst, who'd been rotting away in his old people's home, had died of natural causes at long fucking last. And thankfully there was no family, no children, no partner with whom he might have shared a deathbed confession. On learning that he'd passed, Warner had begun to allow himself the hope that he could start thinking about tidying his desk very soon.

But then, just a few days after Crowhurst had died... there'd been a *ping*. A silken thread of the modest little web that he'd spun in an unassuming corner of the internet had vibrated.

A young man – one of Crowhurst's carers, it seemed – had somehow learned a little too much from the old man and had popped those words into his computer's search engine.

Warner had paid the young man, Adam Cocker, a visit. Adam had turned out to be exceedingly helpful (with a little gentle persuasion) but the visit revealed that there was an even bigger problem to deal with. It wasn't just that a senile old fart had told his carer a little too much. No... things were more complicated than that.

That silly old bitch.... What the fuck had she been thinking?

So she'd had to go too. He'd have liked to have had one last chat with the old dear beforehand, just to unpick why the hell she'd thought it was a good idea to pull this particular skeleton out of the closet and into the daylight.

So the deed was done. James Crowhurst, the old woman and the young carer were now merely three sad, completely unrelated deaths in the unassuming seaside town of Hastings.

Marble Orchard could finally be struck off the watch list.

Or so he'd thought.

Except... that goddamn spider's web had just vibrated again.

15

'Campion House Residential Home. How can I help you?'

Okeke recognised the voice of the receptionist. 'Afternoon. I visited yesterday morning,' she said. 'It's Detective Constable Samantha Okeke.'

'Ah, yes. Hello again,' came the cheerful reply.

'Could you put me through to the manager?' Okeke asked.

'Oh, sorry, Kath's not in today.'

Okeke winced. She needed to put a brake on things, if it wasn't too late. 'What about Megan? Is she in?'

'Megan O'Reilly?'

She'd neglected to take the girl's surname. 'The one who worked alongside Adam. Looking after Mr Crowhurst?' she explained.

'Oh right, yes. You want to speak to her now?' the receptionist asked.

'Please.'

'I'll see if I can find her.' The line clicked over to a warbling and distorted recording of Puccini's 'Nessun

Dorma' – the only bit of opera Jay knew. And, bless him, he sang it loudly and awfully in the shower.

As Okeke waited, her mind circled back to what Karl had told her and Boyd this morning, that she may have triggered a flag for someone, somewhere, simply by landing on that odd, sparse web page.

'I know for a fact that a lot of oppressive regimes use that technique to scoop up journos' and dissidents' IDs,' he'd told them. 'I mean, it's a clunky technique but it works. You'll get some accidental traffic to a page like that, people who've mistyped something or are just messing around. But it's a way to collect a bunch of IPs of folks typing in something like "How to kill Putin".'

Something had drawn Adam Cocker to that page. Or *someone*. It was a reach, for sure, but given that *coincidences* tended to have roots if you pulled them up and examined them... the recent death of James Crowhurst felt like a tendril worth following.

The phone clicked and the warbling opera music mercifully ceased.

'Hello?' came a timid voice. 'Am I in trouble?'

'Is that Megan?'

'Yeah.'

'It's DC Okeke,' she said. 'We spoke yesterday. And no, you're not in any trouble. I just wanted to ask you a couple more things, if that's okay.'

'Sure.'

'The stuff in Jim's room –'

'Oh, I've started clearing that out now,' Megan said.

'Where is it? What've you done with it?' Okeke asked.

'We've still got it. It's all boxed up and waiting for Trevor to take to the recycling centre later on this afternoon.'

'Megan, can you make sure he doesn't?'

'Why?'

Okeke didn't want to say 'evidence'. Evidence of what?

'Look, I just need to go through it all first.'

'But Mrs Bracy said she wants the room cleared out by the end of today,' Megan said.

'All right. How about I talk to her and tell her to keep it, just till tomorrow? I'll try to come over today, if I can. And I may need to take some of it away with me,' Okeke said.

'I suppose so… if Mrs Bracy is OK with that,' Megan said.

'Right, that's sorted, then,' said Okeke. 'And one more thing, Megan. You told me Adam went to Jim's funeral…'

'And me. I went too. We also took a couple of the residents who said they wanted to pay their respects… although, I think Sheila wasn't sure whose funeral it was,' Megan said.

'Do you remember where the funeral was held?' Okeke asked.

'Uh-huh. Grantham Woodland Crematorium.'

∼

OKEKE FOUND the place with a little difficulty. Grantham Woodland Crematorium's entrance was off a winding B-road that was overgrown and all too easily missed. Which she did twice, in fact, despite the satnav's directions.

She drove along a gravel track dappled with patches of sunlight that lanced down through a tunnel of foliage. She emerged at the other end into a kidney-bean-shaped clearing – a parking area for funeral attendees – surrounded by several very modern-looking wooden buildings. One was very much larger than the others; it was clearly the chapel, although absent of the twirls, trappings and symbols of any given faith.

She parked next to the only other car there, outside the site's reception office.

Okeke stepped inside to find a slim man with glasses and a head of woolly dark hair that had been tamed into a side parting.

He looked up from his desk and smiled. 'Can I help you?'

She lifted her lanyard. 'DC Sam Okeke, Hastings CID.'

A pair of eyebrows raised above the frame of his spectacles. 'Oh, good grief, did something awful happen?'

She went over to his desk and, as he stood up, she held out her hand. He shook it and smiled reassuringly.

'There's nothing to worry about. Mr...?'

'Dennis Hague,' he replied. 'I'm the manager.'

On the drive over, Okeke had been questioning herself as to what she hoped to achieve by coming out here. The conclusion she had reached was that she might get lucky and gather some details on who had attended Jim Crowhurst's funeral. Megan had said there hadn't been that many people there. The four of them – two carers, two residents – from the home and maybe half a dozen elderly people who she guessed might have been distant family, cousins perhaps.

'I'm after some information about a service that took place here... about four weeks ago,' she told him.

Dennis nodded, waiting to hear more.

'It was a service for a Mr James Crowhurst,' she said.

The name seemed to ring a bell. 'Ah, yes. A humanist service, if I recall. What specifically did you want to know?' Dennis asked her.

'Well, I'm hoping to find out whether there was a list of attendees.'

'A mourners list?' he offered, then shook his head. 'We

don't have that information in any formal capacity; we just ask for a rough idea of the number of people attending.'

'Ah. I see.' She glanced out of the window at the gravel car park. 'Is there any CCTV out there?'

He shook his head and came around his desk. 'Are you trying to identify someone who might have attended?'

She nodded. Not that she had a specific person in mind, and not that this visit was something she particularly wanted to add to her action log. Because it was 'hunch' policing... the kind of speculative clue-trawling that would cause Sutherland to cough and splutter.

'We film every service we hold in the hall, if that's of any help,' said Dennis. 'Sometimes relatives live too far away to attend in person, so we offer a remote-attendance option. We keep the recording for a couple of months and there's a streaming link that friends and family can use.'

'And the recording shows the guests?' she asked hopefully.

He shrugged. 'The cameras are aimed towards the lectern, the coffin and the woodland view beyond. But you might get lucky. Do you want me to show you?'

Okeke nodded and Dennis led her out of the office, across the car park and into the chapel.

'It's a non-denominational space,' explained Dennis. 'I mean, we *do* hold some religious services here, but there's nothing in here that might cause people of a particular faith any awkwardness, shall we say.'

Okeke looked around. The chapel was a very modern space; most of the walls, floor and sloped ceiling were clad with calming interlocked strips of bright pine wood. The back wall was floor-to-ceiling glass and looked out upon woodland and wild flowers. There were double doors at the bottom and wooden steps led downwards into the wood and out of view.

'Nice,' she found herself saying. 'Restful.'

Dennis nodded as he took in the same view. 'Even atheists can find something spiritually healing from a view like that.'

'I can imagine.'

'Do you mind if I enquire as to what this is about?'

Okeke was still trying to make the case in her own head as to her reason for being here. 'I'm trying to learn a little more about the man whose funeral this was.'

'This Mr Crowhurst?'

She nodded. 'We have very little information about who he was. He was in a residential home for quite some time, and apparently had no meaningful family...'

'Ah, you're trying to identify any next of kin?' said Dennis. 'Presumably for an inheritance issue?'

Okeke decided it was just easier to nod along. 'Yes.' She turned round and spotted a couple of cameras mounted on brackets. 'Those are the cameras?'

'Yes. We use both and sometimes cut between them if a celebrant or a reader moves around or too far away from the lectern.' He walked over to what looked like a pine-veneered raised platform. 'The coffin rests on this... and at the end of the service our bearers carry the coffin out through those glass doors, down the steps and onto a path that winds into the woodland and out of view.'

'To be buried there?'

He shook his head. 'No. It's meant as a symbolic departure, carried away into the trees and wild flowers. To re-join the endless circle of nature, if you see what I mean. Unlike other crematoria, we offer a more purposeful way of saying goodbye to a loved one.'

The Archive

Okeke noticed a small table, not far from the double doors, and a thick leather-bound book resting on it. 'What's that?'

'It's a book of condolences,' he replied. 'As the coffin is carried away and out of view, we invite the mourners to write a thought or a message or a line of poetry, perhaps. Usually, we have a unique one for each funeral, to give to the relatives or loved ones of the deceased, but we have this general book too. Not everyone has someone to whom we can pass on the condolences, but some attendees still want to remember write something, to commemorate the deceased.'

'Do you mind if I...?'

He nodded and led her over. He opened the cover and began to reverentially flip back through the pages. 'Ah, here we are...'

He stepped back to give Okeke a little space. In tidy copperplate handwriting at the top of the page was: *'In memory of James Arnold Crowhurst 11/09/34 – 13/08/23.'*

There just six messages. She saw rounded handwriting that looked vaguely familiar – the same as the imprinted words on the Post-it notepad: *We were all very fond of you, Jim. I loved the stories you shared with me and the time we had together. Rest in peace, my old friend – Adam Cocker.*

Above and below it were bland, perfunctory messages signed with names that meant nothing to her.

But at the bottom, the very last one caught her eye: *And finally, James, someone will share your story.*

Beneath those words, a scrawled signature that was barely legible. Okeke peered closer to unpick the loops and swirls of the handwriting.

Eleanora Baxendale.

16

Okeke struggled to keep her driving speed down to something sensible as she hastened back to the station. She had in her bag a memory stick with Jim Crowhurst's funeral service on it – and that was all, literally all, she wanted to look at right now... She needed a good look at the mourners who'd been gathered around that book of condolences at the end of the service. To see who'd written that final comment.

And finally, James, someone will *share your story.*

All of a sudden, the name Eleanora Baxendale felt to Okeke like the almost-invisible gossamer thread that tied several things together: the woman who'd died in the house fire, Adam Cocker's suicide and Jim Crowhurst's funeral. Both Eleanora and Adam had lived in Ore. Was *that* a connection? Had they known each other? And if those things *were* somehow linked, then either her accidental death or Adam's suicide, or even both, now had to be viewed as potentially suspicious.

And then, of course, there was that creepy-looking web page that was designed to stealthily harvest IP addresses.

She pushed through CID's double doors, just as DCI Flack and his team were all heading out for an end-of-the-day pint. She careered straight into him.

'Whoa!'

'Sorry, sir!'

He smiled and frowned at the same time. 'You all right there, Okeke? Is something urgent going on?'

'Just something I want to get done today... sir.' She glanced at her watch. It was gone five thirty. Campion House would definitely have to wait till tomorrow.

Flack nodded in understanding, and Okeke sidestepped him, hurrying towards her desk. As she logged on and sat down, she looked around. Both Warren and O'Neal appeared to have gone for the day.

She slipped the memory stick into her keyboard's USB port and double-clicked on the file. A media-player window popped up on the screen, showing a view of Grantham Woodland's chapel. A title appeared – 'In Celebration of the Life of' – and it crossfaded to: 'James Arnold Crowhurst'.

Calming classical music played in the background, something she vaguely recognised but wouldn't have a chance in hell of naming. Then she could hear hushed voices, and finally the backs of heads came into view as the mourners arrived and took their place on the wooden chairs set out before the lectern.

A young woman appeared. She took her place behind the lectern and waited patiently for the soft murmuring of voices to cease and the classical music to fade before she began to speak.

'Welcome, everyone, to this celebration of the full and long life of James – Jim to his friends – Crowhurst. My name is Emily, and I'm here this morning as your humanist celebrant, to help you –'

Okeke sped up the video, already irritated by the celebrant's sincere and supposedly soothing voice. The celebrant fast-forward wriggled through her opening dialogue, then a young man stood up and took over from Emily at the lectern.

Adam.

Okeke stopped fast-forwarding as he unfolded a sheet of paper.

'My name's Adam Cocker. I work at the residential home where Jim's been for... well, far longer than me anyway. And over the years that I've been there, I formed a very close friendship with Jim.' She could hear his voice wobbling already: a mixture of grief and probably nerves too.

'I know that Jim lived a very full life, because the clues are there in his room. Photos of his army days; from his time as a teacher in several different boarding schools... pictures of his travels...'

Okeke made a mental note of the time signature and resolved to listen to Adam's words more carefully later, but for now what she desperately wanted to see – and she had her fingers crossed for this – was a clear shot of the woman who'd signed the book of condolences. The woman who was going to be suffocated to death by deadly fumes just weeks later.

The figures on the screen jiggled and fidgeted away at high speed until, at last, six pall-bearers sped into shot, hefted the coffin onto their shoulders and raced the coffin out through the glass doors and down the steps.

She stopped fast-forwarding again. Another piece of classical music she vaguely recognised faded to nothing. The mourners were now on their feet, approaching the glass wall, watching the coffin disappear into the woodland.

Okeke counted nine people. One in a wheelchair being

pushed by Megan. She noticed Adam, his head dipping frequently and a hand coming up to his face. Megan rubbed his shoulders supportively.

Tears. He's crying.

Okeke concentrated on the other figures in view. Old people, all very old, which didn't surprise her. Other than Megan and Adam, it seemed that there was no one below the age of seventy in attendance. And no one who looked like he could be his grandson. So, perhaps she was looking at distant relatives, or old colleagues from the schools he'd worked at...

She saw the celebrant invite them to write in the book of condolences.

Okeke leaned forward, her finger on the mouse button ready to pause and rewind. She watched a stick-thin man, with a fuzz of white hair, write a message, then another one came forward, then Adam... taking his time. He was followed by a couple more people.

Then a woman stepped up. It had to be her. Eleanora Baxendale. Small, round-shouldered, with fine, wavy, snow-white hair held back from her face by an Alice band, she took the pen and leaned over the book.

Okeke paused. Then played, then paused again as the woman finished signing her name, turned round and approached Adam.

Adam's head bobbed as the old woman spoke. Clearly she was comforting him. His eulogy had obviously made an impression on her. Finally, there was a brief awkward hug between them, then the old woman did something else.

She took Adam's hand in hers. It was only for a second or two, and then she turned and walked swiftly away, out of view, out of the hall.

Okeke watched as Adam peered down at whatever the

woman had placed in his hand, then up, perhaps randomly, at the camera.

For a moment, Okeke felt as though the young man was looking directly at her, imploring her to keep going, to keep asking questions, to keep digging...

17

Warren was actually winning, for perhaps the first time ever. *Yes.* This was definitely a first for him – he was right there at the top of the leaderboard, just one kill above the next player down: nOObFix3r.

He could hear this 'Noobfixer' taunting him over the comms; he had an American accent, appalling language, and his voice had been disguised with a baritone filter that made him sound like some booming Nordic deity. (Which, Warren presumed, meant he was barely pubescent and still waiting for 'the boys' to drop).

The bullets were zinging either side of Warren, as he maintained his zig-zagging, bunny-hopping backwards run, while spraying back his own blizzard of bullets. More shots were landing on Noobfixer than on himself, with health bars on both sides in a race to the bottom. And Noobfixer was going to get there first.

That was all that mattered. Warren was going to hand this annoying little brat a teachable moment. He was going to –

The headphones were wrenched off his ears.

'What? Hey... Muuum!'

'Your! Bloody! Phone!'

His mother was looming over him in a bathrobe. Her hair was whipped up into a towel turban – and her still-wet face was florid with exasperation. She had his work phone in one damp hand and thrust it at him.

'Don't leave it in the bathroom again!' she hissed. 'Not when I'm trying to have some peaceful me time!'

He took it from her timidly, and she stomped back up the stairs to the bathroom muttering to herself.

'Ah, fucknuts,' he grunted as he glanced back at the TV screen. He was dead. He looked down at the phone to see who'd just ruined his night.

Only he hadn't missed the call. It was active. He put the phone to his ear. 'Okeke?'

'*Hey, Mu-u-u-u-u-um,*' Okeke whined down the phone at him like a teenage air-raid siren. Then she broke into a phlegmy cackle, sounding very much like an evil witch.

'Hey, Okeke... just piss right off, will you?'

'It'll be "piss right off... *sarge*" soon,' she replied, cackling again.

Warren settled back on his beanbag and watched the leaderboard as 'nOObFix3r' leapfrogged above him.

'What's up? Why're you calling me at home?' he asked.

'I'm calling you on your work phone – which is what they're for, right? In case you don't happen to be *at* work.'

'Fine,' he snapped impatiently. 'Well, what do you want?'

'That house fire you went over to look at...' she began.

'Yeah.' He turned his Xbox off. 'What about it?'

'So, you told me she was called Eleanora Baxendale, the old woman who died.'

'Yeah, that's it. Baxendale. You've got a good memory.' He paused. 'Why?'

'And the fire inspector didn't think the fire was at all suspect?'

'Not so far,' replied Warren. 'But he said he was going to investigate and send me a report. Anyway, why are you asking?'

'And what about the body?' pressed Okeke, clearly ignoring his question. 'You said something about a wheelchair, didn't you?'

'Yeah,' he replied. 'They found one next to her bed. Or what was left of it anyway.'

Warren heard Okeke take a drag on a cigarette, then blow it out. 'Well, I reckon that body they pulled out of the house can't have been Baxendale's.'

'Huh?' Warren straightened up on the beanbag; she had his attention now. 'What? How so?'

He heard Okeke pulling on her cigarette again. 'You and I need to talk. In person.'

'What? Now?'

'Yeah.'

'Uh... no,' he replied firmly. 'I'm home. I'm done for the day. I'm actually in my PJs. Can't it wait?'

'*PJs?* What are you... a toddler? For God's sake, it's not even seven!' she huffed.

Warren bit his bottom lip and balled a fist in his lap. 'I like to get out of my work clothes and kick back when I get home.'

Okeke let out a long sigh. 'Fine. Jesus. First thing tomorrow, then.'

18

Jeremy Warner turned off the country road into the driveway for Downham Manor. The brown road sign marked the entrance and was almost obscured by the low-hanging willow branches looming over it.

He approached the Regency-era building. The CIA staff who worked here had an irritating habit of calling it *Downton* Manor. It was surrounded by well-tended rose bushes and a nicely striped lawn that was good enough to play cricket on. He nodded at one of the old gardeners, Graham, as he passed. Graham had been working the manor's grounds for as long as Warner could remember. Certainly he was there when Warner had started working at Downham. Graham nodded a greeting in return and resumed deadheading the roses.

Warner pulled into his reserved parking spot on the far left of the grand entrance portico. The chief director and the Americans had their more prestigious slots closer to the main entrance, but the majority of the gravel car park was available on a first-come-first-served basis. His might be the most remote reserved spot but, at least it was reserved.

He blipped his BMW with the fob to lock it and then headed inside.

The reception was in the manor's entrance hall, high-ceilinged and naturally lit by the tall windows. On the walls hung a number of large paintings that depicted fox hunts and shooting parties – a procession of chinless nobles in absurdly flamboyant and impractical outdoor wear. As Oscar Wilde once said: 'The unspeakable in pursuit of the uneatable.'

'Good morning, sir.'

He nodded crisply at the receptionist. 'Morning, Daisy.'

The front desk was mainly for show. If some wandering tourist had been seduced by the brown English Heritage sign, Daisy was there to politely inform them the manor was closed today for some much-needed maintenance and that there was actually a very nice English Heritage site a mere half-mile further along the road towards Downham.

Warner pressed his pass against the reader and a light blipped green. There was no gate or turnstile to unlock or swish open, just an acknowledgement that Jeremy Warner, Director of Section Nine, was logged as 'in'.

'Early start?' asked Daisy.

He nodded and returned her friendly smile. 'Bits and pieces, m'dear. The usual bits and bloody pieces.'

She laughed politely. 'Not for much longer, eh?'

Everyone at Downham Manor knew that Jeremy Warner was getting ready to hang up his hat and coat. Partly because it was common knowledge that Section Nine – quaintly referred to the section's dozen staff as the Boutique – was operating on a winding-down budget. The Boutique was a legacy department; the time it had left to run was mapped against the few case files it had left to deal with – or not. Its sole purpose seemed to be to outlive a number of names on a list, then quietly, without any fuss, end itself.

Warner crossed the hall towards a rear doorway that led to what was once Downham Manor's kitchens and pantry. He nodded at one of the other section directors, who was taking the grand stairs up to the first floor: a man half his age, slim, fit, well groomed and, naturally, American. The CIA had a large footprint in the building. Of course they did. In their eyes, the British didn't have the wit to oversee their own clandestine affairs. Supervising adults were required.

Warner stepped through the dark oak door and into the old kitchens, repurposed as the on-site security team's centre of operations.

'Morning, gents,' he said.

The officers on duty waved him an acknowledgement as he produced his pass and waved it at the reader on the door to the old wine-cellar stairs. Section Nine.

The light blipped green, the door clicked, and he stepped down into the clinically lit, subterranean world that had been his day job for the last twenty-five years. He clacked down the stone steps to an open basement space that was punctuated by arches made from crumbling old brick. Dotted around the edges were occasional nooks where oak barrels of mead, ale or wine had once stood. However, the twentieth century had stamped its mark: thick braids of ethernet cables hung in loops from the ceiling, hessian-covered partition screens divided the uneven floor into cubicles, and a water cooler gurgled next to a vending machine that still accepted coins. He nodded to a few of his underlings as he picked his way through the mini labyrinth to his office at the far side.

His office and the briefing room next door were sealed

Perspex boxes, in a thick steel framework, with blinds for privacy. They were the only two spaces in which their dwindling number of operational cases could be openly discussed. The kind of hushed conversations that drifted over the partitions tended to be along the lines of 'Mind if I borrow your hole puncher?'

He waggled his ID again. The reader by his office door flashed green and an unseen bolt slid aside. He stepped in, closed the door behind him, hung his flat cap and jacket on a hook and sat down at his desk.

Even the IT equipment down here was twentieth century. Some of it, at least. His monitor was one of those old beige ones that ate up desk space with their large behinds. His mouse still had a ball and runners in it. He clicked the mouse and logged on to the Boutique's operating portal and headed straight to his inbox.

There were just three emails waiting for him this morning. The first was an alert that one of the watch-list names for case seven, codenamed Queen of Hearts, had gone into hospital for a heart bypass. There was always the chance (and the hope) that the operation would encounter a snag and they could strike another one of those parasitic weasels off the list. What and who they'd glimpsed in the back of that Mercedes-Benz as they chased it through Paris was something the remaining four men were going to take to the grave with them.

One way or another.

The second message had come in from 'above' and was a request for the Boutique's quarterly budget review. Those Who Signed Cheques were very keen to see a steady downward tick in his budget allocation and the eventual retirement of Warner's little fiefdom. Section Nine was a throwback to different times, different methods: frankly an embarrassment to the British Security Service as a whole.

They were down here monitoring the mess left behind from other departments' mistakes. Warner and his shrinking band of merry men (and women) were the long tail-end of 'cleaners' responsible for mopping up operational fuck-ups from the past. And there were many: the double execution in Gibraltar, the false intel cover-up of the *Belgrano*, the Mountbatten coup attempt... and of course, going back... there was *Marble Orchard*.

The third email was a report from Gary Nottridge. Warner had asked young Gary to take a quick look at the recent cluster of 'flies' that had twanged their spider's web. His report listed the incidents, times of occurrence, durations the page had been left open and of course, most usefully, the IP addresses of those that had gone there.

Warner scrutinised the report. There'd been a flurry of activity a few weeks ago. That he knew about, and, of course, it had been recently taken care of. It hadn't been an easy job to authorise truth be told. The hanging of that young man from a tree had been unpleasant. Warner had a lovely nephew his age. But far worse had been dealing with Eleanora.

Ellie had once been the head of the Boutique.

His boss. And, he liked to think, his friend once upon a time too.

He'd been reassured by the pathologist's report that the old woman had died of smoke inhalation and had been found in her bed.

Almost certainly she 'died in her sleep and that should have been an end to it.

So then... why the hell had this Samantha Okeke been visiting his web page?

19

Okeke was in her Datsun thinking about Jay as she waited for the rubbish collection truck to inch its way along the promenade, emptying the wheelie bins for the townhouses and flats along Pelham Crescent.

He'd not called her yesterday to say goodnight. Or even texted her with some dirty innuendo made all right at the end with a kiss. Sure he'd called on the first night, with the sound of a pub and a raucous crowd in the background. But not yesterday, not for the usual final sign-off at ten when he knew she'd be tucked into bed and 'fannying around' on her phone for a few minutes until her eyes had had enough.

It was unlike him. It *wasn't* him. Jay was dependable, predictable like clockwork. They'd been together three and a half years, and every night he'd had to work a late shift at the club, every night he'd been out for a pint with Louis, or over in Brighton for the occasional sleep-over at Karl's, he'd always called her bang on ten.

But last night. Nothing.

She took one last pull on her fag, wound down her

window and dropped the stub onto the road. The car behind her honked. She considered replying with a middle finger, but instead just closed her window.

What's going on there, Jay?

The one thing that had drawn her to him had been his steady, calm demeanour. A stable platform in what had been, back then, her topsy-turvy life. Sometimes he could be a little too predictable, a touch unimaginative, but he was her safe space. Her rock.

In recent months, ever since Louie's murder, she'd noticed him changing. He seemed to be going through some kind of reinvention of himself. He was too young for her to call it a mid-life crisis, but it bore all the same markers: the new interests, the career change, the sudden need to rediscover himself.

Her phone buzzed on the passenger seat. Since it looked as if she wasn't going to be moving for another few minutes, she answered the call. 'DC Okeke.'

'It's Dr Palmer...' came the reply.

'You're early,' Okeke commented.

'Not really. I'm usually in at seven,' Palmer said. She sounded hurried, as though she was keen to press on. 'I took another look at your suicide and also the house fire victim that came in on Monday,' she began, 'and...'I think your suicide... could have been... suspicious.'

'What?' Okeke exclaimed.

'The toxicology report showed significant alcohol in his blood –' Palmer said

'Yes, you mentioned that before,' Okeke cut in, keen to hear the new information.

'Which was masking traces of ketamine. That's the –'

'The date rape drug,' Okeke finished for her.

'Yes. Exactly. It's normally administered by injection... I

had a hunch, so I checked his body, looking for a needle mark, and I found one.'

'Shit.'

'Oh yes,' Palmer agreed. 'It was very cleverly placed. In his neck. I missed it first time round because of the abrasions and bruising caused by the ligature. Whoever injected him did it very deliberately there, knowing that very soon afterwards there would be a noose covering it.'

Okeke felt a spike of adrenaline hit her and she fumbled in her bag for another cigarette. 'So... Adam Cocker was plied with alcohol, sedated, then hung?'

'Hanged,' Palmer corrected. 'But, yes, that's how I'm reading it.'

The rubbish truck edged forward and the cars queuing behind it did the same in its wake. Okeke lit up and slipped into first gear to crawl forward. 'Right. Okay.'

'And the old woman who died in the fire,' said Palmer. 'Eleanora Baxendale...'

'Don't tell me... The same thing?'

'No. She died of smoke inhalation. Nothing suspicious there. Stomach contents and bloods indicated a small amount of alcohol, a very mild sedative... Nytol perhaps. I can confirm, too, that she wasn't able to walk.'

Okeke frowned. 'Actually, she *could*.'

'No, that's not possible,' Palmer said.

'I know for a fact that she could walk,' Okeke said, remembering the video of the woman walking quite steadily to the book of condolences.

Palmer didn't bother asking how she was so certain. 'Well, the woman I examined had chronic osteoporosis in her hips and pelvis. She'd not have been able to stand, let alone walk. So, one of us is wrong.' She paused. 'I know I shouldn't try putting the detective hat on, but... are you sure there hasn't been some sort of a mix-up with the body?'

'The woman was ID'd as Eleanora Baxendale,' said Okeke. 'And a few weeks ago she was perfectly able to walk.'

'ID'd as in "Yep, this is one hundred percent Eleanora Baxendale"? Or...' Palmer paused, aware that she was about to sound rude. 'ID'd as in "This is the name we have for that address – that's good enough"?'

Okeke's first instinct was to snap back with something snarky. But then she remembered the body had gone to Conquest Hospital and then been bumped along to Ellessey due to the pathologist's workload there. It hadn't been considered suspicious... and so the mismatch between the body on the table and the medical records hadn't been picked up on. Until now.

'I'm not pointing a finger at anyone,' continued Dr Palmer. 'I just don't think I have Eleanora Baxendale lying in front of me.'

∼

EMMA OPENED the front door to take out the rubbish and came face to face with Okeke, hand raised and about to knock.

'Oh, hello, Sam.' She peered around her and spotted Warren standing just behind. 'And hello there... Ed. You guys here to see, Dad?'

Okeke nodded. Emma beckoned them in and led them to the lounge. Boyd was spread out on the sofa, toast on a plate that was resting on his belly, crumbs on his chest and wearing a pair of lime-green boxers and a grubby old *Red Dwarf* T-shirt. His hairy feet were on the arm of the sofa and Mia, who was perched beside them, was dutifully giving him a pedicure, licking away at his toes and the gaps between them. Ozzie's focus remained firmly on the toast.

'Visitors,' Emma said cheerfully.

Boyd turned to see his colleagues enter and lurched. 'Jesus!'

He lowered his feet out of sight and sat up, crumbs, crusts and Mia spilling down onto the floor. 'Christ... A bit of warning next time, Ems!' he grumbled as he reached for the remote control and muted *Homes Under the Hammer*.

'Bad timing, guv?' asked Okeke with the ghost of a smile on her lips, as Ozzie and Mia made short work of the scraps on the floor.

'I just... Well, you're not exactly catching me at my best,' said Boyd.

'Relax.' Okeke smiled. 'It's good to see you taking it easy for once.'

Warren offered Boyd a furtive wave. 'How're you doing there, sir? Nice pants!'

Boyd brushed himself down and self-consciously pulled a cushion over his bare, knobbly knees. 'So what is this? Business or...'

'Business,' replied Okeke. 'If that's okay?'

Five minutes later, Boyd had some jogging pants and flip-flops on, and the three of them were in his small study.

'Murdered? Are you sure?'

Okeke and Warren nodded. 'Definitely Adam Cocker. The old woman... I don't know, maybe,' she added. She shared with him what Palmer had told her earlier. 'Teetotal Adam Cocker was force-fed alcohol, sedated with ketamine and then hanged.'

'Right.' Boyd nodded thoughtfully. 'And this old woman... What was her name? Baxter?'

'Baxendale,' said Warren. 'But we believe...' He glanced

at Okeke; she nodded at him to go for it. 'We believe that the body pulled from the house wasn't Eleanora Baxendale but someone else.'

'The dead woman couldn't walk. And Eleanora certainly could,' Okeke told him.

'You know that how?' Boyd asked.

Okeke told him about the footage of the funeral, and seeing the woman, able-bodied, writing in the book and walking away.

'So the body's a friend? Family? Someone staying?' offered Boyd.

Okeke shrugged. 'Probably. We're looking into any friends or family that Eleanora had. But the body that was recovered from the house certainly wasn't Eleanora's.'

'Which begs the question... whose is it?' said Boyd. They both nodded. 'And where's this Baxendale woman?'

'There's something else, guv,' said Okeke. 'I saw her talk to Adam Cocker after the funeral service for Jim Crowhurst.'

Boyd frowned.

'The old man in the residential home/ The one Adam Cocker was particularly close to. The funeral was recorded,' she explained. 'After the service, after the coffin was taken out, the guests were invited to sign a book of condolences. I saw Eleanora Baxendale talking to Adam Cocker. She gave him something.'

'What?' Boyd asked.

'I couldn't see. It was something small. A piece of paper maybe. It could have been her phone number.' Okeke shrugged noncommittally. 'It looked like she was reaching out to Adam.'

'And a few weeks later he winds up dead...' Boyd filled in.

'And then her house burns down and she's seemingly dead too,' added Warren.

'Except, she isn't,' replied Okeke. 'She's missing.'

Boyd glanced at his computer monitor. 'Do you think... she gave him those three words to look up that web page?'

'I don't know,' Okeke replied. 'It's possible.'

'Or maybe she arranged to meet with him later?' offered Warren.

'But the common link between them,' said Okeke, 'is that they both knew Crowhurst.'

'What have you got on him?' asked Boyd.

'His belongings are boxed up at the residential home. And that includes a whole bunch of his notebooks. They look like diaries... journals...'

'Have you been through them yet?' Boyd asked.

She shook her head. 'I need to head over there to get his stuff.'

'So, two murders very possibly linked – and one may be mistaken identity?' Boyd stroked his beard thoughtfully. 'Okay, well you know what to do... This needs to go up to Sutherland and Her Madge.'

20

Chief Superintendent Hatcher took a moment to process what she'd just been presented with, then turned to DSI Sutherland for his thoughts.

'Ian?'

'Well, clearly, we're going to need a more senior officer to SIO this, given it's now a murder enquiry. But Boyd's off and Flack's busy, so...'

'DI's good enough,' said Hatcher.

He puffed his cheeks and let out a deep breath through his lips, almost blowing a raspberry. 'I mean, yes, that rank at the bare minimum. But we've only got two of those available. DI Fox is heading off to Brighton in the next few weeks, and then there's...'

Hatcher closed her eyes. She knew what was coming.

'DI Abbott.'

She sighed. 'Can't we pull someone out of Flack's team?'

Sutherland grimaced. 'That's a tricky one. All his seniors are well and truly embedded in Operation Rosper. If we can pull any out, they'd be DCs.' He nodded at Okeke and Warren. 'And we already have two going spare.'

'What about your floating DS, the aspiring catalogue model?' Hatcher said.

'Minter?' Sutherland shook his head. 'Oh, no, no, no... can't do that to the poor man. He's been hitting the midnight oil for the last week. His inspectors' exam is tomorrow.'

'Then... what about you?' Hatcher asked him.

Sutherland's ruddy face blotched and his mouth flapped open and closed a couple of times. 'I... uh... I suppose I could *oversee* the investigation, but we do need someone at inspector level out and about and running the case.'

'Well, in that case, and it pains me to say this.... DI Abbott it is, then.' Hatcher sighed. 'Is he match-fit to run a murder investigation?' She turned to look at Okeke and Warren, the question addressed to them as well as Sutherland.

'Uhhh...' Okeke managed to squeeze out.

'That doesn't exactly sound like high praise,' said Hatcher. Her eyes settled on Warren, who fidgeted uncomfortably under her gaze. '

I... uh... I'm... errr...'

Hatcher sighed again. 'I'm getting the distinct impression that neither of you have that much confidence in him.'

They looked at each other and then back at Hatcher.

Okeke spoke up. 'He'd need a lot of hand-holding, ma'am.'

'We *do* have to tack a DI or above on for something like this,' said Sutherland. 'However –' he glanced at Okeke – 'for the record, Abbott could be SIO. But if he's kept busy shuffling the paperwork....'

Okeke grinned. DI Abbott could occupy himself with the action log and evidence log, leaving her and Warren to do the heavy lifting.

'Well, let's move forward on that basis,' said Hatcher.

She looked down at her notepad. 'One more question. Are we running this as one case or two?'

'They're definitely linked, ma'am,' said Okeke. 'If we have two teams, two enquiries, we might miss out on anything that falls between them.'

'Right,' said Hatcher. 'You'd better go and get Abbott up to speed. And one more thing… this missing old woman, Baxendale? She's got to be the highest priority. If she's wandering around, I don't know, confused, bewildered…'

'We might need to put something out to the public,' said Sutherland.

'Perhaps a press release?' suggested Okeke. 'Or a press conference?'

'Press conference,' said Hatcher. 'It's been several days now. We don't want it to look as if we're not giving this our A-game.'

'Oh no, not with Abbott doing it, though, for God's sake!' exclaimed Sutherland.

'You could do it, Okeke,' suggested Hatcher. 'If you're up to it?'

～

DI Abbott finished his cheesy puffs, scrunched up the packet and tossed it artfully into his bin. 'So you're saying you think this old boy Crowhurst had something to say? He knew something?'

'Right,' said Okeke. 'He shared something with Adam, and Eleanora seems to know something about his "story", and now Adam's dead and she's missing.'

'Any idea what?' Abbott asked, swiping his fingers down his leg and leaving the faint yellow of artificial colouring on his trousers.

She and Warren both shook their heads.

He glanced at the web page she'd pulled up on his monitor. 'And this website is...'

'Bait,' said Okeke. 'If you tap in those key words, this is what you get. Only, while you're wondering what that weird picture is all about, the website is quietly logging your details.'

DI Abbott reached for his mouse to close the page.

'Relax,' said Okeke. 'It's a screenshot.'

'And you think this Adam provoked his own... murder by looking this up?'

She nodded. 'My working theory is that Baxendale told him something, perhaps just those three words, perhaps a whole lot more. He looked it up, and that's how he ended up dead. And quite possibly that's why someone had a go at Eleanora, too.'

'Someone?' Abbott repeated.

'Someone,' she said again.

Abbott ran a finger back and forth across his chin. 'And Her Madge wants me running this case?'

'As SIO, yeah. Just, you know, keeping tabs on what I can come up with.'

'And me,' said Warren. 'This is *our* case.'

'Things we need to do...' she continued. 'Firstly, properly ID that body in the house. And I need to do a deep dive on Eleanora Baxendale. Also Crowhurst. Who was he? What did he know, if anything? His personal belongings are still at the residential home. I'm going to pick them up this morning.'

'Fire report,' said Warren. 'I need to chase the inspector guy for that.' He glanced at Okeke. 'It *could* have been an unfortunate accident. Just a coincidence?'

Okeke ignored him and continued, 'And Adam Cocker...

he must have had some digital device. A phone, a tablet... something.'

'I can look into that,' said Warren. 'No one leaves a zero presence on the net. That just doesn't happen.'

'Good suggestions, yes,' said Abbott. He leant forward, cracked his knuckles and prepared to take command of his keyboard. 'Well, I suppose I'd better set up a new project space and action log and –'

'One other thing. This woman's old. Really old, in her eighties, perhaps,' said Okeke. 'Hatcher says the first thing we need to do – I mean, our top priority – is make an appeal to the public. Get her photo out there.'

Abbott's face instantly blanched. 'You mean a... press conference?'

Okeke nodded. She could see by the look on his face that she'd just invoked his greatest demon. 'I can handle that bit for you, if you like?'

She wondered if he'd say something along the lines of *'No, very kind of you, Okeke, but as SIO that's probably my responsibility...'*

Instead, his mouth split into a relieved grin and colour began to return to his cheeks. 'That would be great, Okeke. Yes. You... uh... you'd better get that sorted asap.'

'And I'll go chase up the fire guy,' said Warren.

21

There were five boxes of Crowhurst's possessions waiting for Okeke at the residential home. Rather than pick through them there and then, she made the decision to haul them back to the station. One of the boxes contained the Airfix aeroplane models; they'd been stacked carefully by Megan, with bubble wrap around each one. DI Abbott zoomed over to Okeke's desk as soon as he spotted her unwrapping and studying a large four-engine bomber.

'Oooh. That's a Boeing B-17 Flying Fortress, that one,' he offered helpfully. 'I used to have one of those. May I?'

She handed it to him and he turned it over and over, closely inspecting the model like a jeweller.

'Beautiful job,' he said, handing it back to her. 'Is that box all model planes?'

She peered into it. 'I think so.'

'Be careful with the propellors. They break off very easily,' he warned her. 'Oh, and you might as well think about moving those to the Incident Room. We need to start getting set up in there.'

Okeke had no plans to unpack the box; she just wanted to check there was nothing in there that might help her excavate James Crowhurst's past. The next two boxes contained his clothes and shoes. Not a large collection given that he'd been living there for fifteen or so years. The last two boxes contained the books that had lined his shelves, including the leather-bound journals that were filled with his tidy handwriting.

'I'm going to start with Eleanora Baxendale...' Okeke said, closing the boxes back up. 'We'll need a bit more information on her for the press conference this afternoon.'

Abbott nodded eagerly. 'Yes, yes of course. All right, you'd better crack on with that first.'

Okeke shoved the cardboard boxes under her desk; she'd move them to the Incident Room later. Abbott wandered back to his own desk, sat down in front of his screen and began tapping on his keyboard, throwing a peanut M&M into his mouth every four letters or so.

'Right then,' she muttered. 'Who the hell are you, lady?'

She began by searching the main social media platforms for Eleanora Baxendale. She realised this was a little hopeful, given Eleanora's age, but a number of near-misses popped up in LinkedIn, Facebook and Instagram. There was an exact match with someone on TikTok, but a quick check – revealing a page of endless videos of Arianna Grande – confirmed that this was not the Eleanora Baxendale she was after.

On a whim, she went to the Campion House's website and hit the 'staff' link. It showed a page of head-and-shoulder portraits alongside names and roles. Adam Cocker was still on there, and the sight of his cheerful smile and green carer's smock made her pause.

No. It didn't look as though Eleanora had ever worked

The Archive

there. The trouble was definitely going to be her age. Someone of her advanced years would almost certainly have zero footprint on the internet. Okeke could go down the rabbit hole of one of the find-my-loved-ones websites, but she figured her best chance of learning anything about the woman would be to start with her house, her friends and her family.

She put in a request for Eleanora's photo, date of birth and NI number from the DVLA. Next, she navigated to the Online Land Registry's services page and clicked on 'Deeds Search'. She started filling in the online form, then realised that the search result was sitting behind a payment firewall. So she looked around for a contact number and dialled that instead. An hour later, after listening to some god-awful country-and-western on-hold music and being passed around a number of harried-sounding civil servants, she finally arrived at a line manager. After verifying her police credentials, Okeke asked if she could have access to the information immediately.

She heard just one click of a mouse and the manager suddenly, apparently, had everything there in front of her. 'Here we go,' she said cheerfully. 'I'm obviously limited with what I can tell you, but what do you need to know?'

'Well, let's start with the basics. Any contact details beyond her home address. Any next of kin,' Okeke said. It was worth a try.

The manager laughed. 'You can put in a formal request for them or try your own database if that's quicker... but you know I can't give that information out without checking first.'

Okeke rolled her eyes. 'Fair enough. What about the deeds themselves? Is there any information on where those are being held?'

'Let me see... one moment...' The on-hold music was back again.

Fuck's sake.

The music stopped. 'Hello?'

'I'm here,' said Okeke.

'We have the holding solicitors as Burkett and Granger. You want their contact details?'

'Please.'

She jotted those down, thanked the manager and hung up. Then she dialled the solicitor's number. Once again, she found herself explaining who she was and why she was calling. She worked her way through the receptionist to the conveyancing department, on to a solicitor's assistant and finally to the conveyancing solicitor himself.

'Yes, we do hold the deeds for 21 Saddle Road,' he confirmed, 'but these are stored off-site. We'd need twenty-four hours' notice to retrieve them from storage and –'

'I'm not particularly interested in viewing the deed itself,' replied Okeke. 'I'm just wondering if Ms Baxendale had any other dealings with yourselves? Any will? Any power-of-attorney arrangements?'

'Well, that's a different department,' came the reply. 'You'll need to talk to one of the solicit–'

'Yeah, but I have *you* now,' she cut in, exasperated. 'So, rather than start over again, can you just find out who specifically I need to speak to... and just transfer me?'

'Um, not really, Ms....'

'DC Okeke,' she said.

He didn't bother repeating her name. 'I can direct you back to –'

'As I've explained, this is a police enquiry about a missing person. It's quite urgent.'

She heard the man sigh, and she was back on hold, this

time with Rick Astley for company. One insanely irritating verse and chorus later, she was through to a woman who introduced herself as Diane Ryman. Okeke explained who she was and what she was after. Again.

'Yes, Ms Okeke, yes... I can see we do hold a will for Eleanora Baxendale in our storage facility.'

'So, is there a digitised, *scanned* version you could access right now?' Okeke asked.

'Hmmm... looking at our records, the will was lodged with us thirty-one years ago. So, that's quite a while back.'

'Right, I know. But...'

'No,' replied Diane Ryman. 'We don't keep digital records that far back. And, in any case, a will is a sealed document. Only a named executor can open and view it.'

'Do you have a name, there on the screen?' asked Okeke. 'For the executor?'

'Uh-huh,' Diane was sounding flustered now. 'The name I have here is for her sister, Matilda Baxendale.'

Okeke jotted the name down on her pad. 'Is she the sole executor?'

'I think I've told you enough,' Diane said. 'If you want to see the will, you'll have to get approval from the Office of the Public Guardian, make an appointment and then come in.'

Okeke thanked the woman for her help and ended the call. She tapped the name into Google, fully expecting the same disappointing results, but instead there were a couple of hits.

22

'Good evening, everyone. Thanks for turning up at such short notice.'

Okeke glanced at the faces packed into the small press room and wondered what the hell it was with Minter's and Abbott's stage fright. There were fifty people or thereabouts; it wasn't as if she was doing open mic night at Wembley Stadium.

She looked down at the briefing that she, Warren and Abbott had hastily assembled less than an hour ago. There were some phrases she'd have to change on the fly, but nothing she couldn't ad-lib easily enough.

'My name is DC Samantha Okeke from Hasting's CID. We called this press conference at short notice because we now have an ID for the woman who died in the fire on Saddle Road last weekend. In relation to the same incident, we also have an urgent missing persons case...' She took a breath. 'We have reason to believe that it was one Matilda Baxendale who died in the fire, a woman in her eighties who was wheelchair bound. The pathologist's report states that she was overcome by the fumes of the house fire and died of asphyxiation. The report by fire inspection officer, Mark Wells, states that there was evidence of an accelerant near the front door of the house and just inside, clearly indicating that this was an act of arson, and as a result of that information this is now a murder enquiry.'

Okeke glanced down at her crib sheet. 'The property was also occupied by one Eleanora Baxendale, sister to the deceased and owner of the property. Eleanora is a woman in her mid eighties and is believed to have been resident at the house at the time of the fire. She was the full-time carer for her sister. She has not been seen since the incident and is now classed as a missing person and a person of interest.

'Given her age, we are extremely concerned for her welfare, especially as she may be suffering from injuries sustained in the fire, and we ask that any information on her whereabouts be directed to Hastings CID contact line...' She turned to point to a poster on the wall behind her. 'The number's right there but you can also contact us via our website.'

She checked her crib sheet. Done. A doddle. Jesus, literally, a piece of piss.

'I'll now take a couple of questions,' she said, looking confidently at her audience.

∽

BOYD WATCHED the TV screen as Okeke craned her neck and cupped her ear to hear better.

'Sorry could you repeat that?'

'Do the police have any idea of motive with regard to the arson?'

She shook her head. 'At this stage we're keeping our

minds open on motive and on any possible suspects.' She pointed to someone else in the press room. 'Yes?'

Boyd smiled proudly as he watched her confidently fielding the press. He realised he needed to up his game. *She's better than me at this.*

'Could this have evolved from a neighbourhood dispute?'

Okeke tilted her head as though she was giving the question some thought. 'I'd say it's unlikely, but anything is possible. As I said, we are keeping our minds open. Yes?'

'Jack Flynn, *Argus*... Who's the SIO on this case?'

Good bloody question. Boyd wondered who the hell they'd pulled in to run the case, given that Minter was spoken for and DI Fox was clearing his in-tray. Sutherland maybe, deputising downwards? Someone sucked in from a satellite station, perhaps?

'Is it DCI Boyd?' Flynn asked.

Okeke shook her head. 'No.'

Boyd thought he heard a rustle of disappointed sighs. The local press had had fun over the last couple of years with his infamous TV-bleeped expletive, and then the press conference where he'd worn a medical dressing over one ear that had looked like a bra cup stuck to the side of his head. Apparently memes about that on the Hastings community Facebook page still lingered.

'It's DI Abbott,' answered Okeke.

Boyd resisted the urge to plant a hand on his face. All the same, he grimaced.

Charlotte looked at him. 'Is it something Sam said?'

He nodded. 'Abbott's in charge. He's a complete waste of space.'

'That's a bit harsh, isn't it?'

'No, seriously... I honestly don't know how he became a DI in the first place. He's the office motion sensor.'

'Huh?'

Boyd huffed. 'He only stirs to life and starts working when someone passes his desk.'

Charlotte tilted her head back. 'Ahh, I see.'

Okeke was busy answering a follow-on question. '... some leads, but we are obviously very keen to locate Ms Baxendale as soon as possible.' She looked around the room.

'Emma Thorpe, *Eastbourne Gazette*. The missing woman, Eleanora, was she being treated at the time for any mental conditions? Dementia? Alzheimer's?'

Okeke shook her head. 'Not that we're currently aware of. But it's something we'll be looking into.' She nodded at a lady at the back of the room.

'What about CCTV footage? Have the police managed to catch the arsonist in action?'

'That's something else we are... currently looking into,' Okeke replied.

'Is there a photograph we can use in tomorrow's edition?' asked Flynn.

She nodded. 'We have several recent images, which we'll be posting on our press-link web page in the next hour.'

'Oooh.' Charlotte pursed her lips. 'She's very *on it*.'

Boyd nodded. 'She always is.' He reached for his plate of cheese and biscuits, yet more of the hyper-bland white diet he was condemned to for the next few weeks. He sighed. 'She really should be a DI by now. She's a relentless workhorse.'

'Isn't Minter the Hunk going for that rank?' Charlotte asked.

'Yup. And Sam gets to move up to detective sergeant. But quite honestly she's ready for DI.'

'So why can't she apply for that?'

'You can't skip ranks,' he tutted. 'That's just rude.'

Charlotte turned to him. 'Isn't there some sort of fast-tracking process in the police for more capable people?'

He shrugged. 'In some forces there are.'

'But not East Sussex?'

'Nope.'

'Why not?'

He thought about it. He suspected one reason was the fact that rapidly promoted officers tended to be ambitious and impatient to bounce their way up through one transfer after another. Hatcher and Sutherland most likely would rather maintain hold of a small, well-seasoned, lower-ranked (and lower-paid) cohort of detectives than find Hastings station a constantly revolving door for climbers who gained a rank, then transferred somewhere else.

'Okeke's too good at what she does. Rank her up, and she'll be off.'

23

Warner paused the recording of the press conference on his laptop.

'Dammit!' he hissed. He looked up from his monitor to check that the glass door to his office was firmly closed. It was. Not that it mattered. Most of the Boutique's cubicles were empty now. There was just Gary Nottridge, the keen young man still at his terminal, very visibly putting in extra hours to impress him.

Warner looked back at the frozen image on his screen: a black female detective, mouth caught open, mid-answer.

Eleanora's not *dead?*

He skipped back a few seconds and ran the video again...

'*She has not been seen since the incident and is now classed as a missing person...*'

It would perhaps be too easy for him to blame those two bull-necked troglodytes of his, Drummond and Chapps, for not double-checking they'd done the job properly.

But really, they *should have*.

Warner's fingernails scratched at the old rubber mouse

mat, leaving scuff trails.

'Fucking twits!' he muttered. They'd reported back with that swaggering confidence that only long-serving military plods seemed to be blessed with. '*Marble Orchard can be closed now*,' Drummond had arrogantly announced. '*All done with, Mr Warner.*'

Only it wasn't. Not until Eleanora Baxendale's body lay stretched out on a pathologist's shiny metal slab would it be 'all done with'.

His eyes returned to the paused image of the female detective. Gary had placed a file in his in-tray an hour ago with everything he had managed to squirrel up on Detective Constable Samantha Okeke. A woman of Nigerian heritage, with a degree in forensic science, eighteen months of training as a nurse, and five years as a copper: one year in uniform with Kent, another two years in uniform with Sussex Police and, most recently, two as a detective with the same force.

Looking at the woman's surly expression on the screen, he could take a wild guess at what type of copper she was: stubborn, tenacious, quite probably unpleasant and prickly to work alongside. The kind of dogged pain-in-the-rear person who would only double down on something if politely asked to step away from it.

The fact that she'd visited the web page meant she had some kind of information in her possession. But from where? From whom? Even if it was only the three key words that had taken her there. The fact that she'd spent so many minutes on the page, even returned to it several times, suggested she knew it was important. She'd picked up the scent of something, and he very much doubted that she'd give up on it easily.

Drummond and Chapps had reported back to him that

the young care worker had met with Eleanora – they'd got that information out of him before they sedated him. And if he'd met with Ellie, then God knows what she'd shared with him.

Everything?

'Ellie, Ellie, Ellie...'

He found himself sighing. Why the hell had she decided to go rogue' after all this time? After forty years of being the hound, she'd become the fox. But for what reason? She'd run this department for forty years. She'd been his superior for fifteen years before handing him the keys to the Boutique. A lifetime of service, a lifetime of keeping this nation's grubbiest secrets locked away down here in the wine cellar... and now, all of a sudden, she'd decided the whole world *needed to know*? No, the whole world damn well *did not* need to know. What was done was done. And, more to the point, what was done had been done for the right reasons.

He glanced again at Detective Constable Samantha Okeke.

Was she the kind of copper who'd be satisfied with finding the body of the missing old woman and call it case closed? Or would she keep asking questions? Was she the sort of copper who'd continue to pick at a crusty old scab until it began to bleed? He suspected so.

He settled back in his creaking seat and pondered the Must Do's in the order they had to be done. Eleanora needed to be found and dealt with. Quickly.

Then he'd have to seriously evaluate whether this junior officer was going to have to become another unfortunate statistic.

Because some skeletons were best left buried in the past... particularly ones like *Marble Orchard*.

24

Okeke approached her desk and noticed that DI Fox was back from his course. He was slouched in his chair, glassy-eyed and absently scrolling through last night's shift report.

'All right, Foxy?' she called out as she dropped her bag on her desk.

He nodded. 'Saw you on the box last night. Good job.'

'Cheers. How was your refresher course? You got a transfer date yet?'

'Two weeks,' he replied. 'Then I'm getting the hell out of here.'

Okeke pulled a hurt face. 'Come on, Hastings isn't that dull, is it?'

'Just keen to go somewhere new,' he replied, pushing his long hair back out of his face, forming an unintentional quiff on top and two folds of greasy blond hair on either side that looked like little devil horns. 'I'm done with this place: the locals... Rosper... Flack...'

Okeke nodded, then looked around the CID bull pen; it was just the two of them. 'You seen Abbott?' she asked.

He nodded at Sutherland's goldfish bowl. She turned to see Abbott and Sutherland discussing something in his office. Abbott's head was bobbing enthusiastically; Sutherland's, as usual, looked as if it was about to drop off his narrow shoulders onto the desk and roll across into the DI's lap.

'Do you think he's getting bollocked?' asked Okeke.

Fox narrowed his eyes and pursed his lips. 'Dunno. Abbott's looking pretty pleased with himself.'

'How can you tell?'

In her opinion, Abbott had a somewhat limited range of facial expressions: mostly boredom when it came to work, and excitement for breaktimes. Even then it was only the fact you could see the whites of his eyes with the latter that determined which face he was pulling.

The conversation seemed to be coming to an end. Abbott got up and approached the door to Sutherland's office, still nodding as the DSI threw some parting comments his way. He emerged and ambled over towards Okeke and Fox nonchalantly, his hands thrust deep into his trouser pockets.

Fox chuckled. 'The super give you a big spanking for making Okeke face the press?'

Abbott's brows bobbed lazily above his eyes. 'Au contraire, Foxy.' He smiled. *He actually smiled.* Okeke would have sworn his face couldn't do that. 'You're gonna be my bitch until you transfer.'

'What?!'

'He's assigned you to my case.' Abbott's goatee spread wider, showing a tidy row of tiny yellow teeth. 'You're all mine, until you transfer.'

Fox sat up straight. 'You've gotta be fuckin' kidding me!'

'Ahem... that should be "You've gotta be fuckin' kidding

me, *guv*",' Abbott pointed out. He turned his attention to Okeke, the smug grin melting away to his normal dull-eyed stare. 'Thanks for filling in last night, though. Good job.'

She nodded. 'Have we had any calls yet?'

Abbott nodded. 'Half a dozen or so. I may get Warren or O'Neal to listen to the recordings.'

Okeke looked around. It was gone nine. 'Where are they?'

'O'Neal, no idea. Warren... morning fag, at a guess.'

'I guess *I'll* give the calls a listen, if you want?' she offered.

Abbott nodded. 'Yeah, all right.' He turned back to Fox, seemingly far more interested in assigning a task to him. 'Now then, Foxy, sunshine – ' he cracked his knuckles – 'there's a lovely big action log to update. And when you've done that you can...'

∼

OKEKE DONNED her headphones and began to work her way through the recordings. The first three were locals from Hastings, Ore and St Leonards... folks who thought they'd spotted a similar-looking woman to the driving-licence photo on Hasting CID's website in various places. One of them thought they'd spotted her at the end of the pier gazing out to sea.

The fourth was from Hector the Hoaxer – a local character well known to everyone at the station. No one knew who he actually was, nor what he looked like, as he tended to make his prank calls from various phone boxes around the town, and usually after closing time. His slurred Geordie accent was beyond mimicry.

'Hastings Police Station.'

'Oh, aye, pet – ah think ah've got some proper good intel for youse lot.'

A very long one sigh. Then: '*Hello, Hector. How are you doing this evening?*'

'*Fine, doin' jus' fine. Now listen carefully – this is all straight up outta me network o' spies...*'

The file's record showed a runtime of seven minutes. She pitied the poor sod who was on last night manning the line. She decided to skip through the rest of Hector's drunken ramblings.

The next call was short. But it caught her attention. The caller sounded female, though it was a croaky voice that could be mistaken for a higher-register male voice. She played it again.

'Hastings Police Station.'

Pause.

'I need to speak directly to Detective Constable Samantha Okeke.'

'I'm afraid we don't transfer through to individual officers. However, all calls are recorded and then passed on to the...'

The recording ended with a click followed by a *brrrr*.

Okeke listened to it again. Female? Male? She still couldn't be sure, but the caller sounded old, definitely old. The vowels had the prim and proper sounds of an old-school BBC announcer.

She checked the data record for this call. Just like Hector's, it had been made from a public phone booth. The prefix number from the phone booth was one she recognised as being in Sussex, perhaps from Brighton or Eastbourne.

Okeke made a copy of the recording and dropped into

the evidence folder that Abbott had set up yesterday. She then listened to the last two recordings, one from a well-intentioned caller who thought he'd seen Eleanora walking a dog up near Camber Sands, and another caller who was convinced she'd been served soup by the old woman in a teashop. The 'hilarious' way the caller kept saying 'soup' gave Okeke the distinct impression it was another hoax caller.

She decided to switch tasks for a bit and take a look at Crowhurst's journals. She opened the box and stared down at the leather-bound notebooks, all very similar, with dark-blue covers and fire-engine-red spines. They were numbered on the spine, 1 to 9 but number 3 was missing. She quickly checked the other boxes of Crowhurst's possessions but came up with nothing.

Okeke picked up the first volume and started to read it. She didn't know how much time had passed, but a sudden tap on her back made her jump. It was Warren.

She pulled off her headphones. 'What's up?'

'Me and the others are heading down to the pier chippy. You coming?'

Okeke looked at her watch. It was gone one o'clock. 'Shit.'

'You've not been for a fag all morning. Are you feeling okay?' asked Warren.

She nodded at the open book in front of her. 'I just got sort of sucked in.'

'What's all that?' he asked, looking at the stack of journals on her desk.

'They're Jim Crowhurst's diaries,' she told him.

'Anything interesting?'

'Interesting, sure. But nothing that seems relevant so far.'

She looked up at him. 'Can you bring me back a veggie sausage roll, if they're still doing them?'

She watched Warren and Abbott join the mass exodus of Flack's brigade as they emerged from behind their partition and headed out for lunch. Then it was just her and Fox on the CID floor; he was tapping away, one-fingered, at his keyboard with a face like a smacked arse.

She closed the journal and paused to take stock. She'd been reading Crowhurst's spidery writing for a good couple of hours now. It appeared that he'd spent a lot of time in the retirement home recalling and recording everything that he'd done, since he was a little boy. What had she learned about him?

He'd had a normal if somewhat lonely childhood in Broxbourne, Hertfordshire. He'd been the only child of an accountant and a music teacher. Born in 1934, and brought up in a leafy village well clear of London, the Second World War had been nothing more than background noise for him. He had a few vague memories of droning bombers overhead and a damp Anderson shelter at the bottom of the garden, where he was put to bed on nights that the sirens were blaring. He'd attended a nearby grammar school, then Sandhurst to train as an army officer. His childhood, school years and officer training had filled the first journal.

The second one had covered the two years he was stationed in Egypt in charge of a regiment of reluctant and grouchy national servicemen. Then in 1955 he'd requested and had been granted a commission in the 7th Gurkha Rifles and he was assigned to the British garrison in Hong Kong. Crowhurst had seemed to be in his element there: popular with his men and fascinated by the vibrant local culture. The second journal ended in 1959, when he and his garrison were about to redeployed to a new location. Okeke could only assume that the redeployment and subsequent assignments had been recorded in the missing third volume.

The fourth journal revealed that he had moved on from the army to become a history teacher in a prep school. The entries begin at the end of November 1963, and JFK had just been assassinated.

The phone on her desk rang. Okeke looked around and saw that she had the CID floor entirely to herself.

Bloody marvellous.

She set down the journal and picked up the phone. 'CID Hastings?'

The phone line crackled. She thought she could detect a solitary breath being drawn in, or it simply could have been the line rustling with interference. Perhaps even the faint sound of a wave drawing down a beach nearby.

'Hello? You're through to CID Hastings. DC Okeke speaking.'

'Is that... *Samantha* Okeke?' A rasping, feminine voice. There was gravel in her tone and an undercurrent of breathlessness that made her sound like a long-time smoker.

'Who is this?' asked Okeke.

The line continued to crackle, then finally: 'I'm the person you've been looking for.'

'You're Eleanora Bax–'

'No! No names!' the woman hissed quickly. 'No names. They can trigger listening software.'

Okeke found herself lurching in her seat slightly and looking around to check she was still alone. She was. Even so, she found herself lowering her voice. 'Okay. No names. You... it was *your* house that...'

'Was set on fire. Yes.' Another pause. 'And it was my sister who died in it.'

'She was murdered,' Okeke offered.

'Murdered... exactly.'

'You called last night, too, right?' said Okeke.

'I did. But I wanted to speak directly with you... not some silly youngster at a call centre.'

'Okay,' Okeke said. 'Well, you're through to me now. Are you okay? Are you hur–'

'I'm alive, and that's what's important,' Eleanora replied quickly. 'They were after me, to kill me. They killed Mattie instead.'

Okeke felt the hairs on her forearm stir as goosebumps began to surface. *They?*

'Who?'

'I can't say. Not now. Not on this line.'

'But you do know who did this?'

'Yes! Of course I do!' Eleanora exclaimed.

Okeke paused for a second. There was something she wanted to be sure about. Because it was the critical link between what had been Warren's case and hers.

'You went to Jim Crowhurst's funeral.' It was more of a statement than a question.

Eleanora was silent for several seconds. 'Yes... how do you know that?' she asked eventually.

'I just do,' Okeke said. She could explain later, once she'd brought her in. 'How were you related to Crowhurst? Was he family? An old friend? I've got his possessions. Would you –'

'This isn't going to be a long call, Ms Okeke. I'm wary of phones right now. But I do have a question for you.'

'Go on,' Okeke said.

'Do the words *orchard, marble, grapple* mean anything to you?'

Okeke felt the back of her neck and her scalp prickle. 'Yes, as a matter of fact, they do.'

'Where did you come across them?'

Okeke wasn't going to give that away. That was knowledge that, at the moment, only she and Abbott's small team knew about. 'I ,uh... I can't tell you that yet.'

'Well, tell me what you think those words mean?' Eleanora persisted.

Okeke honestly had no idea. 'I originally thought... they might be a location. Have you heard of a thing called What3Words?'

'Yes, yes,' Eleanora replied impatiently. 'Listen to me... They are *not* a location.'

'So what do they mean?' Okeke asked.

'Have you used those three words as a search string? On the internet?'

The question gave Okeke a queasy feeling in her gut. 'I have. The one result took me to a web –'

'Then... I'm sorry,' Eleanora cut in. 'They're onto you, Samantha Okeke.'

The old woman sounded as though she was getting ready to hang up.

'Wait!' Okeke blurted out. 'Who the hell are *they*? And what's this got to do with *orchard, marb–*'

'I will contact you again. But not this way. Be careful. Take precautions.' With that, Eleanora ended the call.

Okeke replaced the phone on its cradle, suddenly feeling as though a laser targeting dot had gently settled on her from afar.

Fuck.

The double doors from the foyer banged open, jolting Okeke back to her senses. She turned to see Warren, Abbott and Fox returning from the pier with their lunch. Warren peeled away from the others and swerved through the maze of office furniture to deposit a paper bag on the corner of her desk.

'One vegan sausage roll,' he announced.

She looked at the grease-stained bag and decided she'd completely gone off the idea of having anything at all for lunch.

25

Okeke spotted Jay as he emerged from Hastings train station. His overnight bag was slung over one shoulder and he was doing that model-like swaggering walk that he did whenever he suspected she might have eyes on him. Checking him out.

She was, at it happened. All things said and done, he was a nice piece of ass... and, God, given that creepy call earlier today, she realised how much she'd missed him.

He pulled open the boot to her car, tossed his bag in and got into the passenger side.

'How's my sexy soon-to-be detective sergeant?' he asked, before planting a kiss on her lips.

'I've got to pass the exam first before you can call me that, babes,' she replied. 'How was your course?'

'Frickin' awesome,' he said, grinning. 'The practical exercise last night was like...' He shook his head as he hunted for the right metaphor, then gave up and settled for his go-to movie reference. 'It was like Jason Bourne. Only we were playing the bad guys.'

'Did they hand out plastic walkie-talkies and truncheons to you all?' she said with a smirk.

He smiled, but ignored her sarcasm. 'There was zero tech – just old-school eyeballs and hand signals.' He squeezed her leg. 'And my team managed to catch the golden goose.'

'That's great, Jay,' she said distractedly. She did a quick scan around the short-wait car park. There'd been a man sitting on a railing earlier, phone to one ear and glancing her way every now and then. She was relieved to see he'd gone. She started the car, pulled out of her slot and exited onto Havelock Road, heading down towards the seafront.

'Did you meet any interesting people?'

'Yeah, a very fit but foul-mouthed American lady who desperately wanted to sleep with me. I had to hold her back with pepper spray,' he told her.

'Very funny,' she replied.

She stopped at the junction facing the sea and waited for the red light to turn green. 'So, did you learn much?'

'Sure. The guys on the course were, like, ex-CIA, KGB, Mossad. Actual real-deal spies. Some of the stories the KGB bloke told were just –' he shook his head – 'toe-curling stuff. Anyway, yesterday they broke down practical on-foot surveillance into three types. So, you've got your one-man shadow, then there's the front-and-follow, and then there's what they call the ABC formation...'

As he gabbled away, Okeke noticed the same man she'd seen back at the train station. He was now at the wheel of the car directly behind them. His eyes met hers in the rear-view mirror. She felt uneasy. There was no one else in the car with him. And he wasn't indicating left or right. Why not?

'Babycakes, you going or what?' Jay prompted.

'Huh?'

He nodded at the green light. 'Good to go?'

'Oh, right... yeah.' She pulled forward, turning right onto Denmark Place. She kept her eyes on the rear-view mirror to see whether the man behind her followed.

He did, slowly, leaving a discreet distance between them.

Jesus. Calm down. Of course he turned right. It was fifty-fifty. Right or left. Okeke shook her head. She needed to get a grip.

Jay was now babbling about how a surveillance team of three or more needed to communicate with each other using a series of pre-arranged hand signals to indicate when the formation would have to do a switcheroo in their roles and employ 'box configuration' to respond to a sudden change of direction by the on-foot target.

They passed by the White Rock Theatre on the right, the pier on the left, heading home to their place just beyond Warrior Square. Okeke drifted into the right-hand lane for the London Road turn-off, and stopped at the next lights. The car behind did exactly the same, also indicating right for London Road. The moment the lights turned green, though, she cancelled her signal and lurched forward, swerving left into the adjacent lane to continue along the coast. This triggered several blaring horns in her wake and a puzzled look from Jay.

'What's up? Where we going? Dinner?' He smiled. 'Thank fuck. I'm starving.'

She checked the rear-view mirror; the car that had been behind her was sluggishly turning right onto London Road and heading inland. Had the man had a moment of hesitation? Had he decided that discretion would be better? Or had he just been too slow to react and follow her?

'Sam?'

She glanced his way. 'Not dinner, no,' she said.

'Uh... so, where're we going?' Jay asked. 'Babes, you want to tell me what's going on?'

She had toyed with the idea of telling him tonight about the web page and the call she'd taken earlier, over a veggie bhuna and a large glass of red wine. She'd wondered how to tell him that there was the remote possibility that some mysterious people might be stalking her, in a way that didn't make her sound like a complete tinfoil-hat-wearing conspiracy crank. She'd even wondered if she could make it sound like a bit of a joke. Like: *It could be something, but honestly, love, it's just another weird day in Hastings CID.*

But the car behind them had genuinely rattled her.

'We're not going home just yet,' she said to Jay.

'What?' he replied, confused.

'We're going to visit Boyd.'

He took that information with a patient nod, watching the sea and the beach slide past them. Finally he turned back to look at her. 'Mind if I ask why?'

Okeke cleared her throat.

'I think I might be in a bit of a... *situation*, love.'

26

Charlotte opened the front door and was somewhat taken aback to find Jay standing there – Okeke, somewhat less so.

'Ah... hello.' She smiled at Okeke. 'Again.'

'Charlotte, I'm really sorry,' Okeke began, 'but we need to –'

'Speak to the guv?' Charlotte finished.

She pressed out a flat and rueful smile. 'I know. And it's work. Again.'

Charlotte stepped back to let them in. 'Emma's just put dinner out on the table, so...'

'Really? That'd be great,' Jay said, entirely missing her meaning. He dipped awkwardly to plant a kiss on Charlotte's cheek. 'Thanks! I'm starving.'

Okeke led the way, down the hall towards the dining room.

'It's nothing exciting,' cautioned Charlotte. 'We're all on the white diet for Bill's tummy. It's just pasta and cheese sauce, I'm afraid.'

Jay grinned as he patted his abdomen. 'Naughty carbs? Perfect.'

Boyd looked at Okeke with the quizzical lift of one brow as she entered the dining room. 'Uh... What's this? Did you catch the aroma of grilled Gouda as you passed by?'

Okeke pulled a spare seat out from the table as she greeted Boyd and Emma, and sat down beside him.

Emma pushed her chair back and got up. 'Can I get you a plate, Sam?'

Okeke nodded and smiled. 'I'm so sorry for dinner-bombing you guys. Um, just one plate for Jay. He's as hungry as a horse. None for me, though.' She turned to Boyd and lowered her voice. 'Can we talk?'

'After dinner perhaps?' said Boyd.

Okeke nodded impatiently. 'Okay. Sure.'

Charlotte came in, leading Jay and the dogs who were weaving between his legs.

'Two more for supper,' she said with a patient, cordial smile that looked as though it was running on fumes. She sat down as Emma came back from the kitchen with a couple more plates and cutlery, and set them out in front of both Jay and Okeke.

Okeke nodded. 'All right. I might, thanks.'

'Whoa, Ems,' said Jay, eyeing Emma's bump. 'Not long to go now, eh?'

'Thirteen weeks if he or she arrives on time,' Emma replied.

'No idea yet?' Jay asked.

'None,' she replied. 'Which is how I want to keep it. A big surprise.'

Emma served up and they ate the whole casserole dish of pasta bake between them, a meal that Charlotte had intended to do the Boyd household for lunch tomorrow too.

As they ate, the two subjects of polite conversation were Emma's coming baby and Jay's spycraft course.

After, as Emma and Charlotte had cleared away, Boyd led Okeke into his study.

'Jay too,' Okeke said. 'I want him in on this.'

Boyd looked surprised. 'On your... sorry, on *Abbott's* case?'

'I think things have escalated a bit,' she said.

Boyd looked at her, concerned, then at Jay, who was hovering uncertainly in the study's doorway. Okeke waved at him to enter.

'Oka-a-y,' said Boyd, 'if you're sure.'

Boyd sat down, watching Okeke curiously as she dropped her shoulder bag in the lounge opposite.

'Jay, your phone...'

'Are you serious?' he asked.

She nodded. As Jay pulled his phone out and handed it to her, she turned to Boyd. 'You too, guv.'

Boyd shrugged and did the same. She placed them on her bag and closed the lounge door, then joined Boyd and Jay in the study, again closing the door firmly.

She wasted no time at all in getting started. 'Guv, I think I'm being watched.'

Both Jay and Boyd reacted the same way. 'Watched?' they chorused.

'That bait web page has triggered something. I'm pretty sure,' she explained.

'How do you know? What have you seen?' asked Boyd.

Okeke told them about the man she thought might have been following her, then about the brief exchange she'd had with Eleanora Baxendale earlier. 'She sounded frightened, Boyd. I mean... genuinely fucking terrified.'

'And you're sure this wasn't a crank call?' Boyd asked.

She shrugged. 'If it was she should get a BAFTA.'

Then she turned to Jay, who looked as though he had a growing queue of questions waiting to spill out of him. 'I think I've stumbled into something I shouldn't have, love.'

'Russians again?' he said warily.

'No. Not Russians. Anyway, they were Georgians, Jay. Not Russians.' She turned back to Boyd. 'The woman who died in the arson attack was Eleanora Baxendale's sister, Matilda. But Eleanora is certain *she* was meant to be the target. And she confirmed that she'd attended Crowhurst's funeral.'

'Did she give a reason for telling you all this?' Boyd asked.

Okeke shook her head. 'The call was super quick. She didn't want to linger...'

Boyd narrowed his eyes. 'Okaay...'

'*Marble, orchard, grapple,*' Okeke cut in. 'She asked me if those three words meant anything.'

Boyd looked at her. 'Okay,' he said again, more seriously this time.

'I told her I'd used them online,' Okeke said, 'and that I'd found that page... and she said...'

'What page?' cut in Jay.

Boyd woke his computer up with a waggle of his mouse, opened a screenshot of the web page. 'This one.'

Jay got up and looked more closely at it as Okeke continued. 'She said they were onto me now.'

Boyd turned to her. '*They* being...'

She shrugged. 'Just *they*', she replied unhelpfully. She leant forward on her seat, elbows resting on her knees. 'I reckon Adam Cocker found that web page after she gave him something at the funeral. A note....'

Jay frowned. 'Funeral?'

Okeke stopped to fill him in, at least up to what Boyd

already knew. 'Whatever *this* is,' she concluded, 'it all begins with Jim Crowhurst's death.'

She told them about the journals she'd been reading and the fact that the third one was missing. 'He was an army officer, about to be redeployed with his men to some unspecified location... then in the next journal, all of a sudden several years have passed and he's a history teacher in a prep school.'

'So how much of a missing chunk of time are we talking about?' asked Boyd.

Okeke pulled her notebook out of her bag and checked it. 'From 1959 to late 1963.'

He thumbed his chin absently. 'And you say that's the only journal that's missing?'

She nodded. 'I've not read the whole lot, just skimmed them, but they're his memories. All the way up to him going into the residential home. Everything's there, except that one volume, containing those five years.'

Jay's attention drifted back to the grainy photograph on Boyd's monitor. 'So what am I looking at?' he asked. 'I mean, I see a bloke looking up at a dead tree.'

'I don't know if the picture itself is significant,' said Okeke. 'But Karl said the page was designed specifically to harvest IP numbers.'

'You spoke to Karl?'

She nodded.

He looked slightly hurt. 'You might have tried me first, babes.'

'Right, because you know all about HTML code?' She rolled her eyes. 'I sent him the link. He looked at the code behind it and said that's what the page does... Logs the IP address of everyone who lands there.'

'And nothing else,' added Boyd. 'There's nothing else to

the website. It's basically a trap to see who's searched for a specific set of key words.'

'That marbly apple orchard thing?' Jay asked.

Boyd nodded.

'*Grapple*,' said Okeke. 'Not *apple*.'

Jay pursed his lips as he evaluated the puzzle before him. 'Well, all right, so it seems to me that it's all about the words, then. You say this Adam had written them down on a pad?'

She nodded. 'And removed the note he'd written it on.' She glanced at Boyd. 'Or *they* did.'

'And presumably *they* have volume three of Crowhurst's memoir as well,' Boyd mused.

'Right,' said Okeke. 'It's possible that Adam had taken it home to read.'

'Or maybe he gave it to the old lady?' suggested Jay. 'If they met to talk after that funeral?'

That was something she hadn't considered. Maybe Eleanora had given Adam a phone number or a time and place to meet her. But there was no way of knowing what she'd placed in his hand.

'So this woman said she was going to contact you again, by another means?' said Boyd.

'Uh-huh.'

'How old is she?' asked Jay.

'Eighty-six,' she replied.

'Christ. And she's gone off-grid?' He glanced at Boyd. 'How the hell does a sweet old dear that age manage to do a James Bond?'

Boyd shrugged.

'Could be an ex-cop?' suggested Okeke.

'Maybe she's a spy?' offered Jay.

Okeke frowned. 'Oh, come on. At her age?'

'A sleeper,' Jay countered. 'From the Cold War?'

'So, she's a sleeper spy in her eighties?' explored Boyd. 'Perhaps Crowhurst's journal blows her cover. She has to silence Adam, then cover her tracks and go on the run.'

'A Russian spy?' sighed Jay. 'So this *is* bloody Russians again.'

This time both Okeke and Boyd looked at him and sighed.

'I mean,' said Boyd, shaking his head. 'Sam, there is a possibility you might have inadvertently stumbled across some sort of MI5 or MI6 operation.'

Okeke frowned. 'Are you actually being serious?'

Boyd shrugged. 'That kind of thing *does* happen, you know?'

Her incredulity deepened. 'Adam Cocker forced booze, sedated, then hanged? An old woman burned to death? By *our* people?'

'Look, it was just a suggestion.' Boyd looked again at the image on the screen. 'I suspect... *our* people can be just as bloody vile and ruthless as anybody else's.'

Okeke exhaled deeply. 'Okay, this isn't really helping me calm the fuck down.'

Jay reached out and rubbed her back. 'Deep breaths, babes.'

She shrugged his hand off. 'Oh, Jesus. I'm not twelve.' She glanced at Boyd. 'What do you think we should do?'

'We?' Boyd turned to look at the study door to check it was properly closed. 'Uh... I'd like to think I'm more of a sounding board here, Sam. A friendly pair of ears.'

Jay looked at him. 'But we're Team Boyd,' he said hopefully.

'Technically, this is DI Abbott's case,' Boyd replied.

'It's not a police case, though, is it?' said Okeke. 'This

shit. It's basically, me potentially on somebody's radar... and, according to you, waiting to find out if some intelligence agency – British or otherwise – want me to have some kind of an accident.'

Boyd sat forward, wincing as the dressing on his side caught. 'If it was me, Sam... I'd make a big show of wrapping things up. *Nothing to see here, folks – one suicide, one house fire, one missing senile old dear. I've got other cases to work on...* That kind of thing.'

Okeke raised a brow. 'But would you, though?'

'Yup. Because I'm not an idiot. Because I learn my lessons from previous cases.'

'So, what literally, do *nothing?*' said Okeke.

'No, I didn't say that. Just go through the motions on the misper for Abbott, then let him decide whether further action's necessary. Knowing him, he'll not want to do much that will take him away from his chair and his lunch.'

'And what if she is just a vulnerable and deluded geriatric out there on her own, and not some valuable asset?'

'Then she'll turn up,' he replied. 'Probably at some A and E or walking barefoot along some hard shoulder. Somebody'll ring in.'

Okeke eyed him suspiciously. 'But you don't think she's just some confused old lady, do you?'

Boyd looked at his monitor. 'That tells me she's not.'

'I could help you,' said Jay.

They both looked at him.

'With what?' Okeke asked.

'With finding stuff out. Finding this old woman, maybe,' he replied.

Boyd nodded. 'That's actually not a bad shout, Jay.'

Jay beamed. 'Thanks, guv,'

'And, Sam,' said Boyd, 'don't do any more digging.' He

nodded at Jay. 'Maybe we could rope in Karl too... to do a little research.'

'Yeah. I'm in,' said Jay, at the same time that Okeke echoed, '*We?*'

Boyd shrugged. 'Well, you seem to be turning up here on a regular basis... Might as well make it official. Unofficially.'

Okeke smiled. 'Thanks.'

'So where do you want to start the *research*, guv?' Jay asked.

Boyd looked at his screen. 'With that image and that page, for starters – and the three key words. Karl might be able to track down who owns the domain.' He leant forward to read the URL. 'It's gibberish to me.'

'We might get something on a reverse-image search,' said Jay. 'And maybe there's some useful info in the image's metadata...'

Okeke looked at Jay, brows up, eyes wide. 'Is that something else you learned this week?'

'I do... *read*, Sam,' he said with a sigh. 'You know... books an' shit?'

'And listen... Sam. Your phone?' Boyd pointed at the door. 'From now on, you've got to think of that as potentially compromised. If your IP address was harvested, then *they* know your name, your address, presumably all your personal data by now. And if a tabloid can do it, I'm sure *they* can do it...'

'Do what?'

'Hack your phone.'

27

Jeremy Warner, like many of his colleagues, both past and present, had become wedded to his career very early on, which had left precious little space in his life for a more conventional marriage. It was a choice faced at the very beginning of one's career when working as a civil servant for a department that technically didn't exist, one of which any cabinet minister could plausibly deny knowing.

The ramifications of such a choice came home to roost as the retirement years began to loom. He had no children and consequently no grandchildren. There was nobody to cuddle on a cold winter's night, or share a bottle of Malbec with on a warm summer's evening.

He was well aware that when the going-to-work part of his life ended, there'd be a huge void to fill. But that had been the choice he'd made many years ago, and if there was a price to pay for being a lifelong spook in retirement, he'd deal with it then.

Eleanora Baxendale had retired ten years ago and, to be honest, it seemed to him that she'd managed to find for herself a very full and active life. Twice a year he'd made the trip to Hastings to catch up with his old boss. She often talked animatedly about the amateur dramatics group she'd joined, the golf club she was a member of and the art classes she was taking.

The last time he'd had coffee with her in a theatre café that overlooked Hastings Pier, about a year ago, she'd asked him about the Boutique and whether any more of their case files had been closed. He hadn't been able to share any details with her, as she was a civilian now, but... the flat smile he'd returned had suggested the answer was no... That it was business as usual. It was the kind of dog-whistle gesture that communicated a great deal between old colleagues and old friends.

He recalled thinking that she'd not looked too well. She'd told him she'd had a pacemaker fitted and was on a basket of drugs to help it do its job. They'd moved on to talk bluntly about current affairs – the war in Ukraine, Trump's chances of a second term – but nothing had suggested she was on the cusp of turning traitor.

She'd been foolishly silly in attending Crowhurst's funeral. Recklessly so. Nothing that remained active down in the wine cellar was worth uncorking. It was rotten grapes to the very bottom of the barrel. What they had left on their books were state secrets that were going to stink forever.

Their only job was to keep them sealed.

So why the fuck, he'd asked himself a dozen or more times recently, *had she suddenly dragged Marble Orchard out into the open?*

28

Eleanora stared out of the small window of her beach hut. The street lamp opposite pierced the night and illuminated a broad circle of the promenade's decorative paving, stealing a little further down onto the top of the shingle beach beyond. Every now and then, she caught the spectral shape of the foam from a particularly energetic wave rolling up the beach and then drawing back into darkness.

The kettle on the electric hob beside her began to gurgle softly. Not for the first time she was relieved that she and Mattie had opted to pay a little extra rent for one of the huts with a power socket. Mattie said the plug socket was essential for her two must-haves: a cup of tea and *The Archers*. (Mattie had been addicted to the radio soap opera for the last forty years.) A day trip down to Seaford simply wouldn't happen if there was any danger she'd miss an episode.

Eleanora looked around the cheerfully decorated hut. Ever since Mattie had moved in with her ten years ago and Eleanora had become her carer (and had to install that wretched nuisance stairlift), they'd come here at least once a week. Even through some of the winter months. The wind-sheltered porch outside was just big enough for Mattie's wheelchair and another deckchair, and they alternated between losing themselves in the pages of whatever books they were reading or floating in the gentle undulations of the sea.

Many pleasant days – balmy hot ones, as well as bracingly fresh – had been spent here, wool-gathering and reading, watching the gulls dive and soar, watching children splash into the surf before coming screaming out of the cold water a moment later. She smiled. Their Seaford beach hut had become her Happy Place.

And when she'd finally surrendered her driving licence at eighty, they'd found Charlie, a Hastings cabbie who was happy to pick them up and drive them over once a week for a mates' rates fare.

In these more recent years, sitting on the porch with a small blanket thrown over her legs and a book in her hands, her mind had idled and drifted back to her past. First to her youth, then to her adult years…

And to the secret things that she knew, and the deeds that she'd done to keep them that way. In that little clutch bag of memories lurked horror. Sights that couldn't be unseen, memories that couldn't be erased.

This little hut, painted a happy cornflower blue inside and out, had been where she'd silently reflected upon her life, her choices, her regret. And now that Mattie was gone – the female police detective had said that she'd mercifully died in her sleep – in between the crying and grieving, Eleanora could voice her thoughts aloud to it.

'I haven't got much time,' she whispered softly.

They were going to find her eventually. She knew that. But far more pressing was the fact that her health was failing. Her poor heart, given a helping hand by a pacemaker, was letting the side down. As a consequence, her lungs were gradually filling up with tiny amounts of fluid; each breath she took was fractionally less effective than the last.

She had drugs for that, of course. But they were in a medicine cabinet that was now locked away inside the soot-covered carcass that had once been her home. The only way to get any more would involve collecting her prescription.

'And Jeremy knows that,' she whispered.

The last time Jeremy Warner had come down to Hastings to visit her, she'd told him about her failing health. They both knew that a lifetime of smoking probably hadn't helped matters.

It was pretty dark in the hut. No candle, no lamp. Just the amber light from the lamp outside spilling in through the scuffed window. These beach huts were not meant to be occupied overnight and Seaford Council kept a beady eye on that; these were beach huts, not budget apartments.

The kettle's gurgling became a soft and steady hiss as the water began to heat up.

As a bolthole, the hut would suffice for now. But eventually either they were going to zero in on her, or she was going to die of pulmonary oedema. Secondary drowning, she believed it was known as: *drowning from the inside.*

'I don't have much time,' she muttered again.

Tomorrow, she reminded herself. Tomorrow she was going to contact that Detective Okeke again. She looked at the small table beside the kettle. On it was a pad of lined paper and her fountain pen... and a dearly valued old hardback that she'd owned since her twenties. A Kipling. She was still deciding whether to vandalise it and tear a page out, or hope this detective was smart enough to figure out what she needed to do.

Eleanora pulled her chair up to the table, carefully opened her book and picked up her pen. Tomorrow... after breakfast. She'd give Charlie a call, not to book a ride back to Hastings but to run an errand for her.

She put pen to paper...

And began to write.

29

Minter was at his desk first thing Friday morning, looking bright-eyed, bushy-tailed and very pleased with himself. Okeke had presumed he'd have taken the day off after the exam to treat himself to a whole day of self-flagellation in the gym.

But instead he'd come in.

'How did it go?' she asked.

'Ah, it wasn't too difficult really, Okeke. I don't know why they do multiple-choice answers because the three wrong ones are so bloody obvious! Sort of like... Henry the Eighth was: A) a Tudor; B) a famous forties jazz musician; C) famous for having only eight toes... and... and...'

'D) had nine wives?' supplied Okeke.

'Right!' Minter nodded. 'Honestly, it was an absolute doddle. I feel a right muppet now for all that time off to get ready for it!'

Okeke was surprised at how relieved she was to have him back at work, even with his scented, well-oiled beard and perfectly conditioned hair.

'How's things been here without me?' Minter asked. 'You cope all right, did you?'

She updated him on the cases that she and Warren had been working on independently before it had become clear that they were entangled in some way – and now they had a single case under DI Abbott's lacklustre supervision.

'You're shitting me?' he replied, eyeing up Abbott, who was sitting at his desk across the floor.

'Nope. To be honest... He's just sort of letting me get on with it.' Okeke's eyes followed Minter's; their ersatz boss stretched back in his seat with a takeaway coffee in one hand and a pastry in the other. '

She was about to excuse herself to go and make a coffee and put her hummus wrap in the fridge when she realised she'd left it in the car. It was another sunny September day and her lunch would cook in its foil on the passenger's seat.

'Oh, bastarding bollocks,' she muttered.

'What's up?' Minter asked.

'My lunch. I left it in my car,' she replied.

Okeke grabbed her car keys, weaved her way to the double doors and stairwell. After last night's paranoia about being followed, she'd begun to feel as though she might have overreacted. *But...* she thought. Her mind wouldn't let her suspicions go.

Those three words. In Adam's flat.

Which Eleanora knew.

Which just happen to lead to a mysterious web page.

Which just happens to quietly collect IP addresses.

As she reached the bottom of the stairs and bleeped through the gate beside the front desk, she realised her anxiety had ramped up again.

'DC Okeke.' It was the desk sergeant calling her. He held

up an envelope and waved it. 'Some bloke just dropped this off for you.'

Okeke went over and took the envelope. On the front, written in perfect copperplate, was her name. 'Some bloke?' He nodded. 'Male. Old. White... and in a bit of a hurry.'

She eased the flap open and peered cautiously inside. There was a sheet of folded, lined paper and nothing more. Mindful – always – that something like this might contain useful forensic evidence, she grabbed a Biro from the front desk and used it to leverage the paper out onto the counter. She carefully unfolded it and held it flat with the top of the pen.

At the top was a dense block of handwritten numbers, broken up by slashes. Beneath that a short message.

DEAR SAMANTHA

If there was a poem that came to mind, from a writer you've undoubtedly encountered recently... what would it be, I wonder?

Eleanora Baxendale

SHE LOOKED up at the desk sergeant. 'You said he *just* dropped it off? How long ago?'

'A couple of minutes, maybe,' he replied.

Okeke crammed the note and envelope into a spare evidence bag, which she slid into her trouser pocket, turned and hurried outside. There was no one to be seen in the car park except for a couple of uniformed officers on a fag break.

'Did either of you see a civvy come in and out again? In the last few minutes?'

They looked at each other for a moment, and one of them finally nodded. 'Yeah... I did, just now.'

'What did he look like? What's he wearing?' she asked.

He shrugged, then puffed out some air. 'Old bloke. White hair. Dark-blue bomber jacket. Dark jeans, I think.'

That was enough.

'Thanks.' She sprinted towards the car park's entrance on Bohemia Road and scanned the uphill pavement, looking towards the site where that old monstrosity of a place, Eagle House, had once stood. She turned left, gazing downhill towards the seafront. At this time of day, as always, the road was still busy, with traffic heading north out of Hastings.

She spotted a man ambling downhill on the other side of the road. He was wearing a dark jacket, dark-ish trousers and an olive-coloured flat cap. There'd been no mention of that, but then he might have just popped it on. The only other pedestrians in sight were both women.

Without further hesitation, Okeke ran downhill after the man in the cap. As soon as she'd started sprinting, he turned right onto Magdalen Road and out of view.

Okeke charged across the road, drawing a honk from a truck descending into Hastings, and darted between the slow-moving uphill traffic. She knew what lay round the corner of Magdalen Road: St Mary's Star of the Sea Catholic Primary School. At this time of the morning, Magdalen Road would be clogged up with parents driving Range Rovers, and the pavement would be rammed with yet more parents pushing buggies and tugging their foot-dragging kids to school. And her old man would be somewhere among them all.

Stopping for a moment to catch her breath, she caught sight of his bobbing flat cap and tufts of white hair. She picked up her pace again, tempted to shout out that she was the police and could someone please stop him. But then he turned onto the road opposite the school – Blomfield Road – and once again she lost sight of him.

'Oh, for crying out...' she wheezed.

He was surprisingly swift on his feet for an old codger. She raced to the corner of Magdalen and Blomfield in time to see him climb into a car. Moments later he was starting the car and pulling away

'Shit, shit shit...' Okeke fumbled for her phone and just managed to grab a couple of pictures of the departing car before it turned at the end of the road and disappeared from view. Impatiently, she opened her photos app to review the images.

She had two blurry pictures of a blue Mondeo and a number plate that began with 'AU'; the rest of it was obscured by another car pulling out.

Okeke drew a deep breath. They weren't great but one of Sully's lot might be able to do something with them. That was something.

And she had something else: the knowledge that Eleanora Baxendale had somebody helping her.

30

Boyd stood there with his front door open, looking puzzled. Ozzie and Mia flanked him, their butts jiggling happily at Okeke's return.

'Back again already?' he said. She seemed a bit puffed out. 'What's happened now?'

Okeke put a finger to her lips and held up her iPhone in the other hand to remind him that it was quite possible the thing had been hacked.

'I just thought I'd check in on you again, guv,' she replied in a way she hoped didn't sound too staged.

He nodded and waved her into his house. 'Oh, that's thoughtful of you, Okeke. I just put the kettle on actually. Fancy a brew?'

She frowned at him. He sounded even more phoney than she had. 'Hey, okay if I dump my stuff in here?' she asked, stepping into his lounge and pointing at her phone.

'Sure.'

She set it down on a side table and gently closed the door on it.

He beckoned her to step into his study.

The Archive

She mouthed, 'Where's yours?' as he shut the door behind her.

'Kitchen,' he replied. 'Okay... so what's new?'

'The plot just thickened.' She pulled the evidence bag out of her trouser pocket and laid it on the desk, as Boyd took a seat at his desk.

He leant forward to look more closely at the brown envelope and a crumpled sheet of lined notepaper. 'What's that?'

'A note from Eleanora. She had some old man hand-deliver it to the station. My name's on the envelope.' She turned it round to show him.

'You had Mags or Sully dust and swab it?'

'Not yet. That's next.' She took a breath. 'I managed to follow the guy out to Magdalen Road but lost him. So I came here. Figured you'd be more help than Abbott.'

'What's in the note?'

Okeke flipped the evidence bag to reveal the note, which Boyd read through the plastic.

'It's a code.'

'That much I managed to work out already,' she replied dryly.

'She mentions a poem,' he said. 'But which poet? Which poem?'

Okeke shook her head. 'I've got no idea. I don't do poets.'

'All right... but this old woman seems pretty sure you know who she's talking about. Someone you've "encountered recently".'

'Honestly, the closest I've come to poetry is singing along to Lewis Capaldi – wait!' She narrowed her eyes. 'Is Kipling a poem guy?'

'As in Rudyard Kipling?' he offered.

'Rudyard?' She shrugged. 'That his first name?'

'Yup. What made you think *him*?'

'Crowhurst. I think it was his favourite writer,' Okeke explained. 'I've been flicking through his journals. Plus, Eleanora knows I've picked up his belongings.'

'All right, so then Kipling it is,' Boyd said.

'Do you know any of his poems?' Okeke asked.

Boyd thought for a moment. 'Didn't Kipling write the "If" one? You know, *If... blah blah blah, blah... then you'll be a man, my son.* Or something to that effect?'

He turned to his computer and typed '*you'll be a man, my son*' into Google. In barely a second, they had their answer.

~

I KNOW you youngsters prefer doing this the modern way. So go to this location. Nurture. Sues. Collapsed. Midday. Sixteenth September. Don't be late. And don't be followed.

OKEKE LOOKED up from the messy page of crossings-out and start-overs. It had taken them just over an hour to turn the batch of numbers separated by slashes into a coherent message, made harder by the fact that Eleanora had counted lines and letters incorrectly on more than a dozen occasions.

'Nurture. Sues. Collapsed,' Okeke read aloud

Boyd was already typing that into What3Words. 'Right. This had better not show us some Norwegian fjord or a patch of Amazonian jungle.'

He hit enter and the screen centred on a road. Beachy Head Road.

'Looks promising,' said Okeke.

Boyd clicked the plus icon to zoom out. 'Okay, so it's near the coast. Not far from Eastbourne.'

Okeke leant over his shoulder. 'May I?'

Boyd gave her control of the mouse, and she toggled on satellite mode. The image flipped from a road map to a mottled patchwork of olive green and sandy brown with a pale thread of grey weaving through it.

'She's picked somewhere in the middle of nowhere,' said Okeke.

'Which makes perfect sense if she's half as jittery as you said she sounded.'

Okeke zoomed back in on the grid location. 'There's absolutely nothing there. I mean, there's a road and some marshland.'

Boyd leant forward and pointed at a pale salmon-coloured square. 'What's that?'

'The roof of something?' She peered closer. 'A bus stop?'

'Nope. A bus stop would be rectangular, wouldn't it?' He paused and said decisively, 'It's a phone box. One of those old-fashioned red ones.' He pointed at the slanted shadow it cast across the road. Tall and thin with tiled gaps.

Okeke took another look. 'Shit, you're right.'

'Damn.' He found himself smiling at this old-school espionage. 'So she's going to call us, then. Tomorrow at midday.'

Okeke raised a brow. 'Us? You're not match-fit for a trip out, guv.'

'I'm not fit to what? Sit in a car?' Boyd said.

'What if there's, you know... *trouble*?' Okeke replied. 'I mean, seriously – Adam Cocker was overpowered, drugged and murdered.'

'Then we'll bring Jay along,' he replied. 'He can do my thumping for me.'

Okeke pointed at Eleanora's words: *Don't be followed*. 'I can't say for sure that I'm not being tailed already. There was the guy I thought might have been following me, remember?'

Boyd nodded. 'Right, you did say. How sure are you?'

'That's the point. I'm *not* sure – I don't know! It could just have been me being jumpy.'

'All right,' he said. 'Well, we're going to need to work something out before tomorrow.'

'Jay's off work today,' Okeke said. 'Since he knows as much we do. It does sort of make sense to bring him along. Anyway, I think it's safe to say he's probably more up to date about cloak-and-dagger stuff than either of us are right now.'

Boyd got up from his seat. 'Give him a call. Let's go and have a pub lunch.' He looked at his watch and corrected himself. 'Pub brunch. You might also want to call CID – let Minter know you're out and about.'

'What about Charlotte? Emma? You going to get some flack from them if...'

'Charlotte's working all day. Emma's seeing Dan.' He stroked his chin. 'Let's see what plan the three of us can put together before they get back.'

31

'A half shandy for the lady, and a Coke for the gent.' Jay passed them out and set down his own pint of lager on the wooden table.

Boyd had suggested the roof terrace of the Bier Garden. The tables were spaced out and the combined sound of gulls, waves and wind, alongside the summer hits playing through the pub's speakers, was loud enough that anyone trying to earwig would have a hard time doing so.

Jay smiled at Okeke. 'I assumed you're ditching your hummus wrap, babes.'

She wrinkled her nose. 'It'll have turned soggy and cheesy by now.'

'Good. Ordered you veggie burger and chips.' Jay turned to Boyd. 'And just chips for you, guv. That right?'

Boyd nodded. 'Yup, keeping it plain and simple for now. I eat anything *exciting* like, I dunno, ketchup, and I'll be –'

'Pissing out your arse?' supplied Jay.

Boyd shrugged. 'Something like that.'

'How's it going?' Jay asked. He'd discreetly avoided the subject at Boyd's dinner table the previous evening.

'Well, it's out,' Boyd replied, referring to the now-removed five centimetres of bowel and the tumour that stuck out of it like a giant gnarly tick. 'I've got a few weeks to recover, then they're going to carpet-bomb me with toxic drugs for six months.'

'That's the chemo?' said Jay.

'Uh-huh. It's a pretty blunt tool. They'll flood me with cell-destroying nasties in the hope they kill any unwanted visitors before the radiation kills me.'

'Jesus. Kind of a scorched-earth policy, I guess' Jay said.

Boyd glanced at their three smartphones in a row beside each other at the end of their table. He picked them up and put them on the next table along.

He sat down and cut to the chase. 'So, Jay? Did you manage to get any research done?'

'Uh, not yet. I had to go into work this morning. Drop off my boss's apartment keys.'

Boyd nodded. 'Has Okeke brought you up to speed on her hand-delivered note?'

'Yeah. The old lady wants to talk to Sam via a phone box in the middle of nowhere.'

'I think she trusts me,' Okeke said.

'But why you?' asked Jay.

'Maybe because I'm trustworthy,' Okeke replied snippily. 'Maybe she liked what she saw when I did the press conference?'

'Maybe it's because she knows you're in the same boat,' said Boyd. 'You're on their radar too.'

'But does this mean *They* think Sam will lead them to this woman?' Jay asked.

Boyd picked up his Coke and took a sip . 'If they really are following Sam, then that suggests to me they're hoping she'll lead them to Baxendale.' He glanced her way. 'I mean, how sure are you?'

'I don't know,' she began. 'That driver – there was eye contact. Several times. He was at the railway station, making like he was waiting for someone. Then seeing him in his car right behind me. No passenger. Then turning the same way I was turning... twice.' She shrugged. 'A lot of creepy shit going on there. Maybe I could put it down to just being randomly weird, but with Baxendale's cloak-and-dagger act? That web page? The arson? A murdered carer?'

'Fair point.' Boyd nodded. 'So then we'll assume the old woman's right. Sam's being watched. Like I say, I'd guess the reason is they want Baxendale, and Sam's their way of finding her. Which begs the question... once they find Eleanora, what's her fate?'

'And what's mine?' cut in Okeke.

'Right,' said Boyd. 'I suppose that depends on how big a thing this is.'

Okeke nodded slowly. 'So, what's the play, then?'

'The only thing I can imagine she wants to do tomorrow is to talk to you in a way that can't be intercepted,' said Boyd. 'Hence the location.'

'Has anyone checked the phone box works?' asked Jay.

'I presume *she* has,' said Boyd. 'She'd need to have visited it to get its number.'

'Or she might have sent someone,' said Okeke. 'That old bloke who dropped the note off, for instance?'

'You know, babycakes, you could use this trip out to Eastbourne to –'

'It's Birling Gap. Beyond Eastbourne,' she said. 'And, Jay... "babycakes"?' She nodded at Boyd. 'We are *literally* sitting across from my boss.'

Jay shrugged. 'The guv doesn't mind – do you, guv?'

Boyd couldn't help smiling at the pair of them. In a way he couldn't quite articulate, the world would somehow be slightly wrong if they weren't with each other.

'As I was saying,' Jay continued, 'you could use this trip out to *Birling Gap* as a test to check if you really are being tailed. It's remote, right?'

Boyd leant forward. 'He's got a point. If you are being watched and you take a sudden and unexpected drive out to nowhere... *They* are going to assume, or hope, at least that you're heading out to meet her. That it's an actual face-to-face.'

'So what? I'm the tethered goat waiting around as bait?' she said.

Boyd looked at their phones on the next table. Since Okeke had first turned up at his place, paranoid that her phone had been hacked, he'd had a quick word with his old colleague Sunny Chandra.

'*Boydy, you're clearly not keeping up on current affairs, bro. There're several total-hack solutions out there on the dark side that can flip your phone into an all-in-one surveillance tool. Pricey, mind. Not for your average pervy stalker.*'

If Okeke's was essentially now a listening device, and all her texts, WhatsApps and emails were being intercepted, then perhaps they could use that to their advantage?

Okeke was still busy processing the thought that her boyfriend was willing to use her as bait. 'But hold up, what if all they're after is for me to go somewhere remote? So they can grab me?'

'Why would they?' asked Boyd. 'You're their only connection to Eleanora. If they follow you out there and see you've been led to a phone box, then I'm pretty sure they'll work out it's so she can talk to you on an untapped phone line.'

'The next step would be for you both to arrange an actual rendezvous,' added Jay.

'Right,' said Boyd. 'In effect, all you'll be doing is actually confirming to them that you're a valuable asset.'

Okeke shook her head. 'I'm not sure about this. I mean... so what happens? I take the call... they're watching me, they can't hear anything I'm hearing over the phone, but they know she's telling me a whole load of stuff. What's to stop them swooping on me the moment I hang up the phone?'

'And do what?' said Boyd. 'Abduct and torture a meeting point out of you?'

She nodded, eyes wide. 'Well... yeah.' She glanced at Jay for some backup. 'I'm going to be a sitting duck out there on my own. It looks pretty deserted.'

'Take your phone into the booth with you,' said Jay. 'If it really has been hacked, they'll be able to hear your side of the conversation, Sam.'

Boyd nodded. 'Jay's right. We could use your phone as a way of feeding them disinformation. Do it right... and you could feed them enough nuggets to persuade them that you're about to hook up in person. That Eleanora's given *most* of what you need to locate her, but not *all*.' He smiled. 'We bait them.'

Jay grabbed her hand. 'Make 'em think that they still need you to take one more call from her before you get her precise location.'

'Christ,' she muttered. 'All at the same time as taking the *actual* call from her?' She shook her head. 'And trying to respond normally?'

'She'll be the one giving information, I'm guessing,' said Boyd. 'So your side of the conversation's going to be a load of 'yep's and 'uh-huh's.'

'But add something like: "*Okay, Eleanora, I will wait for*

that last breadcrumb showing exactly where you are... for next time we speak"?' Okeke rolled her eyes as she spoke.

Jay nodded. 'Yeah, something like that. But maybe find a way to make it sound a bit more natural.'

'Jesus,' she hissed.

'And we'll arrive before you, Sam,' said Jay. 'Won't we, guv?'

Boyd nodded.

Jay squeezed her hand. 'We can find somewhere to lie low and observe, and make a move if anyone dodgy pulls up or looks like they're going to grab you, love.'

'And if they do?' Okeke shook his hand off. 'What are you going to do... use harsh language?'

'I've got my replica gun,' said Jay. 'And Boyd's got that real one in his safe.'

Boyd winced at the suggestion. 'I'm not sure we're quite at the point where I need to be hobbling around with a concealed firearm stuck down my trousers.'

Jay's brows shot up. 'You want to turn up with a tickle stick instead?'

'I just...' Boyd spread his hands, exasperated. 'We're working on a load of stacked assumptions here. Guesses. And having an actual bloody gun in my pocket is not just career-over stuff... It's prison time.'

'Those guesses are adding up, though, guv,' replied Jay.

Okeke shook her head again. 'For fuck's sake, why are we always such an amateur effort? And what if these people are actual, genuine government agents? You know? British? Or even Russian? Won't *they* have guns? And, you know... training? What's the point in bringing a gun, love? That's what gets you bloody well shot!'

'That's why it's important you give them the impression that *now* is not the right time to make a move on you,' said

Jay. 'But if they do...' He looked at Boyd. 'You really want to turn up to a scrap with nothing on you?'

His words hung there for a moment, heavy with an ominous cadence. Superficially they sounded ridiculous, and yet... given the gradually increasing sense that there was more to this than twitchy paranoia...

'I'm not gonna lie,' began Okeke, 'this feels incredibly dumb.'

'We'll be close, Sam,' said Jay. 'Really close. If anyone dodgy turns up...'

She sipped her drink. 'Shit, this would be a lot easier if we knew exactly who we were dealing with. I mean, Eleanora Baxendale didn't sound like your average crazy when I spoke to her. She sounded... competent. Very articulate. Very authentic.'

'Plus, she supplied details that weren't public knowledge,' muttered Boyd.

Okeke nodded. 'She knew *exactly* what the web page was for...'

The squawking sound of seagulls high above them seemed to take on the ominous tone of circling Shakespearean crows.

'If your phone's been hacked in the way Sunny said,' said Boyd after a while, 'then it's got to be a state actor. Which means it could well be our people or –'

'CIA,' said Jay. 'Or FSB? Or Mossad?'

Okeke looked at him. 'That's really not helping my anxiety, baby.'

32

Jay parked his van in the car park for Birling Gap's National Trust visitor centre. Being a pleasant Saturday morning with a clear blue sky, and a couple of degrees warmer than usual for the time of year, the place was busy with folk looking to spend the day at the bottom of the chalk cliffs, on the shingle beach. The souvenir shop was doing a brisk trade in over-priced ice creams, sunscreen, sunshades and windbreaks.

'It's not as quiet and remote as I was expecting,' said Boyd.

'During the week, I bet it's dead,' Jay replied.

'So she picked a Saturday for good reason, then.' Boyd watched a mother lugging an icebox while hustling a noisy family quickly past the shop to the steep wooden steps that led from the clifftop down to the beach.

He glanced back along the coastal road, towards Eastbourne; it curved inland around a gently sloping promontory of rust-coloured gorse and waist-high blackberry bushes that led up to the South Downs. One or two people were walking their dogs among the wild flowers and brambles that spilled over onto the chalk cliffs.

In the distance, a quarter of a mile away, was the faint red smudge of the phone box and a copse of trees just beyond. He and Jay planned to hunker down there. If it looked as if trouble was approaching, they'd be with Okeke in seconds.

'Were your two ladies okay with you coming along on this shout?' Jay asked him.

'Absolutely fine.' Boyd cleared his throat. 'Because I didn't actually tell them.'

Jay's eyes rounded. 'Shit. You didn't?'

'I said that you and Sam wanted to take me out for lunch because you felt sorry for me.'

'Charlotte will tear me and Sam a new arsehole each if she finds out,' said Jay.

'This is on me, Jay. It'll be me she tears into. Not you.'

Jay pulled a tool bag out from behind his seat. Boyd presumed it contained his pretend shotgun.

'Did you bring *yours*?' Jay asked, as if reading his mind.

Boyd nodded.

Reluctantly.

Having the clunky thing jammed into his belt at the back made him feel dirty, like a toerag scrote, like a bent copper. More than that, he suspected he was looking and acting as guiltily as one. Getting the gun out of his safe hadn't been easy. While Charlotte was at work, Emma had been at a loose end, bored and had most annoyingly settled down on his computer for most of the morning. He'd had to find her an errand to run so he could get her out of the study long enough to spin the dial on his safe, whip out the Russian gun, check the safety was on and tuck it away under his jacket.

Then when Okeke had knocked, acting as though she'd dropped by on a whim to take him out for a lunchtime treat, Emma had pleaded to join them. Okeke had had to spin some BS about needing to do a bit of 'confidential work talk' at the same time.

He'd hated the whole act.

'Right,' said Jay, climbing out of his van. 'You going to be okay walking that far?' He pointed towards the copse of trees.

'The consultant said I should do as much walking as I'm comfortable with.' Boyd gazed at the trees, shimmering beyond the heatwaves wafting up from the gorse-covered Downs. 'So let's see.'

Boyd was beginning to regret having lied to Emma. He'd drawn her into his confidence in the past, several times, but this time round she was carrying a little someone who might not want to get tangled up in a murder investigation. And Charlotte? No, she wouldn't tear him a new arsehole, literally or figuratively. But she'd be hurt that he'd kept something from her. She probably already suspected that Okeke had pulled him into something, but until he knew what he was dealing with, what exactly could he tell her?

Jay slammed the door shut and met him at the rear of the van. 'I brought a flask of coffee and a packet of beef jerky. You allowed that?'

'The jerky?'

'Uh-huh.'

'I'm not allowed it,' Boyd replied. 'Not sure I want it either, though.' He shot a glance at the shop. 'Hold on a sec... I might get a Cornetto. You want one?'

~

OKEKE KEPT one eye on her phone and the other on the road ahead. To her left was the serrated edge of Great Britain and a calm English Channel; to her right, at the moment anyway, a rapeseed field, blindingly yellow – Sussex doing its best Ukrainian flag impersonation against the crisp blue sky. The narrow road veered towards the cliff edge, then swung right and inland at the last moment. Just before the road curved left, she noticed a gravel road that snaked off towards a lighthouse: the Belle Tout. A tall and tapering white-washed pillar of Victorian brickwork, it was now no longer a lighthouse but a guesthouse – one with incredible views, no doubt.

She eventually spotted the copse of trees by the phone box. It was the only place where Boyd and Jay could hunker down and make themselves invisible. The rest of the landscape was either gently sloping fields or ankle-high tussocks of gorse.

The red phone booth was a hundred yards beyond the copse, standing entirely alone like some bizarre urban interloper: a Tardis with a fading paint job and clearly lost. She slowed to a halt as she pulled up on the gravel layby beside the phone box.

Instinctively Okeke reached for her phone to call Jay. She wanted to know they were already in place among those trees. She stopped herself when she remembered, yet again, that her phone could well be a tracking and listening device.

Instead, she played the role as assigned: unsuspecting victim of a hacked phone.

She checked her watch. It was 11.57 a.m. 'Right then, Eleanora Baxendale. Let's see if you bother to call.'

Okeke grabbed her phone, stepped out of the car and approached the phone box. Discreetly, her eyes flicked to the nearby cluster of trees. She caught a glimpse of something pale among the foliage, flapping up and down.

A hand.

I see you.

She nodded back at them, reassured. If any men in dark suits and sunglasses rolled up beside her car, Jay and Boyd would be with her in less than a minute.

∼

WARNER HAD PULLED up an office chair to sit beside Gary Nottridge. The young lad had dutifully volunteered to forego his Saturday ju-jitsu class for this morning's surveillance operation. Clearly he wanted to impress his boss and get some active spycraft in before the Boutique closed for business.

'She's stopped,' said Gary. 'I'll zoom in.'

Warner sighed. He'd eaten up a huge chunk of next year's financial pot by applying for a Pegasus licence. They weren't cheap – sixty thousand per target. That equated to two more staff from his dwindling team that he'd have to surrender. All because Eleanora Baxendale has suddenly developed a conscience.

They peered at the satellite image of a winding road snaking between empty fields.

'I presume that's the phone box?' Warner said, pointing at a tiny red square of pixels. Nearby was a small rectangle of dark-brown dots, DC Okeke's car.

'Looks like it, sir,' replied Gary.

Over a speaker, a tinny rustling could be heard. The wind. Then a creaking sound like an unoiled engine hood being lifted.

Clunk.

'She's inside the phone box,' said Gary.

'Where are Drummond and Chapps?' Warner asked.

Gary zoomed out and pointed at another marker on the screen, at a narrow private road in front of a lighthouse. His men were parked up there.

Warner opened the digital comms channel with them. 'Gentlemen, she's parked beside the phone box and has entered. Do you have a line of sight on her?'

He recognised Chapps' nasally voice. 'Not at the moment, sir. There's some trees blocking the view. But apart from that there's nothing out here. If we can see her, then she can see us. You want us to get closer?'

Warner gave that some thought. If Eleanora turned up, then those two bulldogs had orders to speed in and snatch both women. But he seriously doubted she would. It was a phone box; so this was most likely going to be an off-grid conversation. Ellie knew her craft well.

But it wouldn't be entirely off-grid. They would hear Okeke's side of the conversation at the very least. Of course, should the telephone handset be close enough to Okeke's smartphone, there's a chance they could pick up Ellie's voice too. That would be a bonus.

There was another thing to consider, too. Ellie wasn't well. She had a pacemaker and was on meds that she needed to take regularly. Except she'd not been able to take them for the previous week. Moira, his deputy director, had been monitoring her GP's practice. Ellie's records showed that she was due to renew her prescription this week. She might have escaped the fire with some meds but she would need more soon. Very soon. So dear old Ellie was working against a ticking clock.

Which undoubtedly would play into her decision-making.

What the hell is this all about, Ellie?

That ruddy question again. What was she hoping to achieve now this late in the day? To blow the lid on Marble Orchard? To try to parlay a truce? If it was the former, then what the hell did she have anyway? Was it just her story to tell, or did she have hard evidence to back it up? Probably she did. As section leader she'd had access to everything. The files, the footage, the pictures, the medical data.

'Sir?' Chapps was prodding him for an answer.

'Hold your position for now,' said Warner. He checked his watch: 11.59 a.m. One minute to go. 'Let's see how this develops. But be ready to move in on my command.'

'Understood.'

33

Okeke thought about her phone, tucked away in the back pocket of her jeans. Until yesterday it had been her indispensable best friend. Her whole life was on there: her family, friends and their WhatsApp histories. Photos going back years. Even to her time as a trainee nurse. There were pictures of her in NHS scrubs and of her at Hendon Police College, passing out. And pictures from when she and Jay had first started going out.

Rather saucy ones.

If Karl was right... and if Eleanora's paranoia was justified, then she had to assume that all that data had been cloned and was saved on a server somewhere. Everything about her personal life laid out for some faceless, nameless intelligence agents to pick through at their leisure.

Her phone was now a digital traitor, listening to her every word, reporting her location like a snitch, maybe even watching her through the camera lens like a Peeping Tom. She felt an overwhelming urge to toss it out of the booth into the road where hopefully some passing motorhome would turn it into roadkill.

The payphone suddenly jangled to life with the old-fashioned sound of a tiny hammer dinging a bell. She let it ring half a dozen times, breathing deeply to steady her nerves before she finally picked it up.

'Yes?'

A pause. Laboured breathing. And in the background the sound of waves riding up a beach and slowly retreating.

'*To whom am I speaking?*' It was the same raspy female voice as before.

'This is DC Samantha Okeke. Is that you, Eleanora?'

'*Yes. So you managed to decode my Kipling code.*' Okeke thought she detected a smile in the old woman's voice.

'Yes.'

'*Clever girl.*'

'Thank you.' Okeke was mindful that she was going to have to be very careful what she did and *didn't* say.

'*Samantha... may I call you that?*'

'Sam's fine,' Okeke said.

'*All right, Sam. The first thing you must be absolutely clear on is this: you are in danger. As am I.*'

'Who –'

'*We'll get to the "who",*' Eleanora said curtly. '*Firstly, are you alone?*'

'Yes, I'm alone.'

'*Does anyone else know you're talking to me?*'

'No one else knows anything,' she lied. 'It's just me.'

'*That's good. You need to keep it that way for now.*'

'Okay.' Okeke had questions, and plenty of them, all lined up in a queue and eager to be first. 'So, Eleanora, what is this all about? I have a murder case on my hands with the death of your sister –'

'*Two murders, my dear. Don't forget that poor Adam. He didn't commit suicide.*'

'Right.'
'You do understand the two are connected, don't you?'
'Yes,' Okeke replied.
'Matilda's death was supposed to have been mine. Because I've decided it's finally time to speak out,' Eleanora explained.
Careful, Sam, Okeke reminded herself. Be. Very. Careful.
'About what?' she asked.
'Marble Orchard.' Eleanora paused. '*I notice you're not asking me what that is...*'
'Because I'm listening,' said Okeke. 'I'll be honest – I don't know enough about *that* to know what to ask. Why don't you just tell me what you want to tell me?'
'*I'll tell you everything, Sam, but first I would really like to be safe. I need you to come and rescue me, and put me somewhere I can't be found by them.*'
'All right. I can try. We have safe houses. You know, for vulnerable witnesses...'
'Yes, that would be suitable for now.' A dry and humourless laugh rattled out. '*I'm old, I'm tired, my dear... but I'm not yet ready to end up swinging from a tree or burning to death in my own home.*'
'Right. So then, that's something I can look into. I can talk to my seniors about allocating a safe house...'

∽

JEREMY WARNER COULDN'T HELP SMILING. By the sound of it, the stupid old woman had had enough of playing silly buggers and had revealed herself to this copper.

Except it wasn't that fucking simple. Ellie had turned traitor and clearly fancied herself as some crusading whistle-blower. There would be no safe haven for her, certainly not in the UK. If she was harbouring a hope that she could avoid the consequences of attempting to leak the Boutique's deepest darkest secrets, then she was gravely mistaken.

He was desperate to know, though, why on earth had she deemed now to be the right time to air this nation's dirty old laundry? Why, after all these years, did anyone need to know about the difficult decisions that had been made some sixty years ago? Decisions that could have meant the difference between life and death for millions of people if, God forbid, that dreadful day had come to pass.

'*I'm listening*,' they heard the detective say.

It was beyond frustrating; they could just about make out Ellie's rasp. 'Is there any way we can boost her voice?' he asked Gary.

Gary shook his head. 'Not right now. I can try playing around with the recording later. I may be able to filter out some of what we don't want.'

Warner nodded. 'Yes. Yes... let's try that later.'

∼

'THEY WILL KNOW why you're here, dear. That I've contacted you.'

'Are they're watching me now?' Okeke asked.

'*Possibly. I'd be surprised if they weren't already tracking you. They'll know I've led you out to a phone. They'll know you and I have spoken. And* –' Eleanora drew in deeply to recover her breath – '*they know that I have some ghastly stories to tell.*'

'Linked to those three words that you gave to Adam?' she said.

'*How did you know I gave anything to him?*'

Okeke suddenly felt boxed in. She needed to talk freely with the old woman, but was equally all too aware she was probably being listened to. On the fly, without giving the game away, she had to guess how much to say or not say; guess how much *they* knew, and how much to reveal that she already knew.

Fuck it.

'I saw you at Crowhurst's funeral. You handed Adam something.'

'*How observant of you. I gave him my phone number. I wanted to talk with him.*'

'About?'

'*James Crowhurst, of course. You know about him?*'

Again. Caution. 'Yes,' Okeke replied. 'I know a little.'

'*Adam was close to him. James had dementia at the end, but he still had lucid moments. And he shared enough with that young man to make him curious. Adam told me that James, or Jim as he called him, had recounted his memories in a series of notebooks.*' Another deep rattling breath. '*Now, that was something I didn't know. That he'd written it all down.*'

'And?'

'*And I wanted them. The whole story. Not just from my side, but his too. I told Adam just enough to convince him to trust me. That I had Jim's best interests at heart.*'

'Those three words?'

'*A lot more than that. But yes. Those three words – they're code names, you know. Operation Grapple wasn't especially confidential. Plenty about it online. But Operation Marble Orchard that followed... You're going to find absolutely nothing about that. Anywhere.*'

'I think Adam tried to –'

'*Yes. The poor boy made the mistake of sitting at home on his computer and typing those words into a search engine. I should have warned him not to.*'

'I did the same,' said Okeke.

'*Yes. That's why we're now in the same pickle jar, my dear.*'

Okeke heard her attempt a laugh. It sounded dreadful, like some trapped bird fluttering its wings in a canvas bag. '*The reason you're alive still is because they can't find me.*'

Okeke was desperate to know who *They* were.

'*I suspect you want to know who I'm talking about?*'

'Yes,' said Okeke, hoping she wasn't sounding too pushy.

'*A very dark and unpleasant little corner of our intelligence services.*' Eleanora paused. More laboured breathing. '*They're the people who make sure our grisliest skeletons remain locked in the closet.*'

'Ours? As in...'

'*Oh, please don't be naive. You've managed to sound fairly intelligent up until now. The British establishment's caretakers, my dear.*'

'Right. Okay.'

'*So back to the matter of my safety,*' she continued. '*I'm in a bit of a fix. I have money and a rather rudimentary bolthole. But I'm going to need help. I need a particular prescription medication...*'

'All right,' said Okeke. 'What do you want me to do?'

'*I'm going to tell you where you can find me. But not yet. I need you to lose them first. I need you to be absolutely certain you've slipped out of their sights. Can you get away somewhere for a couple of days?*'

Okeke had no idea at all if she could do that. The only advantage she had right now was that *they* didn't know that she suspected her phone had been hacked.

'Yes. Yes I think I can.'

'*Good girl. Get yourself a pay-as-you-go phone. I'm on one right now. I'll give you the number. But only use it on your new phone. Is that clear?*'

'Yes.'

Eleanora read out the number carefully, while Okeke pulled out a pen and scribbled it on the palm of her hand.

'Get yourself a phone and call me. All right?'

'Yes.'

'And then I'll talk you through the next steps. I know how these bastards operate.'

'How?'

'I used to work for them. As a matter of fact, I used to run the very department that wants me dead.'

∼

WARNER GRIMACED. They weren't getting anything useful out of just one wretched side of this conversation. Ellie was doing most of the talking; unless Gary could deploy some technical jiggery-pokery on what they'd managed to record, they were still going to be in the dark.

Dammit. How much has she told this detective? Everything? Nothing? Has she just given her another location?

'The call's ended,' said Gary. 'She's coming out of the phone booth.'

The comms system beeped and this time it was Drummond asking for instructions. 'Sir, do you want us to move in now, or hold back?'

Warner very much wanted them to swoop in. The detective must, at the very least, have a means for re-establishing contact with Eleanora Baxendale.

∼

'YOU TAKE A LOOK.'

Jay handed the binoculars to Boyd, and he trained them on the car that was parked a quarter of a mile away from them. Through the glare of sunlight on its windscreen, he could pick out two men. A couple of thick-set, middle-aged men with scruffy greying hair, one with a pronounced widow's peak and a thick handlebar moustache, and wearing a white polo shirt. His monobrowed partner sported mutton-chop sideburns and wore a pale-blue shirt, sleeves rolled up to his elbows, his forearm sticking out of the passenger-side window.

'What do you think?' asked Jay.

'I think they look suss. I also think they're receiving instructions.'

He could see Handlebar nodding, then reaching for the steering wheel, as Mutton-chops' arm went in. 'Shit. I think they're making a move.'

'What do we do, guv?' Jay asked.

Boyd looked the other way. Okeke was now standing beside her car. He knew she'd be desperately wanting to call him or Jay to update them and ask if they'd spotted anyone. To ask if she was in the clear. Equally he was tempted to call and tell her to drive away like a bat out of hell.

'They're definitely on the move,' said Jay.

Boyd looked back, no longer needing the binoculars. The car readied to pull out onto the winding road. Just before they did so, a car towing a caravan approached from the Eastbourne direction; it passed them at a considerable speed (for a car towing a caravan) as it motored past them, towards Okeke.

For fuck's sake, he willed her. *Get in the bloody car, Sam, and fucking GO! NOW!*

The car rounded the bend, passing the copse of trees. To his relief, the car and caravan pulled over behind Okeke's Datsun. A woman burst out of the back door, holding a toddler as though it was a bomb about to detonate. And the toddler promptly projectile-vomited onto the hard shoulder.

'Oh, thank fuck for that!' wheezed Jay.

Boyd turned to look back at Handlebar and Muttonchops. Instead of coming towards them, it seemed that their car was heading back towards Eastbourne, kicking up a tail of dust and gravel chips into the air behind it.

34

Okeke took a long, hard pull on a cigarette. She held the smoke in for a moment, then blew it out like discharge from a gun barrel. 'Fuck me! Seriously?'

Jay nodded. 'Two of 'em. Just around the bend in the road. Out of your line of sight.'

She glanced over to where her car and Jay's van were side by side in the packed service-station car park, phones still in their vehicles. Shaken by the whole experience, Okeke had disabled her location setting, then turned the thing off completely.

Even though the seats outside Costa were busy with irritable parents, surly teenagers and grizzling kids, they felt safe enough to talk openly.

'You're sure?' she asked.

Boyd nodded. 'Pretty sure. I thought they were getting ready to close in on you and then that caravan pulled over.'

Okeke made a face. 'I didn't realise kids that size had that much in them.' She stubbed her cigarette out. 'And these guys just went back the way they came?'

Boyd nodded again. 'The caravan saved you.'

Okeke realised she was actually trembling.

'So...' said Boyd, nudging her gently. 'What did she say?'

'Well, as we suspected, they're spooks.'

'British ones?' asked Jay.

She nodded. 'Nasty British ones.'

'And did she say why they're after her?' prompted Boyd.

Okeke shrugged. 'She's got something she wants to make public. Marble, orchard and grapple – they're all code names. She said Operation Grapple wasn't especially confidential, which I suppose means we could just Wiki it.'

'And the other two?' asked Jay.

'Other *one*. Operation Marble Orchard. Apparently we won't find anything on that. Anywhere.'

'Did she give an idea what it was about?' Boyd asked.

Okeke paused to think. 'Her exact words were "Operation Marble Orchard that followed" but that's all. So I'm guessing maybe the operations were linked, and that Marble Orchard came after Grapple. Perhaps not long after? I dunno.' She shook her head. 'It was all so bloody cryptic.'

While Boyd mulled that over, she pulled the cheap pay-as-you-go phone out of its plastic blister pack. She slipped off its back and slotted in the SIM card that had come with it.

Jay spotted the smudged numbers on her palm. 'Please tell me that's not her phone number.'

'Uh... yeah. It is. I didn't have anything else to hand.'

'Shit. If they'd grabbed you, Sam...' He shook his head. 'Christ, they wouldn't even have needed to beat it out of you... All they'd need is your cold, dead hand.'

She looked up at him. 'Your concern for my welfare is genuinely touching, my love.'

'So how does she want to proceed now?' asked Boyd.

Okeke held the phone up. 'We'll talk again. She definitely wants to meet in person before she gives up any more info. But she said I've got to lose the spooks. I mean... *properly* lose them before we do. Get away for a couple of days, even.'

Jay shrugged. 'Well, maybe I can help a little there...'

She pulled a face. 'Babes, you did a four-day entry-level course.'

'It was a training course,' he returned snippily. 'And it was more than entry level.'

Boyd raised his hands. 'All right, all right. Look, any knowledge is going to be helpful right now, isn't it?'

'She said she knows exactly how they operate. And who they are,' Okeke said. She paused. 'Because she used to run their department.'

Jay dribbled hot coffee onto his lip. He wiped his mouth. 'What?!'

'Yeah. That's what she said. She was their boss... a while back.' Okeke powered on the phone. 'Sounds like an ex-MI5 section leader who's gone rogue.'

'Bloody hell, no wonder they want her so badly,' said Boyd.

Okeke checked the smudged number on her palm and tapped it into the phone, saving the contact as 'Mum'. 'There... she's in.'

Boyd checked the time. 'It's two o'clock. I should probably get back, otherwise Emma and Charlotte will be on my case.'

'Oh, I think Em's already on it,' said Okeke. 'I'm not sure she totally bought into my treat-you-to-lunch act.'

'I'll grab a tinny of beer from the shop,' said Boyd, standing up. 'So I smell of booze when I get back.'

'Guv?' said Okeke. 'What's our next move?'

'I don't know. Maybe we need to start by finding out exactly what Operation Grapple was.'

35

'How was lunch?' asked Emma grumpily. 'Because all I had was last night's cold leftovers.'

'Uh, yeah. We had a pub lunch. Burger and chips. Nice.'

'Had a few, did you?' she asked, sniffing the air in his wake as he headed for the kitchen.

'I stuck to Coke, I'll have you know,' he replied casually.

He still had the Russian gun tucked into the back of his trousers and was keen to put it away before it either tumbled out onto the floor or Emma spotted the slight bulge through his jacket.

'Charlotte called from work to ask where you were,' said Emma, following him into the kitchen, Ozzie and Mia in tow. 'You weren't replying to her texts.'

Boyd slapped the kettle on. 'Coffee?'

She nodded. 'I think she suspects you're sneaking some naughty work in.'

Ozzie was circling Boyd's legs, his nose twitching frantically as he hoovered away at the cuffs of his trousers.

The Archive

'What is it, Oz Bear?' she asked. 'Did Daddy not take you out with him, either?'

God, it was stuffy in the kitchen. He desperately wanted to shed his jacket and... the gun. But he needed to get rid of Emma first. He really, *really* wanted to shove that vile thing away in the safe as soon as possible.

'Okeke just wanted to ask me a couple of procedural questions. She's got her sergeants' exam coming up in a couple of weeks,' he said.

Emma picked at something on his shoulder. 'They have Velcro weeds in this pub, do they?' She pulled a sticky cleavers stem off his jacket and held it out for him to see.

'Hmmph. The pub garden was a bit overgrown. They obviously didn't get the memo that No Mow May is well and truly over.'

She narrowed her eyes. 'Must have been quite the jungle.'

Ozzie's interest focused a little higher. He was sniffing at Boyd's butt now.

'Oz, that's enough, buddy,' he said, pushing him away.

Boyd reached up to pull the coffee jar out of the cupboard and, as he did so, he felt Ozzie's heavy front paws land on his arse – and his cold wet nose dived under the back of his jacket.

'Ozzie, no!' Boyd shouted.

Ozzie dropped onto all fours, just as Boyd realised that the bulk tucked into his belt had gone. 'Fuck's sake!' he said.

Emma froze in place as she stared down at the dark ridged metal of the weapon's grip protruding from Ozzie's mouth.

Boyd bent down slowly. 'Give it back, buddy – there's a good boy.'

Ozzie's tail started wagging.

'Nooo... we're not playing ball.' Boyd gently eased the gun out of Ozzie's jaws, checked the safety was still on and wiped the slobber onto his trousers. 'Good lad,' he said.

'Dad...' Emma's face had blanched.

Boyd looked up at her, ready to deliver a lie, or at least a half-truth.

'Please... tell me this isn't about those Russians?' she said.

∽

HALF AN HOUR LATER, the gun was back in the safe and they were sat at his desk in the study.

He had given Emma pretty much the whole truth, because, try as he might, she wasn't prepared to accept a watered-down bullshit version of events. She studied the grainy image of a man staring up at a bare tree.

'So... how um... how *concerned* should I be?' She frowned. 'Fuck that. How frickin' shit-scared should I be that someone else is going to crash though our front door in the middle of the night?'

'Sam's the one who needs to double lock her doors right now, Ems. Not us,' he said, trying to reassure her.

'But if she's got you involved, which she clearly has... then won't that affect us too?'

Boyd shook his head. 'If this is about some old national security issue, then I can't imagine MI5 are going to crash into our house with their guns blazing, can you?'

'But what about the care worker you said was found hanging?' Emma pointed out. 'And the woman who died in the fire?' Absently she rubbed her hands over her swollen belly. 'If what you're saying is right, they've already killed two people! Why wouldn't they be happy to kill another three? Four? Five?'

Boyd really couldn't imagine that the UK's intelligence agencies would want to attract a whole load of attention by leaving a trail of bodies in and around Hastings. Surely, anybody who might be affected by it being leaked – a minister, a secret agent, a department head –would be dead or at least well into retirement by now? But, perhaps, whatever Operation Marble Orchard was, it still had some sort of strategic relevance, even now? It was hard to imagine that, though. Soviet Russia no longer existed and the eternal game players of intelligence and counter-intelligence had bigger fish to fry right now: the war in Ukraine; the power struggle that was going on in Moscow; China's increasing pressure on Taiwan, and on and on.

'Emma, this isn't Saudi Arabia, okay? We're not North Korea.'

'Dad! You said they hanged that young man! They burned an old woman to death! They're after this Baxter woman. If they've already actually killed someone, surely they're now fully committed.' She glanced again at the screenshot of the web page. 'Whatever THAT is, they've killed twice because someone got curious about those three words. What makes you think they would stop there?'

She had a point.

'And you had an actual, proper gun, tucked into your trousers!' she added. 'So don't tell me there's nothing to get worried about.'

Emma grabbed the keyboard.

'Hey. Just be careful what you tap in, Ems.' Even though Sunny had installed an IP blocker on his PC, he wasn't a hundred per cent sure that the wrong kind of search wouldn't result in his name and address popping up somewhere.

"Operation Grapple, right?' she said, as she typed it into Google.

Almost instantly, the results popped up.

'Oh my God,' she whispered. 'A *thousand* times more powerful than the Hiroshima bomb...'

36

'Baby... this is serious,' said Jay.

Okeke turned in her seat to look at him. 'Oh, you think?'

He gazed out of the dusty windscreen of his van at the weekenders milling around Pelham Arcade, some playing crazy golf, others queuing for 99 Flakes and freshly fried doughnuts. None of them, it seemed, had a care in the world. Neither he nor Sam had wanted to go back home after dropping Boyd off. He couldn't help wondering if their home was stuffed to the gills with bugs and cameras by now. The thought made him feel queasy.

'I mean this is worse than the Salikov thing,' he continued. 'It's not just some dodgy Russian criminal gang... We're talking proper James Bond-type people.'

She let out a sigh. 'I know, I know.'

'So why don't you just pass it uphill?'

'To who? DI Abbott? To Sutherland?'

'Yeah.'

She knew that she ought to. But then what? If she

started spreading what she knew across Hastings CID, would that not make her an even bigger problem in their eyes?

Her new burner phone buzzed in her lap and she jolted. It was an unknown number. She showed it to Jay. 'Shit. Do I answer this?'

He nodded. 'They can't have got your number. Only the guv knows it,' he pointed out.

Okeke thumbed the phone. 'Yes? Who's this?' she asked.

'It's Boyd.'

She let out a sigh of relief. Then immediately sucked it back in. 'Shit. Wait! You're not using your –'

'Relax, it's Emma's phone. I'm going to pick up a pay-as-you-go. In fact, we're heading up to Tesco now to buy one.'

'We?' Okeke asked.

'Yeah... Emma knows.'

'What?' Okeke exclaimed. 'Why?'

'Ozzie decided to investigate,' Boyd told her. 'He sniffed out my gun as soon as I got home and let's just say it all got very awkward, very quickly.'

Okeke turned to Jay. 'Emma knows.' To which he rolled his eyes.

'Listen, Sam,' Boyd continued, 'we just googled Operation Grapple. Have you had a chance to do that yet?'

She shook a cigarette out of the packet. 'No, we've not gone home yet.'

'Where are you?' he asked.

'Pelham Arcade. Watching the tourists and debating whether to pack our bags and run for the hills.' She was only half joking. 'What did you find out?'

'Operation Grapple,' Boyd replied, 'was the testing programme for British H-bombs in the Pacific. You know, those big hydrogen ones.' There was an edge to his voice. 'If Marble Orchard has something to do with Grapple, but it's *not* a matter of public records then... you know what I'm saying?'

'You think it might be something like a test that went wrong?' she cut in. 'Some kind of a cover-up? A clean-up operation?'

'Yup. Something like that. Which may mean something truly fucking horrific. I dunno... wrong test location, several thousand Polynesians incinerated?'

'Shit.'

'Right. And that's the bit that's really spooking me. If it was a balls-up, then I'm guessing it would have been a pretty big one. Enough of a clusterfuck that after all this time it would be literally impossible they could go public with it.'

He sounded rattled. But she could also hear dogs barking in the background. 'You're taking the dogs to Tesco?'

'Hardly,' he replied. 'We're going to collect Charlotte from work...and then we are pissing off. I suggest we take Eleanora's advice and get away. I don't want to take any chances. The sooner we know how big a deal this could be, the better.'

'Right,' said Okeke. She paused for a moment. 'Guv? You're seriously at this level of what-the-fuck?'

'Definitely.'

'Where are you going?'

'I dunno... we'll book an Airbnb or a hotel or something using one of Charlotte or Emma's credit cards.' He paused. 'Look, I'll call you when we've found somewhere and give you the details. All right?'

'Sure,' she replied.

'OK, we'll speak in a bit.' With that, Boyd hung up.

Jay was staring impatiently at her, eyebrows raised, waiting to hear what Boyd had had to say. 'And?'

She lit up her cigarette, rolled down the window on her side and blew out a swirling cloud. 'I'm not sure who's more paranoid now,' she said. 'Me or him.'

37

Jeremy Warner was well aware that Saturdays – particularly such lovely warm September ones as this – were not a day to discuss shop, especially not with the NPSA's senior director, Aubrey Dutton.

Warner had managed to persuade the weekend secretary at Thames House to put a call through to his private number. Within the hour, the senior director had agreed to take thirty minutes out of his 'invaluable family time' to listen to Warner's concerns, provided he made his way over from Downham Manor to Dutton's home in Richmond upon Thames.

Because Warner hated driving anywhere near London and no pool drivers were available at Downham, he'd had Gary drive him over in his grubby Mini Cooper, the young man pink-faced and apologising profusely all the way round the M25 about the messy state of his car.

At quarter past six, they pulled up outside Dutton's home on Petersham Road. It was a three-storey Edwardian townhouse with a small front drive, already clogged by half a dozen cars.

'You stay here, Gary,' Warner instructed.

'I can't! I'm on double yellows,' Gary replied.

'You're an intelligence officer. Improvise, lad,' Warner told him as he climbed out and slammed the passenger-side door. His shoes crunched across the gravel as he squeezed between the expensive sports cars and made his way up the steps to the front door. He pressed the bell and waited.

As he did, the muted sounds of a party in the back garden drifted around the side of the building. He pressed the bell button again and almost immediately the door opened. A breathless, flustered woman in a Peppa Pig kitchen apron stared back at him.

'Sorry, it's a bit of a yomp up from the back garden.' She looked him over quickly, then her face wilted. 'Oh dear. Don't tell me it's work?'

He nodded. 'I'm afraid so, Mrs Dutton. I'm here to see your husband.'

She stepped back and waved him in. 'I'll get him,' she said with a sigh. 'You can wait in his study.'

She led Warner down a high-ceilinged hallway with half-height cream-coloured wood panelling and air-force blue walls. She opened a door on the left.

'Here we are. But don't get too comfortable. I'm going to tell him he can discuss work for ten minutes and no more.'

Warner stepped inside and she closed the door on him. The room was small, but again high-ceilinged. Beyond a rosewood desk was a tall bay window. Curious, he wandered over to it and found himself looking down on Dutton's long, narrow back garden that led to the Thames River beyond. Some sort of family gathering seemed to be in full swing: a barbeque pit was belching a plume of smoke up into an overhanging willow tree, a long trestle table was covered in used plates and cutlery, and sheets of foil rested upon whatever hadn't quite been finished.

He recognised Aubrey Dutton wearing khaki shorts and a pale-yellow shirt. He was apologetically extracting himself from a family game of charades, his full head of silver hair scooped back above a ruddy forehead. He'd clearly caught some of the sun this afternoon.

Warner stepped back from the window so that Dutton wouldn't spot him being nosy as he came up the side path. He planted himself at a respectable distance from the desk, in the middle of the room, waiting for the director.

'Warner, isn't it?' said Dutton as he entered.

'Yes, Mr Dutton. Jeremy Warner, Director of Section Nine.'

'For God's sake, this had better be important.' He looked thoroughly irritated. 'We're in the middle of my daughter's leaving barbeque, man. She's off to York University on Monday.' Not bothering to wait for an apology, Dutton continued, 'Now, Section Nine. Your lot are the mole people down in the basement at Downham, aren't they?'

Warner nodded. 'Legacy cases.'

'That's right, the old dirty laundry. So what the hell is so bloody urgent that it couldn't wait until Monday morning?'

'A potential leak, sir.'

'Okay, well... plug it. That's what you're there for,' Dutton said, turning towards the door.

'Sir.' Warner took a breath. 'We have a developing situation that requires increased resources.'

'As far as I'm aware, your job is to keep tabs on a bunch of old codgers until they pop their clogs,' Dutton said. 'How many watch-list targets do you even have left?'

'We've seven active cases, sir,' Warner said. 'That's sixteen people left on our various watch lists.'

'So then, one unlucky OAPs' coach trip to Brighton could render your Boutique obsolete, couldn't it?' Aubrey Dutton smiled. He obviously thought he was being hilarious.

Warner remained silent. Unamused.

'Fine, so what is so important that you're here now?'

'Like I said, sir, a potential leak. I have already taken some action, but... *complications* have developed.'

Dutton wandered over to the window and gazed down ruefully at his grown-up kids and their friends continuing the game of charades. 'A complication, eh? Such as...'

'The previous director of Section Nine, Eleanora Baxendale.'

He smiled. 'Uh... yes, I remember Ellie. The old girl still with us, is she?'

'She's gone rogue,' said Warner.

That caught Dutton's attention. He turned round. 'I'm sorry, what?'

'I believe she intends to go public with one of our older, more sensitive cases.'

'What the hell? Why, for Christ's sake?'

Warner shook his head. 'I don't know her reasons. Perhaps to absolve her conscience before she dies?'

Dutton nodded. 'Is she writing a book?'

'Not to my knowledge,' Warner replied.

Dutton perched on the corner of his desk. 'So, what then?'

'One of our watch-lists targets living in a residential home recently died of natural causes. It appears, though, that he shared sensitive information with a care worker there, then either the care worker contacted Eleanora, or vice versa. The situation was showing signs of escalating. So... we contained it. Starting with the care worker.'

Dutton raised a hand, indicating that he didn't want nor need to hear any specifics.

'We also had to make a move on Eleanora,' Warner went on, 'but that... well, it went a little pear-shaped.'

'How *pear-shaped*?' Dutton asked.

'Quite, sir.' Warner told him about Drummond and Chapps' bungled misidentification. 'Too much haste and not enough thought,' he concluded.

'And now Ellie's in hiding, is she?' said Dutton.

Warner nodded.

'So, what you're telling me is that your little department's lost one dotty old woman, and you need *more resources* to find her?'

'But she's not a dotty old lady, is she?' replied Warner. 'She's one of us. She knows how we do things. There's another thing...' He cleared his throat. 'The local police force in Hastings are involved. Well, one particular detective. We know she's established contact with Ellie. There may be an attempt to meet her.'

'And you need some strings pulled?' Dutton guessed.

Warner nodded. 'That would, of course, help. But mainly what I need are extra people. The manpower to run a twenty-four-hour surveillance cycle on this detective.'

Dutton felt like leaning over and slapping the man sensible. That would mean well-trained agents being pulled off other ongoing operations. The agency was already stretched thin, monitoring various other, far more important miscreants. 'For fuck's sake, Warner... she's a frail old woman. Just deal with it!'

'Sir, you're aware of the cases we're still responsible for?'

Dutton was aware of a few of them: the Kelly thing, the Arthur Sutton incident, the Paris pursuit, the Iranian embassy, Lockerbie. 'Yes.'

'Are you aware of Operation Marble Orchard?'

'No,' Dutton replied. 'I can't say I'm familiar with that one.'

Warner took a step forward, pulled out a pen, leant over his desk and scribbled the operation name down on his blotting pad. 'Then may I suggest you familiarise yourself with it as soon as possible?'

38

'Let me get this straight in my head,' said Charlotte, gripping the dashboard as Boyd rounded a tight country corner. 'Just to check I'm not completely losing my grip on reality.'

'Go on,' he replied.

'Having only recently greatly annoyed a Russian criminal gang, you've now decided to make an enemy of the British secret service?'

Boyd hunched his shoulders. 'Not *all* of it,' he replied. 'Just a bit of it.'

'A bit,' she repeated. 'But this *bit* of British intelligence is after you because you've stumbled upon some big state secret that might have something to do with H-bomb testing back in the fifties?'

'That's the gist of it,' Emma replied from the back seat.

Charlotte nodded slowly. 'And so we're now effectively on the run?'

'Right,' Boyd said, taking another blind bend uncomfortably quickly.

'Along with Sam and Jay,' added Emma.

Charlotte nodded again, taking a moment to calmly form her next question. 'So, what is this big state secret?'

'That I don't know,' replied Boyd. 'All we've got is a code name.'

'And some old lady who used to work for this... *bit* that's after Okeke,' said Emma. 'Because this woman *does* know.'

'And we're heading off to meet her?' Charlotte asked.

'No. We're heading to... Where is it again, Emma?'

'Kintbury Lock,' Emma said. 'We've rented a narrowboat.'

Charlotte twisted round in her seat. 'We're going to stay on a –'

'Houseboat, a barge-like thing,' Emma replied. 'It's the only place I could find on Airbnb at short notice that would allow dogs.'

Charlotte turned to look at Boyd. 'Bill... please tell me this is a hilarious cover story concocted by the pair of you to whisk me away for a surprise romantic weekend break.'

'Well, it wouldn't exactly be romantic with Ems and the dogs in the back seat, would it?' Boyd pointed out.

Charlotte settled back, her brows knitted together. 'Oh God.'

'Next right, Dad,' Emma said. 'Coming up, two hundred yards.'

Boyd rounded the next bend and then turned onto an even narrower single-lane road flanked by high bushes and trees leaning in from either side to form a tunnel of foliage.

Emma was staring at her phone. 'The next bit's a short section of A-road, then we're back on Bs again.'

Boyd glanced in the rear-view mirror. 'We're sticking to B-roads where we can. I want to avoid any traffic cameras. Well... as many as possible,' he explained.

'Oh God,' Charlotte said again softly.

'I've got to say –' he glanced at her quickly – 'you're, uh, taking this remarkably well.'

'Bill, I'm hovering midway somewhere between utter confoundment... and sheer unbridled terror,' she said.

'It'll pass,' said Emma. Charlotte met her eyes in the rear-view mirror. She was grinning, a little manically. 'I'm not gonna lie,' Emma added. 'It's kind of exciting.'

'And there's some sort of a plan, I hope, Bill?' Charlotte said. 'Other than just hiding away on a boat?'

'Of sorts,' Boyd replied, slowing down for a T-junction.

'Left, Dad,' said Emma. 'Left, then first right.'

He signalled and turned. 'We meet this old lady. We find out what this is all about, then we decide what we're going to do with it,' he told her.

'If we blast it out onto the internet, or to a newspaper, to anyone who'll listen, basically... then there'll be no point in them coming after us,' Emma said. 'I mean, once it's out there, it's out, right?'

'Uh-huh,' Boyd grunted as he took a sharp right. 'That's the idea.'

'This is going to take a few days to sort out, isn't it?' said Charlotte. 'I'm going to need to call in sick tomorrow.'

Boyd glanced her way. 'Seriously? You're worrying about –'

Charlotte cocked her head. 'It's not all about you, Bill.'

∽

THEY ARRIVED at Kintbury Lock at ten past nine in the evening. Kintbury was a small village centred around a lock on the Kennet and Avon Canal. There was a small boatyard with narrowboats on chocks, in various stages of repair and maintenance, and a pub imaginatively called the Wheelhouse.

Boyd manoeuvred his Captur into a space at the furthest end of the pub's car park, in case the building had external CCTV cameras. He parked under the overhanging branches of a horse-chestnut tree, mindful that most of its conkers appeared to have already dropped. He was pretty sure, despite Emma's concerns, that satellite technology wasn't being pulled into service to try to spot them from low orbit. That kind of nonsense happened to Jason Bourne, not Bill Boyd. All the same... he made sure as much of his car as possible was obscured by the sprawling foliage.

They grabbed the dogs and the few bags of supplies and belongings they'd quickly scraped together at home and headed along the canal's towpath. The sun was gone but the sky was still a dull blue-grey, and by the waning light Boyd found the narrowboat, moored exactly where the owner had described. Boyd found the padlocked cabinet in the cockpit and entered the code Emma had been given. The padlock pinged open and inside the wooden cabinet they found the boat's keys.

'Shall I check on the others?' Emma asked.

Boyd nodded. Emma almost dialled Okeke's iPhone, but stopped herself in time, and used her new number instead.

'Emma?' Okeke replied after a couple of rings.

'Yeah. Where are you and Jay?'

'We're five, ten minutes away.'

'Cool. We're parked in a pub car park. The Wheelhouse. Our boat's just along the canal beside it. I'll keep an eye out for you,' Emma said.

Fifteen minutes later, Okeke and Jay joined them just as Boyd had figured out how to switch on the boat's electrics, light the galley stove and put the kettle on to make a brew.

'Guv,' Okeke said as she took the galley steps down from the cockpit.

He turned to greet her. In a moment of relief at seeing him, she reached out and hugged him tightly.

'This is fucking insane,' she mumbled into his shoulder. He patted her and let her go.

'Are you all right there, Sam?'

'I'm bloody stressed out,' she replied. 'All the way up, I kept fixating on cars behind that I thought were following us.'

Boyd nodded. 'Me too. The paranoia's exhausting, isn't it?'

He could hear Jay's deep voice as he greeted Emma and Charlotte, accompanied by Ozzie and Mia barking their hellos, then the clunk of his shoes coming down the galley steps. 'All right, guv?'

Boyd reached out and grasped Jay's hand firmly. 'Yeah, good. You two up for a coffee? I just stuck the kettle on.'

'Sure,' Jay replied.

Okeke returned to the galley steps and poked her head out into the cockpit. 'Emma, I recognised your number. You used your iPhone to call me,' she said.

'Yeah. It was just a quick –' Emma began.

'It was a dumb thing to do. You shouldn't have!'

'Hey,' Emma replied, still smiling, unsure if Okeke was being serious or not. 'Bit rude.'

'It was dumb,' repeated Okeke without smiling back. 'My iPhone's being tracked.'

'Yeah, but I didn't call your iPhone,' Emma pointed out. 'And Dad used it to call you before.'

'That's not the point. Your dad should have known better,' said Okeke, glaring at Boyd. '*Your* phone might have been hacked as well!'

Jay stepped away from Boyd and placed a hand on Okeke's back. 'Easy there, babes. She's just –'

Okeke shook his hand off. 'Jesus! We don't know anything for sure, though, do we?' Her eyes met his, then flicked to Boyd's. 'Seriously. We have no idea how big a deal we're mixed up in, and no fucking clue how much effort they're willing to put into shutting it down! If they managed to hack into my phone, that means they have all my contact details. Which means your phone, guv. Yours, Jay. Yours, Ems... Charlotte. Any of our phones could be compromised. Maybe even all of them!'

She took a deep breath and glanced back at Emma. 'No more phones. No more googling anything, or just checking something. We have two pay-as-you-go phones. That's it! They're all we can use from now on.'

Okeke's voice was sharp and ragged. And Emma looked as though she was on the verge of tears.

'Okay, fair point, Sam,' Boyd said calmly. 'Fair point, well made. Everything stays off from now on. As in off-off. If we need to look something up, we find an internet café or look at a book.' He looked at Charlotte. 'And maybe no calling in sick tomorrow. For anyone.'

He realised Okeke was quite right. They had no idea how wide a net had been cast in order to wrest control of this situation. Or, as Okeke had mentioned, how big a deal this was.

The kettle on the gas stove began to whistle softly.

39

Ten minutes later, they were all sitting outside in the open cockpit. The September evening sky had finally gone fully dark and they were gathered around the flickering light of a fake- flame electric lantern on the cockpit's floor. It cast leaping shadows between their legs and up into the low branches of the canal-side trees beyond the towpath.

'Oh, we really should do this more often,' said Charlotte mock cheerfully.

It triggered a nervous chuckle from the others. An owl hooted a reply from above.

'So, the real reason I brought you all here –' Boyd attempted a smile – 'is for a team-building exercise.'

The joke, for what it was, fell flat.

'Okay, look, fine. I panicked when I read the words "nuclear weapons tests",' he said. 'And I'm well aware it's a reach to presume that Marble Orchard is the name of some weapons-test balls-up recovery operation.' He sighed. 'So if I've panicked unnecessarily, everyone, I'm sorry.'

'But that shit happens,' chipped in Jay. 'There's stuff that happens all the time that governments cover up for, you know, ever. History's full of it.'

Charlotte looked at him sceptically. 'Such as?'

Jay shuffled uncomfortably under her gaze. 'Well, for starters... 9/11. That was a big set-up job, wasn't it? And...' He frowned for a moment as he tried to dig up other examples. 'Oh yeah. Weapons of mass destruction. Right? How many people died for that porkie? Then there's the Lockerbie disaster...'

Boyd wasn't sure if Jay's defence was helping him. He decided to step back in. 'Look, what I'm saying is, as far as I'm aware, governments tend to be really prickly about arse-covering cover-ups. And even more prickly about covering up the cover-ups.'

'*Kill people* prickly?' said Charlotte.

'Sometimes.'

'But all that testing happened back in the fifties,' she pressed.

'Like I said, maybe something went horribly wrong after Operation Grapple? You've got to remember this was the Cold War. Pretty tense time.'

'What if they bombed the wrong Pacific island?' said Emma.

'I don't see how you could hush that up,' said Okeke.

'There was no internet back then. I bet there's a lot that's been hushed up in the past,' replied Emma.

'Like the Yanks not landing on the moon, for example,' said Jay.

They all looked at him. He grinned. 'Just kidding.'

'So,' continued Boyd. 'Marble Orchard, then – *possibly* linked to Operation Grapple, which is public knowledge – was something that was kept top secret, for whatever reason.' He shrugged. 'A mistake? Something more sinister?'

'Why would today's government be so concerned about hushing up something that another government, literally in another *century*, was responsible for?' Emma asked.

'Sometimes it's not the original deed that's the problem,' said Charlotte. She glanced at Boyd. He wondered whether she was beginning to see his point. 'It's the lying about it for decades afterwards. It's the hushing-up bit that comes back and bites you on the bottom.'

Boyd nodded. 'If, say, several thousand innocent island dwellers were accidentally nuked, I could see that being a problem if it came to light today.'

'You think Eleanora was part of it?' asked Jay. 'Involved in whatever originally happened, or the cover-up after?'

Okeke nodded. 'I think so. Maybe the cover-up bit. I mean, she's in her late eighties, right? She'd have been in her twenties – maybe she had some kind of junior role?.'

'Which department was she in?' asked Jay. 'I mean, does it have a name? What does it do?'

Boyd and Okeke exchanged a glance.

'She didn't say. But,' said Okeke, 'she was pretty clear that she's been a British spook for some time.'

They all sat in silence for a while, listening to the water lap gently against the narrowboat's hull.

'Do you think we've over-reacted?' asked Charlotte. 'By that, I mean... does running away like this make us all look guilty of something?'

'Charlotte's got a point,' said Jay. 'If they try to blame those two deaths on us, we've just made ourselves look guilty as fuck.'

Boyd shook his head. 'Honestly? It would probably be easier for them to take us all out than try to frame us.' He looked around. 'A boating accident? A butane hob that was faulty? A gas leak...'

Emma's face fell. 'Dad...'

He stopped. 'Yeah. Okay. Sorry.'

'I guess the question isn't whether we've over-reacted,' said Okeke, 'but are we fooling ourselves that we've done enough?'

'I think we're ready to call her back,' said Boyd. 'She'll be waiting.'

'She said not until I'm absolutely sure I'm not being tracked.'

Boyd gestured at the narrowboat, the canal and the surrounding trees. 'We're as off-grid as we can possibly get in the UK.'

'Umm,' Jay said. 'We're sitting in the middle of Berkshire. It's not exactly some Tibetan mountaintop.'

'We're as sure as we can be,' said Boyd. 'I mean, that's the point, isn't it? You can never be absolutely certain.' He nodded at the tree-lined towpath. 'They could be squatting in those trees right now, watching us...'

'Jesus, Dad...'

He changed tack. 'But the new phones –' he smiled for Emma's benefit – 'now, there's no way they could have anything on them.'

'*Yet*,' said Okeke.

'Well, the sooner we use them, the better, then,' replied Boyd. 'We should call her.'

Okeke nodded. 'All right. Let's get it done.' She pulled her phone out and dialled the one number stored on it. 'Here goes....'

The phone rang once before it was answered.

'*Sam?*'

'Yes, it is.'

'*Are you safe now? Are you alone?*'

'I'm safe, but I'm not alone.'

Eleanora paused. '*Who's there with you?*'

'My boss, DCI Bill Boyd. His partner. His daughter. My boyfriend.'

'*Good God. Anyone else? Your second cousin twice removed, perhaps?*'

'No, that's it. We... we're all basically lying low in a –'

'*No details please!*' Eleanora cut in.

'Okay. So, we're all, you know, getting pretty jumpy. These are good people, Eleanora. I trust them. You can trust them.'

'*Well... I suppose I don't have much choice in the matter, now,*' she replied. They listened to her draw in a long rattling breath.

'How are you doing?' Okeke asked her.

'*Not particularly well.*'

'Can I put you on speakerphone? So the others can hear?'

Another pause. Then: '*If you must.*'

Okeke set the phone on her knees and tapped the loudspeaker icon. 'So, we all know about Operation Grapple. The H-bomb tests.'

'*That's good. Then you'll have a sense of how serious this is.*'

Boyd leant forward. 'Eleanora? This is DCI Bill Boyd. Sam's one of my regular team. We work very closely together. Myself and her boyfriend, Jay, were watching Sam's back when she took that call in the phone box. She'd been followed. We spotted two men in a car, watching her from a distance.'

'*Were they white? Middle-aged? Hairy faces? Like those stupid Hairy Bikers?*'

He smiled; she was spot on. 'Yes.'

'That'll be Drummond and Chapps. Both ex-military police. They were our dirty hands, so to speak.'

'Dirty hands,' echoed Boyd. 'You mean...?'

'Use your imagination.' She sighed. 'Yes, hitmen. Quite ruthless and dangerous, the pair of them. I'd have thought they'd both retired by now.'

'Eleanora,' said Okeke, 'so, like I said, I think we're off the radar. But –'

'Think? You're not sure?'

Okeke glanced at Boyd before replying, 'We don't know for certain. All I can say is we think so.'

'Good. Because you can never can be sure. But... there are a few little tricks you can use to check.'

'Such as?'

'Bait and trigger.'

Jay nodded. 'I know that one. That's the thing where you force whoever's tailing you to commit and move in.'

'That's right. Sam's young man, I presume?' said Eleanora. 'It incites a must-act-now scenario. Terror cells use it. They'll send one of their chaps out, looking like he's primed and ready to act, backpack and all.' She took a deep breath, then continued. 'If there's suspicion of an imminent act of terror, we have to respond. And then, of course, the rest of the cell know they're being watched.'

'So who's the bait' asked Boyd. 'Sam?'

'Well, obviously. Sorry, dear, but they're hoping you're going to lead them to me.'

Okeke wilted. 'Great.'

'You'll want to set up a situation that will force them to make a knee-jerk decision.'

'Such as?' said Okeke.

'Walking into one of those internet cafés with a memory stick in one hand might do it if they have eyes on. If they see you logging on and pushing the memory stick into a socket, they will presume you've managed to get something from me.'

'Great, and they'll all descend on me?'

'Yes. Like a herd of elephants. If I were Jeremy, that's the order I'd probably give.'

'Who's Jeremy?' asked Boyd.

'Jeremy Warner. My successor at Section Nine.'

'What's that?' Boyd asked.

At the other end of the line, Eleanora was overcome by a bout of rattling coughs, followed by laboured wheezing.

'Are you okay?' said Okeke.

'No. I need this situation resolved... quickly.' Eleanora took a few deep breaths, then carried on. 'Section Nine is a lesser known nook of MI5 – there to make sure that some rather dubious mistakes made in the past quietly wither away.'

'What's Marble Orchard?' asked Emma, before adding, 'Sorry, this is Emma. Bill's daughter.'

'That, my dear... is the million-pound question,' she replied. 'Emma, my dear, we did something wrong back in 1962. Something terribly wrong.'

A long pause. No one dared speak, eager to hear more.

'No,' she said finally. 'I'm not going to explain all that over the phone. When I'm safe... then we'll discuss it.'

'How does Jim Crowhurst tie into this?' asked Okeke.

'That will have to wait too. All I'll say for now is that Captain James Crowhurst was a true hero. And we treated the poor man appallingly.' There was more coughing and wheezing. 'Look, you can probably hear I'm struggling, so... try what I suggested. Bait them and see what happens.' They heard her issue a wheezy cackle. 'If you're all alive and in one piece afterwards, then give me a call.'

'Okay,' replied Okeke. 'We'll give it a go.'

'Please... do it quickly, though,' urged Eleanora. 'I'm really *not sure how much longer I can last without my wretched pills.*' She hung up.

The five of them sat in thoughtful silence, listening to the trees along the canal whisper to each other, then finally Charlotte spoke.

'She seemed rather nice, didn't she?'

40

The first thing next morning, Jay drove his van over to Newbury, just a few miles away. He parked on the outskirts and walked into the small market town with the peak of his trusty baseball cap pulled down low to hide his face.

And after half an hour of exploring, he found what he was looking for – a suitable candidate in his 'professional' opinion. Assad's, an internet café that was sandwiched between a newsagent's and a Vapez store on Magpie Lane, a mini pedestrian-only precinct of shops off Northbrook Street.

The narrow thoroughfare was perfect for what they needed: long and thin, only one way in and one way out. He was pretty sure no daft bugger would even try a hit down there. No access for vehicles meant there'd be no quick grab-and-bundle into the back of an unmarked van. If they swooped on Sam, they'd have to carry her, kicking and screaming, all the way up Magpie Lane to Northbrook Street, past a Greggs that had tables and chairs set outside for the summer months... and hopefully would be busy later on this morning.

He had Boyd's burner phone on him and used it to call Okeke. 'I think I've found the perfect place to set up our trap.'

'Please tell me it's very public,' Okeke replied.

'It will be.' It was not yet nine. And it was a Sunday. He *assumed* the small precinct would be busier later. 'It's looking like it'll be a nice day, so...'

'Shit, I can't believe I'm doing this,' muttered Okeke.

'Honestly, babes. I've assessed it and it looks pretty good. It's a bottleneck. Me and Boyd can park our arses at the end. If shit goes down, they'll have to come through us. You'll be perfectly safe, love.'

'Oh, you know that, do you?'

He smiled. 'I've got this.'

'With all your recently acquired expertise?'

'Babes, trust me.' He gave her a more detailed description. 'If anyone tries to grab you, just scream that you're being kidnapped. I'm sure there'll be enough have-a-go heroes to help me and Boyd out. I mean... good-looking chick, like you?'

'Great, love,' she replied drily. 'That's so very reassuring.'

~

'THIS IS PRETTY GOOD,' said Boyd, looking around. 'Nice and busy too.'

Jay took a bite out of his Greggs sausage roll. 'It'll be a complete shit-show if they try to grab Sam here.'

Boyd nodded. From where they sat outside Greggs, there was a clear line of sight down the pedestrian way to the internet café at the far end. If Okeke perched herself right next to the window, to any spooks who might be watching, it would be clear as day exactly what she was attempting to do.

Emma and Charlotte were further down Magpie Lane, where it widened into a small square. They were sitting on a bench directly outside a charity shop. They had an even clearer view of the inside of the internet café, as well as eyes on anyone who might suddenly make a frantic move towards it.

The plan, if that wasn't too grand a term for what they had cobbled together, was that Emma and Charlotte would sit there, idling and chatting, while watching out for any suspicious-looking *lurkers* and anyone entering Assad's directly after Okeke.

Should they see anything that looked like the start of a response, Charlotte would signal Boyd by standing up and stretching her arms. He and Jay could then wade in. He had his Russian gun, tucked once again into the belt of his trousers. This morning he was actually glad to have it on him; if it came to it, he'd pull it out and fire a warning shot in the air.

If it came to it, he'd decided last night, he wouldn't hesitate to aim the thing at one of *them* and use it.

He checked his watch: two minutes to eleven. They'd all agreed on eleven as showtime. This was when Okeke would turn into Magpie Lane from Northbrook Street and enter the small precinct, walking with purpose and a hint of furtive paranoia down the length of the precinct towards Assad's.

'Don't overdo the acting, Sam,' Jay had advised her.

'Babes, I won't be acting,' she'd replied edgily. 'I will be genuinely shitting myself.'

Boyd looked around. 'So many people for a Sunday,' he muttered. 'Thank god for that.'

'Well, that's good... and bad,' said Jay. 'There are lots of witnesses if something goes down... but then there's more folks for us to keep an eye on.'

Boyd nodded. 'I think with this whole private-eye thing, you may have found your calling.'

'Tell Sam that.' Jay sighed. 'She still thinks I'm trying to be a pretend cop.'

∽

'So REMIND ME AGAIN... What were those clues to look out for that Jay mentioned?' asked Charlotte.

'Headphones on. Supposedly listening to music,' replied Emma, 'but actually listening for instructions.'

Charlotte frowned. 'Headphones? Hmm, well, that's about half the people wandering around here, then.'

'Hand signals. Folks looking around a lot. Acting edgy.' Emma ticked the clues off on her fingers.

Charlotte pursed her lips. 'Edgy? How does one define edgy? Are we talking twitchy? Sweaty?'

'I dunno.' Emma shrugged. 'I guess you only know it when you see it.'

'Right.' Charlotte looked around, trying to zero in on anyone who appeared out of place, or who had no clear reason to be lingering. She suspected she probably resembled a big-eyed meerkat, flicking her head in one direction, then the other, checking for predators.

'See, now *you're* looking edgy,' said Emma as she idly flicked through a magazine. 'Maybe we should just make out like we're talking to each other, you know... rather than being look-outs?'

Charlotte nodded. That seemed like a smarter idea. 'I do hope the dogs aren't making a big racket aboard the boat.'

'We should have left them some chew bones to keep them busy,' muttered Emma.

Charlotte cast around for something else to say. 'So, how are things going with you and Dan?'

Emma looked up at her. 'We're having *that* conversation? *Now?*'

Charlotte shrugged. 'He hasn't been around for several weeks. I just wondered if...'

'He's touring with his band, remember? They got that small slot at the festival over in Cornwall.'

'Of course I remember,' Charlotte hissed. 'I just can't think of anything else to say. It's too stressful.'

Emma shook her head. 'Okay, so their gig went down really well apparently. They've started getting calls from booking agents. Dan said there was even a chance they might be supporting PepperBoy in a couple of months' time.'

Charlotte nodded as though the name meant something to her. 'Ooh, that all sounds rather exciting.'

'Yeah, he's pretty stoked about it all.' She looked at her watch. 'Eleven,' she said softly.

'Right. Yes.' Charlotte nodded sombrely. 'Showtime.'

∽

OKEKE PAUSED on Northbrook Street beside the entrance to Magpie Lane. She took a deep breath to steady her nerves as she eyed the narrow passage, punctuated by a pair of bollards that were clearly designed to withstand the impact of a Challenger tank. If she was already being watched, then fine... Her genuine display of anxiety would only suggest to them that she was about to do something radical.

Jay was right. It was – thank God – busy. From where she stood, she could see the internet café at the far end. Magpie Lane led towards it like an ominous gauntlet that she was going to have to purposefully stride down, giving the impression all the way that she was confident no one had the slightest bit of interest in who she was and what she was up to.

She tried not to look at Jay and Boyd ahead and to her right, sitting outside the Greggs with the air of two bored tradesmen taking a break. Instead, she picked up her pace, trying her best to channel the vibes of an intrepid reporter with a sensational story that was burning a hole in her pocket.

As she passed Jay and Boyd, she pulled out her iPhone and held it to her ear.

'Okay, any spooks out there, this is Detective Constable Samantha Okeke with Marble Orchard , your big fucking secret', she muttered to herself. 'And guess what... I'm about to upload everything I have and spam the internet with it.'

If there were any spooks present right now, they'd be in a loose diamond-shaped configuration Jay had explained to her last night: one ahead, one behind, and one either side. The volume within was 'the box', and they'd be doing their damnedest to keep her inside it. The rest would be in a van, and now, because of the bollards, they were going to be kept on Northbrook Street but ready to spill out at a moment's notice.

She fumbled in her jacket pocket as she approached Assad's Internet Café and pulled out the memory stick that they'd bought in a garage on the way in this morning. Maybe she was acting a bit too overtly, but perhaps that wasn't a bad thing. The point of the exercise was to trigger a response, to tease some unseen team leader into making a split-second decision and calling out a 'go' command.

She wondered if holding the memory stick in her left hand had triggered a flurry of murmured communications into phones and pinhole mics. She couldn't help a quick look around to see if she could spot anyone talking to themselves.

And, bingo, there was one. A portly man in his fifties with sideburns and frizzy grey hair pulled back into a scruffy ponytail. He was ever so slightly behind her, to her left, and heading in the same direction as he held a phone to his ear. He wore a denim shirt and waistcoat, like a grizzled old roadie, and a pair of old-fashioned Walkman headphones.

Fuck.

He wasn't talking. Just listening. Suspicious in itself. His eyes met hers for a split second before she looked ahead again. What was it Jay had said? *If someone makes eye contact once. It's random. Twice, take caution. Three times... you're being followed.* She took another couple of strides and glanced over her shoulder. And again they made eye contact.

Fuckity fuck.

All of a sudden, this plan felt like the dumbest plan ever. She was quite literally walking herself, deliberately, into a trap. Forcing their hand. If it triggered nothing, then great, wonderful – she'd shaken their tail and there'd be high-fives all around. But on the other hand... five minutes from now she could find herself trussed up and gagged in the back of a van, with that ugly bastard sitting on top of her.

She clocked Emma as she approached the internet café, one hand resting on her rounded belly, the other flicking through a magazine. And Charlotte sitting beside her, as stiff as a board, wide eyes darting around anxiously.

Christ.

Okeke took a deep, steadying breath, and pocketed her phone as she stepped inside Assad's Internet Café. The place reeked of old coffee beans and stale sweat, with a lingering trace of cigarette smoke. It was largely empty: a couple of booths were occupied by men tapping away furiously.

She approached the old man standing behind the counter. 'A terminal please.'

'Five pound an hour,' he replied.

She pulled a note out of her bag and handed it over. 'Anywhere?' she asked, gesturing at the vacant booths.

He nodded as he tore a ticket from a roll and handed it to her. 'No TikTok, Instagram, Snapchat. No computer games.'

She nodded and headed over to a window booth. Through the grubby glass, she could see Emma and Charlotte. Charlotte still looked as though she'd just sat down on a sharp spike. At the far end of Magpie Lane, she could just about make out Jay and Boyd and the passing traffic on Northbrook Street. No one had followed her into the café, which meant Mr Roadie could just have been an innocent civilian, and Okeke was just being paranoid...

Or he'd recognised that he'd been clocked and pulled himself out from the surveillance box.

The overwhelming sense of paranoia was draining. Everyone she could see through the window could easily be mistaken for a spy. She could understand the mental exhaustion that undercover officers often suffered. A couple of DCI Flack's team had recently had to take a break from their covert work on Operation Rosper and she'd sarcastically quipped to Warren that it must be hard work having to shoot pool and talk shit all day long with a bunch of scrotes.

Maybe she'd been unfair.

She took a deep breath – part acting the role of would-be whistle-blower, part releasing genuine nerves – and then logged onto the internet terminal. Again, she looked outside for any hint of a knee-jerk response.

'Okay... well, here goes,' she muttered.

Very slowly and deliberately, she slotted the memory stick into the USB port beneath the monitor.

41

Margaret Hatcher was so focused on deadheading her roses that she didn't hear the car pull up in her front driveway, nor did she hear the footsteps as the two men came round the side.

'Chief Superintendent Margaret Hatcher?' A well-spoken male voice broke the peace of her back garden.

She stood up straight, shears in hand, and turned to see two men: one old, pale and stick-thin in a grey suit – he reminded her of the John Major puppet from *Spitting Image*; the other, a youthful-looking middle-aged man in a maroon blazer, polo shirt and chinos with foppish silver-coloured hair slicked back above a sunburnt forehead and panda eyes.

'Yes?' she replied. 'And you gentlemen are…'

The younger man stepped forward and offered his hand. 'Aubrey Dutton. And this is Jeremy Warner.'

Hatcher shook his hand. Dutton looked and sounded as though he should be valuing someone's collection of Spode pottery on the *Antiques Roadshow*. He was all plummy vowels and Oxbridge charm.

The Archive

'We're from MI5.' Dutton pulled a self-effacing smile. 'His Majesty's Secret Service.' He laughed. 'It's always fun to say that bit.'

Hatcher set the shears down on the top of her cuttings bucket. 'Oh?'

She'd been half expecting a home visit from them ever since the Arthur Sutton incident. And *fully* expecting a visit from them in the aftermath of the Salikov encounter last year.

'MI5 is a rather broad church,' she replied. 'Specifically which department?'

'The NPSA,' replied Dutton.

'Ah, the National Protective Security Authority.' She raised her eyebrows, inviting him to elaborate.

Dutton seemed a little flustered under her gaze. 'I wonder, could we have a little chat with you?'

She gestured at her garden and the round wooden table and chairs on the patio. 'It's quiet out here.' She added, 'My son's home, but he makes rather a racket with his music inside.'

Hatcher led them over to the patio, and they all took a seat at the table.

'So, what can I help you with?' she asked.

'Well,' started Dutton, 'we have a somewhat awkward situation going on at the moment... One of the sections under my departmental umbrella has the role of safeguarding legacy state secrets.' He smiled. 'Our dusty old skeletons, so to speak.'

Hatcher couldn't help but notice that Warner grimaced at that. He obviously disliked his boss's rather dismissive description. 'They are national security cases that are still very much top secret,' Warner added.

'All right,' said Hatcher. 'And what has this to do with me?'

Arthur Sutton. It has to be. Or the Salikovs.

'My colleague here, Jeremy, runs the section,' said Dutton, gesturing to him. 'Jerry... would you go ahead and explain?'

Warner nodded and cleared his throat. 'My predecessor, Eleanora Baxendale, retired from the post ten years ago. And we understand your force's CID may be working on a case that's linked to her.'

Baxendale – the name rang a distant bell for Hatcher. It was a very distinct name. Then it came to her: DC Okeke's press briefing on Wednesday. The arson attack... and the misper.

Hatcher nodded. 'Yes. A house fire. We're looking at a likely case of arson and of course manslaughter... because, I presume you're aware, there was a fatality. Her sister.'

Dutton nodded sombrely. 'Nasty business.'

'Indeed,' said Hatcher. 'And Eleanora Baxendale, who owned the house in question, is missing and someone whom we'd very much like to find.'

'As do we,' said Dutton. 'Because, you see, we're very concerned about her welfare.'

Warner nodded. 'She's in her late eighties and not very well.'

'More to the point,' added Dutton, 'we believe she may be in some considerable danger.'

'How so?' Hatcher asked.

'She may be on an FSB hit list.'

'FSB? I'm sorry... *Russian* intelligence?'

Warner shot a glance at his superior; Dutton nodded and took over. 'We have reason to believe Eleanora was a long-term sleeper agent for the Soviets... and potentially a recruiter for them. Which means she would, of course, know the names of a number of moles among our people...'

'So, I'm presuming she'd be an incredible asset to you,' replied Hatcher.

'As far as we've managed to piece together, she was toying with the idea of going public, naming names... Exposing the lot of them,' Dutton told her.

'And why would she do that?' Hatcher asked.

He shrugged. 'Guilt? Remorse? An act of atonement? Perhaps she no longer likes what the Russians have become in recent years? I really don't know. But, you are right, that makes her an incredibly valuable intelligence asset.'

Warner stepped in again. 'We suspect the FSB somehow caught wind of what she was intending. The house fire may have been an attempt on her life and... well, here we are.'

Hatcher crossed her arms and sat back. 'This seems like a particularly *candid* briefing to be giving to someone outside of your little club.' She smiled cynically. 'A mere provincial chief superintendent.'

Dutton returned her smile. 'Well, yes, quite. We don't normally do home visits on a Sunday either, but... this is very time critical, I'm afraid. The reason why we're talking to you like this is Eleanora. We really do want to help the poor woman. She's vulnerable out there; she's elderly and unwell.'

'And let's not forget valuable,' added Hatcher drily.

'Very,' replied Dutton.

'But we're also aware,' said Warner, 'that she managed to contact one of your detectives for help.'

Warner paused, obviously waiting for her response to that. Hatcher remained perfectly silent, her gaze steady.

'It was a Detective Constable Samantha Okeke,' said Warner, fiddling with the knot of his tie. 'She made a public appeal, which of course you know about, and we think Eleanora saw it and responded to it. Directly.'

'We believe your detective may be in continued contact with her, helping her to stay in hiding,' cut in Dutton. 'DC Okeke may have a perfectly valid reason for doing so, but that very much puts her in danger too. We are concerned for the safety of both women.'

'We need to know everything about Samantha Okeke,' resumed Warner. 'Family, friends, contacts, close colleagues. Places she might use to help Eleanora hide. But probably most helpful would be to have a chat with her closest colleagues.'

'Well, that would be DCI Boyd,' Hatcher replied.

Warner's head tilted at the mention of his name. 'Could you...'

'I can give you his phone number if you want to speak with him. The rest you can find out for yourselves.'

42

They all returned to the narrowboat in a jubilant mood. Okeke especially. Nothing had happened in Newbury. Nobody had swooped in to grab her. She'd sat in the window of the internet café for ten minutes, tapping away on the keyboard as if she was in some frantic text exchange with Julian Assange or Ed Snowden... and still nothing had happened.

Boyd stepped aboard the narrowboat and stopped at the cabin door. 'I just need to get my jacket and then I suggest we go and make use of that pub,' he said, nodding towards the Wheelhouse. 'I think we've all earned a pint, don't you?'

'Hells, yeah,' said Jay.

Boyd spun the lock, opened the door and then froze. Someone had been there while they were out. The bench-seat cushions were in disarray; various cupboard doors were wide open, their contents pulled out and scattered on the floor. The communal area had the look of a very thorough, very frantic search conducted with little care for discretion.

'Somebody's ransacked the place!' snapped Boyd.

Then another concern hit him. There was no barking. No Ozzie. No Mia. The long interior was still and silent.

'Everyone off!' he shouted over his shoulder as he reached under the back of his jacket to retrieve the gun.

If they've been here, they could be close by. Even aboard still.

From the foot of the galley steps, he listened as the others scrambled onto the towpath. He waited for silence to descend before he slowly advanced into the galley, towards the far bulkhead and the door that led to the forecabins, gun held out in front of him, breath held steady.

The narrowboat swayed gently beneath his weight, causing the cupboard doors to clatter softly against their clasps. As he neared the door, he heard the heavy rapid breathing of someone who'd been exerting effort very recently and was unable to hold their breath to stay silent.

Then a thud. Perhaps something heavy in a forecabin falling from a shelf or one of the bunks.

Boyd raised his aim and kicked the door inwards...

... to reveal Ozzie with a pillow in his mouth, the material torn and goose feathers stuck to his nose. Behind him Mia balanced on her hind legs, her head and front paws poking around inside a storage locker.

'Oh, for fuck's sake.'

43

Eleanora stirred her mint tea slowly as she looked out at the families playing on the beach. It was lovely golden sand here at Seaford. Better than the wretched pebbles that largely carpeted the beach at Hastings. The sound of circling seagulls, happy children and gentle waves made for an idyllic sonic landscape. A soothing, reassuring balm for her jangled nerves.

Frankie's Beach Café was one of those perfectly located little establishments. The hut itself might look a little scruffy, with its guano-dappled lead roof and wobbly, weatherworn wooden seats and tables, but the location was just perfect, absolutely perfect, right on the edge of the beach.

From where she sat, Eleanora could see the row of brightly coloured beach huts, including her cheerful cornflower-blue one, which had been her home for the last week. Frankie's – or more accurately Frankie's toilet – had been a life-saver.

As she watched two little girls industriously assembling a wonky sandcastle, her mind fluttered back to her own childhood years, and a day like today, down on the beach.

She'd been there with Mattie, Mummy, Nanny and the dogs. They'd had beautiful sun-kissed, endless summer days, even though there was a war going on somewhere beyond the rippling blue English Channel.

Then, as the afternoon cooled, it would be back home to Barnham House, Mummy's family home, for tea and toasted crumpets, and finally the evening would be spent playing with Mattie. She had a magnificent doll's house in her room, a miniature replica of their grand home, complete with miniature versions of Mummy's favourite pieces of furniture. There was even a tiny version of Mummy herself and themselves, and even some of the staff: Nanny, Mr Wilson and Lottie.

There had been no miniature Daddy, though.

Daddy hadn't come back from France during the war. They'd received a letter and a medal but nothing more. And without Daddy to look after them all, things had gone downhill. The money dried up, Barnham House was taken over by the army during the remaining years of the war, and by the time they could have it back, Mummy had had to sell it to pay off debts that had mounted in the meantime.

Eleanora's mind fluttered back to the present, like a homing pigeon returning to its loft.

Only a handful of times throughout her life had she returned to Barnham House. Each time it had been a horrendously painful experience, seeing what the passage of time had done to the once-grand building and well-tended grounds. It was derelict now. Sections of the heavy slate roof had caved in as the oak beams holding them up had perished.

The last time she'd visited had been the day after she'd retired from the Boutique. It had been a nostalgic road trip for her and Mattie to see the old place once more. In fact, to say a final goodbye to it. Mattie's chronic condition had progressed to the point where she'd soon need a wheelchair, and the uneven floors of Barnham House were a perilous terrain for her to traverse with only the aid of her walking stick.

It had been a fleeting visit. To say goodbye but also to find mementos they could take back with them to Eleanora's house in Ore.

Eleanora had gone up the grand stairs to the first floor – foolhardy, really, given its unsteady creaking condition – to visit her old bedroom and then to look in on Mattie's. Mercifully, the doll's house had fared better over the years than the house it had been fashioned after, having been shoved into a nook and forgotten about.

It had fared better than either of them, truth be told. Not long after that visit, Mattie's osteoporosis had rendered her bed-ridden. And Eleanora's weak heart made it near impossible for her to lift Mattie out of bed. The only time she could get Mattie into the wheelchair was when their home help visited every other day.

And now that Mattie was gone, Eleanora was the last of the Baxendales. There were no children or grandchildren, no nieces or nephews. The Baxendales had had an august lineage of ministers and dukes, admirals and generals, lords and ladies... and now it concluded with her: a fragile old lady living in a hut on a beach.

Not just fragile but dying. In fact, dead if she didn't get her hands on her wretched pills soon.

She caught a glimpse of her reflection in the café's glass windbreak. Her snow-white hair, gossamer fine and distressingly thin, fluttered lifelessly in the breeze, along with her summer cardigan and skirt. Her ankles, God help her, were swollen to the point where they looked like the legs of a pool table. Once, a very long time ago, she'd been an attractive young woman. Even into her sixties and early seventies, while she'd still been working at Downham, she had been referred to as both striking and handsome (with 'for her age' tacked on at the end).

Now, the woman staring back at her looked like some wretched old bag lady.

44

'Well, that's going to cost me,' said Boyd, tidying up the last of the destruction. 'The bedding's ruined. The pillows are ruined.' He looked at Ozzie and Mia, both staring at him guiltily from the corner of the galley.

Charlotte tutted as she picked up the gurgling kettle and prepared a round of coffees. 'Bill, given the current situation, maybe that's something to fuss over later?'

'Hmm, maybe,' he said, shooting daggers at the miscreants. 'I'll give you a hand.'

He took three mugs from the counter and clumsily made his way up the steps to the cockpit. 'Milk, sugar and biscuits coming,' he announced as he handed them out.

Charlotte came up behind him with a tray and set it down on one of the bench seats.

'So,' she started as she sat down, 'how certain are we that we've managed to get the better of the British secret service, then? Because,' she said, holding the plate of Hobnobs out, 'that really did feel a tad too easy. I can't help but wonder if they're... I don't know, bluffing us. Trying to make us *think* we're home and dry...'

'We did as she suggested,' said Okeke. 'I mean, she's the expert, right? I guess we have to assume that the coast is clear if we're going to try to meet her.' She looked at Boyd. 'Seriously... it needs to be soon. She needs to be in a hospital.'

'So, are we going to call her now?' asked Emma. 'Tell her we're ready to come and get her?'

Boyd nodded. 'That's the next step. But after that we need to figure out how to keep her safe? They obviously want her. There's probably an alert set for the moment she's admitted into a hospital.'

'So then what about walking her into the nearest BBC news studio?' said Jay. 'I mean, you know, get someone like Fiona Bruce or Clive Myrie to do a big-ass, breaking-news interview? Blow this shit wide open.'

'Be that as it may, but we still don't know what it is she wants to reveal,' said Boyd. 'All we have is the code name Marble Orchard and our own theories about what it could be.'

'I bet we're right, though,' said Emma. 'They bombed the wrong island.'

Boyd shook his head. 'I'm not sure it was done like that, Ems... from a plane.'

'The point is,' continued Jay, 'once it's out there, it's out there. No point those spooks coming after us any more.'

'No point... *if* it gets out there,' said Okeke. 'I think the government's pretty handy at muzzling a bad news story, isn't it?'

'And nobody's going to print or broadcast a whistle-blower without some kind of evidence,' added Boyd. 'I don't think this is sorted if we just hand her over to the Beeb and say, "Go on, then, love – tell these nice people what this is all about."' He sighed and took a sip of his coffee. 'There's no way Sam and I get to keep our jobs after this. We'll be done as police officers.'

She frowned sceptically. 'Come on. I'm sure we've done worse!'

'Her Madge will be leant on to make an example of us. We're going to be complicit in leaking a state secret. I don't think, as a rule, the police take too kindly to that.'

Okeke shrugged. 'Well, anyway, Emma's right. We should call her and let her know we think we're ready to meet.'

∼

ELEANORA'S PHONE buzzed noisily in her bag, jerking her from her meandering thoughts. There was only one person who had her number. The young black detective, Ms Okeke.

'Yes?' she answered cautiously.

'Eleanora?'

It was her knight in shining armour. 'Sam,' she replied, smiling. 'You're safe, I presume.'

'I am. We did exactly what you suggested.'

'The bait and trigger?'

'Yes. I sat in a window seat of an internet café. Made a big deal of pushing a memory stick into the computer and tapping away.'

'And?'

'Absolutely nothing,' replied Okeke.

Eleanora heaved a sigh of relief. There was no way Jeremy would have let that happen if he had eyes on her.

'All right.' Her need for medication was getting desperate. She could hear and feel her lungs crackling with each deep, rattling breath she took. 'I think we can have a go at this.'

'Eleanora, how are you doing?' asked Okeke. 'Your breathing doesn't sound too good.'

'It sounds worse than it is, m'dear,' she replied. 'Obviously, the sooner this wretched nonsense is concluded, the sooner I can get back on my ruddy pills.'

'Okay. So... we should arrange to meet?'

'Oh, yes. Yes. There's no point muddling around any longer. Now, I have an address. Are you ready?'

'Hang on – let me grab a pen.'

Eleanora sighed. 'In my day, you'd have to remember things. Directions. Addresses. Numbers. Ciphers.'

'Sorry... I –'

'Not to worry, dear. Those were different times,' Eleanora wheezed. 'So, listen very carefully... Don't make me repeat myself.'

45

'Here's Boyd's phone,' said Drummond, handing it to Warner. 'He left it here. It was plugged in and charging.'

Warner nodded. 'At home and left on. Clever.'

He looked around the small study. A scruffy man cave that belonged to a regular bloke, neither cultured nor a troglodyte. Just an ordinary man. novels lined the shelves alongside dusty VHS boxes and DVD slipcases. Admittedly the books weren't classics, but at least they weren't vanity coffee-table tomes.

He could pay for another Pegasus licence to open up DCI Boyd's phone, but the fact that he'd left it behind told Warner two things: firstly, that Boyd was well aware that his iPhone was a potential liability – an essential daily gadget that could be manipulated into a powerful surveillance tool. And secondly, that he knew enough to run.

Drummond nodded. 'Looks like he left in a hurry. And he's taken his dogs and family with him.'

Warner went to investigate the house's generous lounge, its large bay window looked out onto a small front yard. He surveilled the sloping street, the rooftops opposite and a pleasing sliver of glinting sea beyond.

A very nice place for a mid-rank copper. It was nicer than his place. Which irked him somewhat.

'I want every bit of digital tech, anything written down...' he announced to Drummond. 'And don't worry about being discreet. Pull this place apart. If he's done a runner, then he already knows we're onto him.'

'Yes, sir.'

He left Drummond to pass on that message to Chapps and the rest of the search team and returned to Boyd's study. 'I want everything that's on or in that desk,' Warner called out, noticing a pad of paper beside the monitor.

'Yes, sir.'

He scanned the room once more: in addition to the desk, a small sofa bristled with white dog hairs, an IKEA shelving unit cluttered with books, CDs and DVDs, and a Gordian knot of cables, adaptors and extension leads spilled from a wicker basket.

Then something else caught his eye. It was tucked into the corner beneath a low shelf, next to the sofa. 'There's a safe. Let's have that as well.'

Warner went upstairs to check the bedrooms. DC Okeke's terraced house in St Leonards-on-Sea – their previous stop – had displayed similar evidence of a hasty departure. Clothes pulled from drawers, underwear and pop socks scattered across the bed. No sign of her iPhone, though. Either she'd dumped it or she had the device with her but powered down completely.

Not that they needed it to gather intel – everything that was on that phone had already been cloned and dumped onto the Boutique's server. They knew everything about Detective Constable Samantha Okeke. Where her family lived, that she cohabited with a man called Jason Turner, that she was looking forward to a promotion to detective sergeant. Even the more granular details: for instance, the most listened-to tracks on her phone were by someone called Dua Lipa. She was a member of several Facebook groups, including 'Hastings and St Leonards Marketplace', 'Overheard in The Nelson', 'Hastings and Bexhill Labour' and 'Below Decks Addicts'

He wandered back downstairs and into the dining room, where one of the team was going through recent post.

'Anything?'

'Uh, bank statements, utility bills for William Boyd. Also post for an Emma Boyd... And there's a *Reader's Digest* subscription for a Charlotte Bellefois.'

Warner's phone buzzed in his pocket. He pulled it out; the caller was Aubrey Dutton. He answered it immediately.

'How's it going?' asked Dutton.

'Boyd is undoubtedly in on this with Okeke,' Warner replied.

'Dammit. If she's reached out to him for help, then who else knows?'

'She has a partner. Jason Turner. I would say almost certainly him too.'

'Bloody wonderful,' Dutton muttered.

Warner could hear female voices in the background and the thunk of a cork being pulled from a bottle. Dutton, he guessed, was now back home in Richmond with his family, keen to be there for his daughter's last Sunday roast before she headed off to university. But also, he suspected, Dutton was keen to place himself a healthy distance away from the grubby work of intelligence gathering.

'We have Boyd's iPhone. He left it at home. Very deliberately,' Warner said.

'Then I would suggest he's left nothing on it that could help us,' Dutton replied.

'My thoughts exactly –'

'Extract what you can from it anyway,' Dutton ordered. 'He may have been careless enough to leave us a clue.'

'We can try,' said Warner.

'Listen, I don't want this operation escalating any further. You understand? Do what you can. You should have enough to fix this.'

Warner understood completely. Dutton's helping hand with more manpower would provide him with enough resources to plug the leak, but if not – and if Eleanora managed to tell all to the world – then the senior director wanted the wriggle room to claim he had no idea what Jeremy Warner and his rogue department had been up to.

'I have to go,' said Dutton firmly. 'All I need to hear from you is when the situation has been successfully resolved. Preferably in the next twenty-four hours.' With that, he hung up.

The slippery bastard was mitigating his involvement. Probably even constructing his alibi for possible later use: '*I can assure the committee that I was giving my daughter a grand send-off to university at the very time these alleged events occurred...*' It was always the same. Always letting some chump lower down the ladder to take the blame.

Warner pocketed his phone and wandered into the kitchen. It was tiny – there was barely room to swing a cat. At least *his* kitchen was bigger.

He went to open the back door but was stopped by a polite 'Sir?'

One of Dutton's contingent of fresh manpower was holding a sheet of paper. 'Phone bill, Mr Warner.'

Warner shrugged. 'So? We have William Boyd's phone right here. It's of no use –'

'His daughter's, sir. And we can't find her phone anywhere. I've turned her room over. Twice.'

Warner found himself smiling.

The silly girl's taken it with her.

46

'It looks very, um, ruined,' said Charlotte, zooming in on the Google Earth image. She passed Emma's phone back to her.

'That's the address she gave,' said Okeke. 'Barnham House.'

'Okay, that's enough,' cut in Boyd. 'Turn your phone off, Ems.'

She rolled her eyes at him. 'I took the SIM card out last night. I'm on the pub's Wi-Fi.'

'That's still a risk,' he said. 'We know where we're going now, so switch it off.'

Emma sighed and did as she was asked.

They were in the Wheelhouse' beer garden, which overlooked the canal and the towpath. The outdoor area was deserted apart from them. It was lovely and warm, even though the sun was settling on the horizon like a blob of wax and would be gone soon. Ozzie and Mia's attention was firmly on a pair of swans idling on the water, just a few yards away.

It was an idyllic scene worthy of a Constable canvas.

'Question is,' said Jay, between chomps of cheesy chips, 'do we go there tonight or tomorrow?'

'She sounded pretty bad,' said Okeke. 'I mean, really short of breath and wheezy. She definitely needs medical attention. I say, we head there as soon as we've eaten.'

'She'll be okay for one more night, surely?' said Boyd.

'I don't know,' she replied. 'If she's struggling to breathe, has a pacemaker, is under extreme stress *and* for God's sake let's not forget her age, she could have a stroke or go into cardiac arrest at any moment.'

'If we go now, we'll be arriving late,' said Charlotte. 'If it *is* a ruin, do we really want to be stumbling around it in the dark?'

Okeke shrugged. 'That's what torches are for.'

'And I'm also concerned about being led into a trap.' Boyd picked up a saggy chip. 'I'd prefer to arrive in daylight so we can pull up nearby and look it over before we go wandering inside. The last thing I want is to bump into those two spooks in the dark.'

'The Hairy Bikers,' Jay chuckled to himself.

'All right,' said Okeke. 'But we get up early, right?'

Boyd nodded. 'As soon as it's light. It's a two-hour drive, give or take. We can be with her by, let's say, nine.'

'And what then?' asked Charlotte. 'I'm guessing we'll need to take her straight to the nearest hospital. But I'm guessing the alert will be triggered if they pull up her medical records...'

'She can give a false name,' said Emma.

'Or no name at all,' added Boyd. 'We can say we found her wandering around. Say she's got no idea what her name is. She'll play along with that, I'm sure. So long as they get her some oxygen and give her whatever drug she needs.'

'Will that be enough?' said Charlotte.

Boyd looked her way. 'I don't know. But the first priority has to be keeping her alive.'

'You know, on Monday morning,' said Okeke, 'if I don't call in, Abbott, then Sutherland, then Hatcher will be on my case.'

'Me too,' said Charlotte. 'Bernard will be wondering what's happened to me if I don't drop him a line.'

'Also me,' said Jay. 'I've got the keys to my boss's flat still. He'll be wondering –'

Boyd shook his head. 'We're going to have to play this one day at a time. Let's see where things stand tomorrow morning.'

The possible outcomes for tomorrow ranged from dire to uncertain. It could be an elaborate trap... or it could be genuine. If so, and they managed to get to a hospital, what then? What evidence did she have other than her words? Was it even plausible that they could just contact some news editor, dump the story on them and then go home? He doubted that very much.

Emma looked at Boyd. 'Dad? Do you think we're going to be watched for the rest of our lives?'

Again, Boyd had no idea. 'I've got a nasty suspicion that once you're on someone's database, it's bloody impossible to get back off it,' was all he could say.

Ozzie and Mia suddenly let out a volley of barks as one of the swans scaled the grassy bank – and it seemed to have a beeline for the food on their table.

'Um, Bill... the dogs?' said Charlotte, reining in Mia. 'I'm pretty sure the swan's going to win if they get into a ding-dong.'

Boyd got up, grabbed Ozzie and Mia's leads and dragged both barking dogs to the other side of the beer garden.

Charlotte, Emma and Okeke stood up too, wary of the approaching swan.

Jay, however, remained where he was, not prepared to surrender his evening snack. 'Err... you lot? It's just a bloody bird.'

'A rather big one,' said Emma.

Jay put a defensive arm around his plate as the swan, now only a few feet away, lifted its long neck and spread its wings with a challenge display.

'Nope!' replied Jay. 'They're mine! So, piss off, you overgrown seagull!'

The swan hissed, feathers splaying along its wings and up its neck, making itself look even larger.

'Yeah, yeah –'

The bird hissed again, then, without warning, it lunged, its beak going straight for Jay's forearm.

'Ow!' Jay jerked backwards, rubbing the bottom of his forearm frantically. The bird was poised to have another go, but Jay decided he'd had enough. He scrambled off the bench and backed away to join the others.

'Bloody thing *bit* me!' he said.

'Pecked you,' corrected Okeke.

He showed her the red welt as it began to form on his arm, while the swan calmly helped itself to the bread baps at their table, Charlotte nudged Boyd's side.

'It's normally you that ends up arguing with the birds.'

'Hmm.' He nodded. 'Makes a pleasant change.'

47

Warner had never seen so many people crammed down here in the Boutique, not in the entire twenty-five years he'd worked for the Boutique. The glass-walled briefing room was standing-room only, with thirty personnel jostling for elbow space, eleven of them his regulars, the rest drawn from MI5's pool of digital and practical surveillance officers, courtesy of Dutton's string-pulling.

'I just want to start by saying good work so far, everyone,' Warner began. 'I know it's a Sunday, it's late and you all have families you want to get home to, but... we're very close to drawing a line under this leak threat. We may even be able to resolve things tonight.'

Warner wished he had the room to pace. It was intimidating to have this many faces so close. He felt hemmed in by them and the digital whiteboard behind him. It glowed with the faces of DC Samantha Okeke and her partner, Jason Turner, DCI William Boyd and his daughter, Emma. And Charlotte Bellefois, believed to be Boyd's partner. All of them most likely in transit or lying low. Also very possibly together.

'The intel gathered earlier this afternoon from the daughter's phone has given us a feast of information,' he said, smiling. It wasn't an infectious smile, and he was met with thirty deadpan faces, every one of them keen to get a result in the next twenty-four hours and escape this cramped and gloomy last-minute secondment.

'We have Boyd's and Turner's vehicle details and registration numbers, which the police have entered onto their national ANPR alert list. This group may be using both vehicles or just the one.'

'What's the cover story?' asked one of the new faces.

'With Boyd, corruption and involvement with a Georgian OCG. Turner is wanted for a violent assault on a minor. If either are pulled over by traffic police, the call will be redirected to Section Nine. And if you're the one to take the external call, we're the NPRRT: the National Police Rapid Response Taskforce.'

'Which doesn't exist,' grunted Drummond. 'So, chief, if the copper asks?'

Warner disliked the scruffy man intensely. As a field operative, the look was probably an essential disguise, but he suspected Drummond maintained the has-been Hell's Angel image in his spare time.

'You tell them it's a recently established southern counties interforce asset. It's being trialled... It's all very, very new and we're still trying to find our feet,' Warner told him.

There wouldn't be an issue, Sussex Force's Margaret Hatcher had assured him. The local forces were constantly setting up short-lived cooperative initiatives with their own impossible-to-remember acronyms.

'Next.' Warner pressed the whiteboard's clicker and the screen displayed photographs taken earlier this afternoon.

'The intel gathering at Boyd's house has given us some surprisingly useful Easter eggs tucked away in his safe. A severed ear in a jar...'

A number of the faces before him grimaced slightly at the image on the screen.

'Two wads of twenties, totalling ten thousand pounds. One of them has some blood spattered on the top few. Also, a handwritten message...'

A scribbled note appeared on the screen.

BOYD, *I am in your debt. You ever need help, you contact me –*
Rovshan.

'ROVSHAN SALIKOV,' explained Warner. 'Ex-KGB money man and OCG boss, now working with our colleagues in MI6 to identify and locate dirty Russian money and assets. But that doesn't mean he's turned over a new leaf and isn't still making money from criminal activities abroad; it just means *he* can't be touched.' Warner turned to look at the whiteboard. 'This note, however, along with the money found in the safe means Boyd can be apprehended. By associating with Salikov, he's fair game.'

'Any useful finds on Turner?' asked another new officer.

Warner shook his head. 'Clean. But, given the look of him, I'm sure any arresting officer will believe he's got a criminal history. As I said, we've put a flag against his name for a violent assault on a minor, so if an arresting officer wants to run a quick check, they'll find a warrant for arrest.'

'But this, ladies and gents, is the grand prize.' He clicked to next page to reveal a number of screenshots. 'Emma

Boyd's iPhone. And we got the green light for another Pegasus licence.'

Relief rippled through the crowded room. Maybe they would, after all, be heading back to their regular desks tomorrow or Tuesday morning.

Warner turned to Gary Nottridge, who was standing at the side. 'Gary, do you want to tell everyone exactly what we've got?'

He noticed the young man's jug ears suddenly turn pink with embarrassment. Clearly he hadn't been expecting to deliver a performance this evening.

'Uhh... right. Yeah,' Gary mumbled. 'So, we remotely installed Pegasus on her iPhone earlier and, you know, obviously, we have complete access to everything on it now.'

Warner stepped over to him, gently held his elbow and pulled him towards the whiteboard, turning him to face the room. 'Loud and clear, please, Gary, so they can hear you at the back.'

Gary cleared his throat and started over. 'We've installed Pegasus and now have complete access and partial control of her phone. We don't have firmware control –'

'Do you want to explain that, Gary?' prompted Warner,

'Sure. Uh, so basically it means that if the phone is switched off, we can't do anything about it. However, it was on, briefly, this afternoon and that was enough for us to extract this data.'

Gary pointed at the screenshots behind him, then clicked to the next screen: an Airbnb booking screen. 'So, Emma Boyd booked this place yesterday. It's a narrowboat on the Kennet and Avon canal in Berkshire. The booking's for five nights, starting last night. So...' Gary looked back at his boss for help. 'Um, that's where... she – I mean, they are... maybe...'

Warner took over. 'Clearly they're using the boat to lie low and this isn't some planned holiday getaway. Which indicates that they're aware that they may under surveillance.' He nodded at the screen. 'The fact that the daughter took her phone *and used it* means they aren't as surveillance-alert as we thought. All the same, they will undoubtedly be extremely cautious and equally jumpy. So, we need to move quickly.'

He turned to his deputy. 'Moira, would you like to brief the field teams?'

Moira Cullen took the whiteboard's clicker from Warner and began to walk everyone through the operation.

Warner left her to get on with it and edged his way out of the stuffy briefing room and into the cooler space outside. He caught his reflection in the glass and noticed his tie was askew. As he adjusted it, he gave thought to what should happen once they had this motley band of amateur spies in containment. By tomorrow midday he should have extracted Eleanora Baxendale's location out of them, and hopefully by teatime he'd be sitting with her, ready to find out how much damage she'd done and her reasons for doing so.

Then after that? For his ex-boss, the options would– by necessity – be bleak. She had to already know that.

But the others…

'*When tying a knot for good, Jerry,*' Ellie had once told him, '*we use a proper bowline, not some lazy reef knot.*'

48

Two 'JMS Plumbers' vans pulled into adjacent spaces in the car park at just after three in the morning. They weren't the only vehicles there. In one corner, tucked beneath a horse chestnut tree was a dark-blue Renault Captur. In the other corner, next to a pub's gated beer garden was a scruffy van with 'CLEAN ME!!!' finger-written into the dirt on one side.

The van engines were switched off. All was still and silent in the darkness.

∼

'Zulu, Zulu – this is Alpha. We now have eyes on Boyd's car.'

'Zulu, Zulu – this is Bravo. Confirmed. Reg number is a match. We've got him. Over.'

Warner smiled at the use of 'over'. The Bravo team leader sounded as though he was a generation older than the rest of them and used to analogue radio protocols. The youngsters in his team, he surmised, had only known digital comms.

He leaned into the desk mic. 'All units – this is Zulu. Let's make this happen as quickly and quietly as possible. Green to proceed.'

He settled back in his seat and sipped the awful lukewarm coffee that the Boutique's vending machine had spat out. He stretched wearily, then turned to look at Drummond and Chapps sitting nearby. Both of them had faces like smacked arses.

For God's sake, he thought, *sulking like bloody children because they're stuck here.*

Drummond was shaking his head irritably, while Chapps stared at the phone in his hand, swiping every now and then with his finger. Those two miserable buggers were fossils, relics from a time when spycraft was more of a blunt instrument, all shoe leather and hard knuckles. They'd argued that they ought to be leading the teams, but Moira had shot them down – rather brutally, truth be told – saying that neither would be fit enough if the operation became a pursuit on foot. Far better to use the experienced (and fitter) field teams that Dutton had seconded for them.

He was saving Drummond and Chapps for later, when Boyd and his gang were restrained and holed up in a safe house. Aubrey Dutton had made sure there was one available not too far away from Kintbury. Not a safe house in the usual police sense – a building with basic amenities, tucked away in a remote location with a duty officer to keep them safe and run errands to the nearest grocery store. No. 'Safe' meant undiscoverable, inescapable and sound-proofed. In this case, a derelict nuclear bunker from the Cold War era. It was on a mothballed US airfield in Kent and had been repurposed by the CIA in 2004 to hold and interrogate persons of interest during George Bush's 'war on terror'. The British Security Service had inherited it, complete with all the necessary tools and equipment to extract intelligence. Drummond and Chapps would have their chance to contribute their skills and play with those toys later.

'*Zulu, Zulu, Alpha – approaching canal. Narrowboat in view. Repeat, narrowboat in view. Hundred yards to our left. No lights on.*'

Warner sat forward again. 'Bravo, Bravo, Zulu – report.'

'*Zulu, Zulu, Bravo – slow progress…*'

Warner could hear the soft crackle of twigs underfoot and the rustle of leaves as the team leader kept his channel open. Finally: '*This is Bravo. We're on the towpath. Narrowboat in view. No lights on. Over.*'

Warner nodded. The team had been briefed that there were likely two dogs on board. Now that the boat was in their sights, he'd keep comms to a minimum. The age of the dogs – and thus the sensitivity of their hearing – was an unknown.

The plan was straightforward: find an open window on the towpath side of the boat, ease in a hose and pump in aerosolised fentanyl. Next, wait for three minutes, then step aboard, restrain the people and euthanise the dogs. Done correctly, there shouldn't be a single bark or raised voice from beginning to end.

Of course, if these folk were as paranoid as he suspected they might be, there could well be someone awake and on watch. In which case, Plan B was quick and noisy: storm the boat, shoot the dogs and drag their targets to the vans, kicking and screaming.

'*This is Alpha – ready to approach.*'

'*This is Bravo – also ready. Over.*'

'All units, proceed.' Warner put the handset down on the desk, then picked up his paper cup of coffee.

Gary looked at him. 'Sir?'

'Yes?'

'What's going to happen to them?'

The young man's look of concern made him realise how much self-gaslighting played a part in how the younger members of staff justified what they did for a job: statistics analysis, listening in on calls, monitoring trends on social media, tracking the movement of high-value targets, installing hacking software on phones, assembling compromising material on individuals to use as leverage packages. Any one of those tasks could be their specialism, and that specialism would be all that they knew, or chose to know.

But rarely, it seemed to Warner, did they pause to take a long hard look at the bigger picture – to consider *why* they performed their specialism for an above-average, inflation-proof civil-service salary and a generous pension packet at the end. The *why* was for higher pay grades. For the grown-ups to worry about.

So what was the big picture? *To control the sheeple.* To keep the herd moving along in the right direction. Whether they were marching the herd towards a cliff edge or sunlit pastures was a debate for politicians or historians, but for Warner the job was keeping all the sheep facing in the same direction. Even if it meant having to cull a few curious outliers.

As Ellie had once said to him: '*Sometimes you have to break an egg or two to make an omelette, Jerry. And our job? Our job is to hide those broken eggshells.*'

'We'll find out what they know, Gary,' he said finally. 'Show them the error of their ways,' he added with a reassuring smile. 'And send them on their way.'

The comms line crackled. '*This is Alpha – we're aboard the boat.*'

'Job done?' asked Warren.

'*No, sir. There's no one here.*'

∼

BOYD GROANED with pain as he continued to lean into the turn. It seemed like Jay was negotiating the world's largest roundabout.

'You okay, Bill?' asked Charlotte.

He nodded and gently rubbed his side. 'Just a bit sore...' He looked at Okeke. 'Tell your other half to slow down a bit, will you? We're sliding around all over the place.'

Okeke rapped her knuckles on the van's front partition, and Emma's face appeared in the open hatch. 'You lot okay back there?'

'Tell Jay to slow it down a bit.'

'He's only doing about fifty,' she replied.

'Yeah, but we don't have seat belts.'

'Or seats,' called out Boyd.

'That's fair,' said Emma. 'Will do.'

Boyd was also feeling a touch car-sick with there being no proper windows in the back, and, by the look of Ozzie, licking his lips repeatedly and hanging his head low, so was he.

'Guv?' Okeke piped up.

'Boyd,' he replied. 'We're not at work.'

'I think we should check in on Eleanora when we do a pit stop.'

'Use a payphone,' he told her.

'She may not answer if she doesn't recognise the number,' Okeke pointed out.

He sighed. 'Fine.'

'I also want to see if there's anywhere I can buy an oximeter,' she said. 'An oxygen monitor,' she added, seeing

Boyd's confused expression. 'One of those clip things you put on your finger.'

Boyd pulled a face. 'At a service station?'

Okeke nodded. 'You'd be surprised what you can pick up at a service station these days.'

'Germs mainly,' Boyd huffed.

The van braked heavily, causing the dogs to scrabble and panic, and for everyone else to sway and lurch in unison.

'Jesus,' Boyd grumbled, clutching his side. 'I'm beginning to regret this decision.'

As they'd vacated the boat in complete darkness, he'd suggested using Jay's van and leaving his Captur behind. No point driving two vehicles that could be clocked on ANPR. Plus Jay's van was filthy, which made the carefully deployed mud on the rear number plate slightly more plausible.

'I think it was the right move to set off early,' said Okeke. 'Get there before rush hour hits. And time's an issue.'

'She can't be that close to death, surely?'

'If she's got fluid building up in her lungs, then she's got a reduced capacity to oxygenate her blood. That's a condition that can go downhill fast. I may have to call an ambulance when we get there.'

'Great,' Boyd said.

'Maybe that would be a helpful thing?' said Charlotte. 'I mean, Bill, you mentioned the alert, but surely government spooks are hardly likely to snatch us in the middle of a busy hospital?' She looked from Boyd to Okeke. 'Or are they?'

~

EMMA HAD the unwieldy road map spread out across her thighs, her protruding tummy holding it in place like a bowling-ball-sized paperweight. She was reading it by the light of her iPhone's torch.

'So, there's a turn-off south of Swindon, which gets us off the M4 and puts us on the B4005.'

Jay nodded. 'Heading?'

'Um... south. Yeah, all the way down to....' Her finger traced the motorway. 'Tidworth. Then we can wiggle our way back east towards – '

'Hold on – we've been driving *west* for the last half an hour?!'

'I know. I know. I just realised I... Got confused with this bloody map.'

'Ems!'

'I'm sorry! I'm used to, like, using digital maps. We need to go east.'

'Ah shit-sticks.' He shot a frustrated glance her way. 'Your phone's on, Emma, even if you're just using the torch function. You know that, right?'

'It's okay I switched it to aeroplane mode. It's a just a torch right now.'

'All the same,' Jay said, 'The guv's right... you probably need to keep that thing *off*-off.'

Emma puffed her cheeks and then held the phone's side button until the screen went dark.

Jay looked her way and offered her a placatory smile. 'Torture, eh? Not being able to use your phone?'

She gazed out at the phasing motorway floodlights, throwing alternating waves of sickly orange glow, then shadow, then orange glow again. 'Actually, it's kinda refreshing. I've been doing way too much doom-scrolling over the last few months.'

'You looking forward to becoming a momma?' Jay asked.

She pulled a face. 'I think I'm excited and terrified in

equal amounts.'

'It's a big old thing,' said Jay. 'Something I wanna do one day. Be a dad.'

'And when's one day going to be?' Emma asked, glancing across at him.

'Good question,' he said with a sigh. 'Me and Sam are both in our thirties. She's determined to build her career, reach DCI before she gets to fifty. And I just started out on my career. I'm not sure exactly when we're going to manage to squeeze out a sprog.'

'How's the private investigator thing going?' she asked.

He smiled. 'I'm loving it. It's like being a copper but with no paperwork and no rules. Well, not *no rules*, but, just less.'

She nodded. 'That's what drives Dad mad. All the paperwork that comes at the arse end of a case when it's passed to the prosecution. He said it always feels like it's the end of the case when you've got the suspect... but then, actually, that's kind of where it all starts, I think.'

Jay nodded. 'Yeah, Sam's told me that even if you've got the paperwork done right, the CPS can still drop it at any point if they can't *guarantee* a win in court.' He shook his head. 'Sounds bloody crazy to me.'

Emma looked out of the windscreen. The motorway was virtually empty, an endless straight sweep of tarmac bathed in pools of amber light.

'How much, actual danger are we in, Jay?' she asked after a while. 'Do you know?'

He sucked air between his teeth. 'I think *a lot* if we don't manage to get to this old dear in time. I mean, if she knows something important, then *that* could be the only thing that's going to get us out of trouble.'

'And if we don't get to her in time?'

Jay shrugged. 'I don't know, Emma. I really dunno.'

49

'Mr Warner?'

He pulled his third paper cup of coffee out from the vending machine and turned to see Gary Nottridge. 'Yes, Gary.'

'Emma Boyd's phone was active. We've got a live location, sir. She thinks she's still dark, but she doesn't know we've deactivated aeroplane mode.'

Warner hurried back to Gary's cubicle with his steaming coffee. 'So where are they now?'

Gary sat down and showed him the road map on his screen. A green marker pulsed as it slowly inched its way along a motorway. 'They're just south of Swindon. It looks like they're getting ready to come off the M4.'

'They're on a ruddy motorway? How come the ANPR cameras on there haven't flagged them up?'

Gary shrugged. That wasn't his area. 'I don't know, sir.'

'Where are our people?' Warner asked.

Gary scrolled the map until two more pulsing green markers came into view. 'Alpha team. Bravo team. They're on their way back here.'

Immediately, Warner picked up the comms headset. 'All units – this is Zulu. We've have a live location. They're currently on the M4, south of Swindon, heading west....'

Gary zoomed in on the map. The marker looked as if it was sitting static at the slip road off the motorway. 'They've stopped.'

'Standby,' said Warner, then leaned in to look more closely. 'What's there?'

'Service station. A Holiday Inn. A McDonald's.'

'I don't think they'd be stopping for a ruddy Big Mac,' muttered Warner.

The marker began to move again, inching slowly down the screen. 'They've gone onto a B-road, sir. They're heading south now.'

Warner squinted at the screen. 'All right, ladies and gents – they're now heading south on the B4005.'

The two team leaders acknowledged him.

'This is Alpha. Can you give us a rallying point ahead of them to tap in our end?'

Gary zoomed out the map to give Warner a wider canvas to work with. 'They're heading into the North Wessex Downs,' he said.

Warner tapped the screen at what he thought was a good point. Gary nodded in agreement.

'Marlborough,' said Warner. 'If they change course, I'll update you.'

'*Understood*,' came the reply. '*It would be helpful to have constant updates... sir, so we can trim our –*'

'I can do that,' said Gary.

Warner shook his head. He needed the young man on something more important.

He looked around and caught the eyes of one of Dutton's

extras, a woman currently monitoring police radio traffic.

'Hey! You are?'

'Penny Holmes,' the woman replied.

He waved her over and pointed at the live markers on the screen. 'Those two are our field teams. That's the target. They're trying to make up the distance. Keep them updated on where the target is heading. Got that?'

She nodded. 'Yes, sir.'

He cocked a finger at Gary to walk with him. The young man followed his boss to an empty cubicle further along.

'I'm not entirely convinced we're not being played with,' said Warner. 'If that's Emma Boyd's phone, how do we know she hasn't just thrown it into onto the back of a flatbed truck?'

'Well, we *can't* be sure, sir.'

'You got a data dump from her phone, didn't you?'

'Not a complete one. Partial, sir. But now we can control it, I can use Pegasus to extract everything.'

'And she'll have no idea her phone's on and doing that?'

'Not unless she gets a text from someone. It'll buzz or ring. I can switch aeroplane mode on first, so nothing'll come through.'

'Do it.'

The young man hurried back to his cubicle. Warner watched him shove the young woman to one side to get to his keyboard and started tapping away at it.

Warner sank into the seat in the vacant cubicle, the partition walls providing him enough privacy so that he could rest his tired eyes for a moment or two.

∼

EMMA GAZED out of the passenger-side window at darkness. Now they were off the motorway and thrown into pitch-black darkness, the only lights she could see were blinking red ones every now and then, from the tops of phone masts – or they could have been turbines. The early hours of the morning whizzed past her as a blurred zoetrope of stone croft walls and patches of gorse caught in the headlights of the van. All the while, her mind flip-flopped between the mundane and the ominous. One moment pondering what shade of blue to paint the nursery ceiling, and the next wondering whether she was ever going to see her home again.

Dad had a gun on him. Jay had a sawn-off shotgun replica. Sam, usually so calm, collected and full of dry wit, was now quick-tempered and taut with stress: a hollowed-out shadow of herself. The only person who seemed largely fine was Charlotte. Emma wondered if she was putting on a show of it'll-work-out-in-the-end stiff-upper-lip forebearance for her and Dad's benefit, or was genuinely the kind of person who faced stress with an unbreakable brick wall of stoic well-it-could-be-worse optimism.

We could end up in prison. Or dead.

She didn't know much about high treason, but wasn't leaking a national secret just that? She reached into her jacket pocket to pull out her phone and google it, to find out what kind of sentence she'd face if that charge was thrown at her, but quickly stopped herself.

It stays off, she reminded herself. It was all too easy, she noted, to unthinkingly rouse one's phone for a quick look at this or that. She let go of her phone like it was a hot brick.

The phone settled back to the bottom of her pocket, screen still dark. And yet behind that façade of dormant inactivity, it was busy, betraying her secrets, sharing her contacts, revealing her whereabouts, telling a young man several miles away everything it knew about her.

∼

'SIR!'

Warner blinked his tired eyes open. He must have dozed off for a moment. Gary was standing over him. He looked like a metal detectorist who'd discovered a stack of buried Roman coins.

'Sir... I think I've tracked down the number for Baxendale's burner phone.'

'What?' The adrenaline of that news hit Warner like a hammer and he was wide awake once more. 'How?'

'It's on Emma Boyd's recent call list. It was a new number that she's never dialled before. I got the provider. It's a pay-as-you-go. Jiraffe.com.'

'And what does that do?'

'They're on our back-door database. I managed to look up the details. The SIM was activated on Saturday, so I deduced that this was DC's Okeke's burner phone. I investigated Okeke's SIM and it's logged as calling only one number. Twice. On Saturday evening and Sunday. The phone mast both calls routed through was just outside Kintbury.'

'Where the narrowboat is.'

Gary nodded.

'And now all of a sudden they're headed back south again,' Warner mused. 'In the middle of the night and leaving one vehicle behind as bait for us.' He turned to Gary. 'That's got to be her... It's got to be Eleanora. She's finally given them a place to meet her!'

Gary nodded. 'I think you could be right, sir.'

50

Eleanora was trying to distract herself from the burbling sound in her chest, the constant sensation of needing to chase after much-needed oxygen, to grab yet another big, gulping breath. As she stared out at the dark sky and the gradually multiplying pinpricks of stars, her mind drifted back to when she was in her early twenties, a young woman full of confidence, armed with her first-class degree in history and certain she was destined for Great Things as she relocated from Wiltshire to London.

Her confidence had driven her to respond to an intriguingly worded advert in the *Daily Telegraph* soon after she'd settled into her digs. An advert that had led her to a dusty hall off Wardour Street, which held scratched old-school desks and a host of fellow bewildered people and an exam of extraordinarily odd questions. Then, finally, a few days later, she'd had an interview with two well-spoken gentlemen who explained they were from the Home Office.

They'd enquired about her views on politics, on the current prime minister, Harold Macmillan, her thoughts on the Suez Crisis and the Russians sending those two dogs, Belka and Strelka, into space. And they seemed to already know so much about her background and her family connections, including the tragic tale of her family's dwindling circumstances.

She may have answered all their questions in the correct fashion, but she was certain it was her quick mind and self-confidence – bordering on haughtiness – that had resulted in them inviting her to join Her Majesty's Security Service.

Within a year of joining – manning desks, taking minutes of meetings in shorthand and filing index cards in filing cabinets that would slam mercilessly shut on her fingertips and chip her nails – she found herself seconded to a top-secret project.

A project code-named Marble Orchard.

For several months she was told absolutely nothing about it, only that Marble Orchard was an undertaking of the utmost importance. She was given the task of sourcing the materials and equipment needed to set up a field hospital on a remote offshore platform ten miles out from the coast of Essex. She learned the platform was one of a number of Maunsell forts that had been constructed during the Second World War to provide early detection of German bombing raids.

She recalled feeling both thrilled and terrified at the prospect of being responsible for constructing a hospital atop an old, creaking radar platform that shuddered and groaned with the impact of every wave. She had no medical knowledge, no experience of procuring medical machinery, but being young, savvy, well-educated and keen to learn fast, her newly assigned department director had confidence that she was more than up to the challenge.

The result was a modern, well-equipped field hospital,

assembled within two months, generously resourced with medicines and dressings, trolleys and machines, courtesy of the wonderful now-established NHS. A stunning achievement of which she'd been so immensely proud at the time, as she inspected it on its opening in February 1962.

Then the first patients had arrived –

The stubby Nokia in her lap buzzed noisily, jerking her out from her reverie. She picked it up, hoping to see DC Okeke's familiar number.

Her thumb froze above the 'receive call' button.

Unknown.

It could be one of those annoying AI spambots cycling through random numbers to tell her that she'd been mis-sold a pension and was due a tidy sum in compensation if she just tapped *1 after the bleep. Or it could be DC Okeke. Maybe she'd bought herself a new phone, just to be on the safe side? In which case, clever girl.

But if not, then...

The phone continued to buzz.

What if Jeremy and his team had managed to get hold of the woman and extracted her number from Okeke's phone? She shuddered at the thought of the things Drummond and Chapps would have gleefully done to get it.

Eleanora might have been a decade out of date with current phone-tracking technology, but she certainly knew that answering a call meant establishing a traceable link through strings of phone masts to her approximate location. And even approximate would be far too close for comfort.

The phone finally stopped buzzing and lay still.

∼

'NO ANSWER,' said Gary.

'Dammit,' whispered Warner.

'I could clone Okeke's SIM,' said Gary. 'Should take about ten minutes. It'll mean that our number will appear as Okeke's.'

Warner suspected the old woman was desperately waiting to hear from the detective and quite sensibly wasn't going to answer a call from anyone else. All they needed from her was to accept their call, nothing more.

The various service providers' traffic-logging software was now primed to alert them the moment her phone connected. Even if she hung up immediately, it would still be job done... They'd have a phone mast identified and a modest search radius to zero in on.

Warner nodded at Gary, his fingers poised and flexing above the keyboard, and as eager as a greyhound in its starting trap, waiting to be released.

'Proceed.'

～

ELEANORA SURMISED it was probably a random spam-bot call. Her mind drifted back once again to 1962 – and the patients...

They came over the course of three days, arriving by naval helicopter and accompanied by medical personnel dressed in white all-in-one hooded suits, which she much later learned were called hazardous material, or hazmat, suits.

The first patients to arrive were horrifically injured third-degree burn victims: fingers gone, often noses and lips too. Eyes swollen shut but extruding like blackened peaches. Their hands and feet were little more than stumps. Their whole bodies were covered in creams and weeping dressings, and they were dosed heavily on sedatives and morphine. Even so, their screams echoed off the metal bulkheads and walls of the pristine ward that she had been responsible for assembling.

The second tranche of patients arrived the next day. They had less severe injuries, mostly second-degree burns to their arms and faces, their skin livid purple. Most of them, curiously, had no burn damage around their eyes, giving them the appearance of panda eyes. These men – and they were all men, young men – were less distressing to receive, their pain and discomfort successfully suppressed with analgesic creams and oral medication.

The final group arrived on the third day, men with little or no burn damage at all and apparently in good health, able to disembark from the helicopters without any assistance.

She realised, looking at this final intake, that all the patients were brown-skinned – those that still had skin at least. She later learned they were all Ghurkhas.

Her director, Andrew Bonham-Carr, informed her that her role now was to film the men. To record and document everything: their behaviour, their levels of pain, the dose amounts of the various medications they received. He gave her a Standard 8 camera, the size of a lunch box, and told her to record what was happening with each patient every hour, on the hour, and each filming session had to begin with a card that displayed the time and date.

The first batch of patients only lasted a few days and Eleanora dutifully filmed as each one of them was checked for signs of life by medical staff in protective suits, then wrapped up tightly in their sheets, slid into thick, black plastic bags and taken away by helicopter.

The second and third batch of young men lasted a lot

longer. Several weeks, in fact. The minor burns of the earlier group seemed to heal easily and at one point she'd been convinced that all the remaining men were going to make a full recovery and leave the platform. But then, one by one, they began to fall sick.

The phone in her lap buzzed once again and this time she didn't lurch in her seat. This time she was relieved to be yanked back to the present. This time it *was* DC Okeke's number.

She and her friends had to be getting close now and Okeke, undoubtedly concerned, must have been calling to ask how she was feeling again.

Awful, she'd reply without hesitation. Eleanora was pretty sure she'd gone so far downhill that she was going to need hospital attention as soon as they arrived, that her struggling pacemaker and fluid-filled lungs were in danger of failing her at any moment.

'Samantha...' she wheezed breathlessly as she accepted the call. 'Is that you?'

There was no answer.

'DC Okeke?' she tried again. She thought she heard a male voice in the background. A vaguely familiar voice softly murmuring, '*That will do.*'

The call ended abruptly, leaving the phone humming in her ear.

'Oh my God,' she whispered to herself. 'They've found me.'

~

Gary pointed at the monitor. 'There! That's the first one in the 5G chain.' He looked up at his director. 'She'll be within five hundred yards of that point.'

Warner scanned the network map. 'Shit! I should have known! Dammit! We could have picked her up days ago!'

He turned to Drummond and Chapps. Both had now tucked their phones away and looked ready and relieved to finally have something to do.

'Get a ruddy car, will you?' Warner shouted, and they leapt up and headed for the stairs.

'Wait for me outside. I'm coming with you!' he called out after them, then looked around at the remaining personnel in the wine cellar. He picked out Moira Cullen.

'Moira, I want you as police and emergency services liaison. This is a red-level op – maximum threat. If anyone asks: yes, it's terror-related. The rest of you are on call, monitoring and redirection. I want a clear path to her... and a response void around that phone mast! Gary... brief Moira on the location.'

He raised his voice so that all the new faces could hear him. 'Everything goes through Moira. Is that clear, everyone?'

Heads nodded as Warner grabbed his jacket off the back of a chair and pulled it on, before hurrying up the steps after his two attack dogs, Drummond and Chapps.

51

It was still pitch-black when they arrived at the location Eleanora Baxendale had given them. A blink-and-you'd-miss-it turn off the winding country lane they'd been on since they leaving the A31.

The van's headlights picked out an ornate wrought-iron gate that was mostly rust held together by encrustations of lichen, and flanked by eroded brick pillars that looked as though they'd been sandblasted by the passing of time.

Emma climbed out of the van and slid the side door open. 'We're here,' she announced.

Boyd, Charlotte and Okeke climbed out stiffly, while Ozzie and Mia leapt down to the weed-strewn ground and began to sniff for suitable places to empty their bladders.

Boyd looked up at the waning moon, nearing the end of its night shift and heading for a treeline. 'Christ, anyone here getting *Woman in Black* vibes?' he muttered.

Jay walked around the front of the van, torch in hand, and tried the gate. It rattled open with ease, shedding a small cascade of rusty flakes.

'Well, at least we won't have to climb over it.' He pushed

both gates wide open and then aimed the beam of light ahead. In the stark light and the dancing shadows, they could make out a long, straight driveway among a sea of knee-high weeds and drooping heads of cow parsley.

Jay sucked his teeth. 'My van's suspension ain't gonna like that.'

'It looks worse than it is,' said Okeke. 'You're not off-roading... There's a driveway beneath all that.'

'There could be debris,' said Jay, 'and I won't know until I thump into it or go over it.'

'Driveway's a generous word,' said Boyd. 'To be fair.'

Jay raised his beam of light and something glinted in the gloom. 'There's something up ahead, let's take a look.'

Charlotte herded the dogs back into the van and shut them in.

'Just a thought,' she said as she approached the gate. 'Does that look like terrain that a frail old lady could cross easily?'

Boyd nodded. She was right. If Jay's van couldn't hack it, he doubted Eleanor Baxendale could.

'I can't see any recent signs of a vehicle carving through those weeds,' said Jay. 'Are we sure this is the right place?'

Emma nodded. 'According to the instructions she gave us.'

'Call her,' said Boyd.

Okeke pulled her burner out and tried Eleanora's number. She waited out a dozen rings before disconnecting. 'No answer.' It was super early, but she was sure that Eleanor would have answered no matter the time. She looked at Boyd. 'I'm really worried about her.'

'Then maybe let's hurry?' prompted Emma, nodding at the darkness before them.

'Yup, okay,' said Boyd. 'But stealthily. No headlights.'

Jay glanced his way. 'Umm... mate, there's no stealthy with my van. It's a diesel.'

'And if the spooks are already here, Bill, and lying in wait,' added Charlotte, 'don't they have fancy gizmos for seeing things in the dark?'

Boyd realised they were both right. If this was some kind of trap, they were already caught in it.

'We're here now,' he said after a moment. 'Let's go.'

∽

ELEANORA STARED AT HER PHONE. That last call had been Jeremy trying to ping her location again, she was sure of it. She tried to guess what that meant. Did they have her rough location and needed a more precise indication? Did that mean his people were in the area now?

She shuddered in the darkness. Over the last few days, her fear of being found by him had begun to wane. If they found her, yes, she'd be a dead woman. But she and Jeremy had history. A long professional friendship. In fact, she was the one who had recruited him back in the late nineties.

Jeremy, of course, would want to know what compromising materials she'd managed to smuggle out of the Boutique's filing cabinets and what she'd done with them. Were they in some hiding place? Lodged with a friend? In an envelope in some solicitor's filing cabinet to be opened on the occasion of her death?

And he would almost certainly extract that information from her before he was done. She was no hero when it came to pain. But, having got what he wanted, he'd ensure she wasn't dealt with cruelly. The Boutique weren't the Gestapo or the KGB. There'd be a sedative, more likely a flask of whisky, then whatever manner of death that could be made to look the least suspicious.

Given how bad her breathing was, how laboured every breath sounded, that wasn't going to be too difficult.

∞

Boyd's eyes had grown accustomed to the darkness. The moon was still tiptoeing above the treetops and casting oblique slivers of light across the building before them.

'So, basically, it's a creepy old haunted mansion,' muttered Emma as she got out of the van.

'Shhh...' hissed Okeke. She was on her phone again, willing Eleanora to pick up. Hopeful that in the perfect stillness they might even hear the buzz of it coming from somewhere within. 'No answer,' she whispered again. 'Something's happened to her, I'm sure.'

'Or she's being very cautious,' said Boyd. 'Which is good.'

'So what's the deal?' asked Jay. 'Do we call out for her? Do we go inside?'

'Fuck it,' said Okeke. She stomped up the front steps and pushed the large main door. It creaked loudly as it swung inwards. She stepped inside. 'Eleanora! Are you in here? Are you okay?'

Without hesitating, Jay followed her.

Boyd turned to look at the other two. 'Charlotte, Emma? Stay with the van and the dogs.'

'Oh, Bill,' replied Charlotte. 'This isn't an episode of... of *Scooby Doo.*'

'I want you two with the van,' he said. 'Just in case we need to make a hasty departure.' Make sure we've got an exit.'

'I can drive it. I'll stay,' said Emma. She looked at Charlotte. 'But I'm not staying alone.'

Charlotte turned to Boyd. 'You shouldn't be clumping around inside a ruin. For God's sake, you have stitches in you still. And what if there *are* bad guys waiting in there?'

'There won't be,' Boyd replied. 'Maybe some foxes. A deer or two... but nothing worse.'

'How do you know?' Charlotte asked.

'Eleanora's been careful. We've been careful. I'm sure no one has any idea we're here.'

'Plus, Dad's got his gun,' added Emma.

Charlotte's eyebrows shot up. 'What?'

'Christ, thanks Ems,' Boyd grunted.

'You have an actual *gun*?' Charlotte looked horrified.

Jay's face appeared in the open doorway. 'Guv, you coming?' Echoing from inside the derelict building, they all heard Okeke calling out for Eleanora. 'She's going off on one,' said Jay, an edge creeping into his voice.

Boyd nodded, then he turned to Charlotte. 'I'll just be five minutes, okay? We've got to find her. We may need to carry the old girl out if she's had a stroke or a fall or something.'

Charlotte lasered him with a look that said they were going to have things to talk about later, then she nodded. 'Just be careful, Bill.'

∼

ELEANORA REGISTERED the approaching footsteps first. Then her name being called out softly, almost lost amid the rumbling sea breeze, the sound of waves gently thumping onto the beach and the few early-riser gulls circling overhead.

'Ellie? We know you're here – come on out.'

That was a voice she remembered all too well: thin and reedy, and right now stretched with a vaguely theatrical, singsong tone to it.

'It's over, Ellie. This silly little game of yours is over,' called Jeremy Warner.

It *was* over. She'd known her game of hide-and-seek wasn't going to last much longer. One way or another he'd have eventually discovered she kept a beach hut in Seaford. The secret to evasion was to keep moving, never staying put in one place for too long. And that was a young person's game.

The only good news was that if Jeremy and his people were here, they weren't *there*. Which meant the game wasn't quite over. Not just yet.

She looked down at the phone in her lap. Samantha and her friends must be at Barnham House by now. Perhaps the second call she'd just missed was Okeke to say, '*We're here, what do we do now?*'

From outside, it sounded as though Warner and his minions were further down the promenade, just a few dozen yards away. She heard her one-time colleague calling out softly to her again.

'Now, which one of these ridiculous beach huts are you hiding in? Do we have to kick in every wretched door or can we do this in a more grown-up manner?'

She swiped her phone's screen in the darkness, aware that its tiny screen would wink on, quite possibly spilling light out of the small window of her hut, giving her away.

She only had a few seconds...

∽

OKEKE PANNED her torch around Barnham House's once-grand entrance hall. It was empty. Pale squares on the walls hinted at large framed paintings that had once hung there. Scuff marks on the wooden floor suggested heavy items of furniture that had been removed with little care for the building itself.

Above her hung a length of dusty electrical flex and a thick chain of wrought-iron links that presumably had once suspended a grand chandelier many decades ago.

She cupped her mouth. 'Eleanora! It's Sam! If you're somewhere here, if you can't raise your voice, just make a noise! Knock on a wall!'

She heard Jay's footsteps as he crossed the hall to join her. 'Some crib, eh?'

'Shhh,' she hissed, then raised a finger to her lips. 'I'm listening for her.'

'Maybe she isn't here,' he said after a few moment's silence. 'Maybe...'

Okeke's phone suddenly began to vibrate in her jacket pocket. She glanced at Jay and smiled. 'See? She must have heard me.'

She pulled her phone out – it was Eleanora. 'It's Sam,' she began, 'where –'

'Stop!' Eleanora hissed frantically. 'I don't have much time... Listen! It's right there! It's in the house!'

'What is?' Okeke asked her, momentarily confused.

'The archive,' Eleanora rasped. 'Everything I smuggled out. Everything you need –' she drew a long laboured breath – 'to tell the story. Marble Orchard. What we did to –' A loud bang cut her off. Like the crack of wood splintering.

'It's in her house,' Eleanora said urgently. 'In the fireplace. All of it!'

Okeke looked around. In a house this big, there were going to be many fireplaces. 'Which room, El–'

'Sam!' Eleanora pressed. 'You have to tell every–'

Okeke heard several muffled voices and the clunk of the phone being dropped, followed by the sound of scraping feet and the whimpering feeble cry of an old woman.

The call ended.

Okeke looked up and saw that Boyd had just joined them.

'Was that her? Was that Eleanora?' he asked.

'They've got her,' said Okeke. 'The fuckers got her.'

52

Warner sat down carefully in the only other chair in the hut: a foldable canvas beach chair that creaked as he lowered himself into it.

'That was Mattie's,' whispered Eleanora. 'There was hardly any weight to her.' She gestured at the frail wooden frame. 'I can't vouch for it taking yours.'

Warner nodded slowly. Finally he spoke. 'I'm very sorry about what happened to her, Ellie. I want you to know that she passed in her sleep. She died of smoke inhalation.'

'You're certain of that, are you?' she replied. 'Certain that she didn't burn to death? Awake? In agony?'

'I've seen her post-mortem. It was definitely smoke inhalation. She was found in her bed. She wouldn't have been aware of anything,' Warner said.

'And what about –' Eleanora took a deep rasping breath – 'that poor boy?'

Warner shook his head. 'You know better than anyone, Ellie, this business isn't always nice.'

He reached for her phone. 'Now, I'm going to presume if

I dial the one number you have on this that it will be DC Okeke's number?'

She remained silent, staring defiantly at him.

'And if I ring, she probably won't answer now because you just warned her not to?'

'I don't know who you're talking about,' she managed to say with a tight smile.

He returned it. 'Of course you don't. The thing is, Ellie, we hacked the phones. We know DC Okeke, her fellow detective Boyd, her boyfriend and a couple of others are on their way to your ancestral home. I expect they're already there by now.'

Eleanora maintained her poker face, pressing her lips together, which produced a barcode of deep wrinkles along her top lip.

'I have two teams closing in on them.' Warner sighed. 'They're not going to get away, I'm sad to say. So, why don't we talk about why you sent them there and what it is you're hoping they're going to retrieve for you?'

~

'Say it again... exactly like she said it,' said Boyd.

'It's right there. It's in the house. In the fireplace,' Okeke repeated.

Jay panned his torch around the drawing room to the left of the entrance hall. There was a grand fireplace right there.

'And what are we looking for?' he said as he squatted in front of it and aimed his torch into the dark, soot-covered recess.

'An archive,' said Okeke.

'Which consists of what? asked Boyd.

She shrugged. 'No idea.'

'Files?' called out Jay. 'Documents? Notebooks? Pictures?'

'Film cannisters? Hard drives?' added Boyd.

'Look, she didn't say,' Okeke snapped. 'Maybe Crowhurst's missing journal? I have no idea.'

Jay leant forward, one hand in the grate, the other aiming his torch up into the chimney flue. He began to prod and poke at the soot-clad bricks he could reach, hoping to dislodge a loose one.

'This is a big place,' said Boyd. 'God knows how many fireplaces it has.'

'So then we spread out,' Okeke replied. 'Take a floor each. Let's get Emma and Charlotte helping.'

Boyd nodded. All hands on deck made sense. 'I'll get Charlotte, but Emma's staying with the van. I want her to keep an eye out. Just in case...'

～

'JERRY, I think you know exactly what I've squirrelled away...'

Warner narrowed his eyes. 'Marble Orchard?'

She nodded. 'Everything that I filmed.'

'The medical observations, the notes... the treatments?'

'All of it... Those poor men... Dying, one after the other... I filmed them all.'

Warner shrugged. 'You were part of it, Ellie. You were complicit.'

'I know.' She took another couple of deep, burbling breaths. 'And I've had to live with that.'

'You shouldn't be so hard on yourself,' he replied. 'That was important work, back then.'

Critical research work, in fact. If the Cold War had turned hot – and, good God, it nearly did over Cuba later that year – then Britain's nuclear weapons would have been dispatched without question. Thanks to the earlier tests in the Pacific, the incineration radius and the blast-damage radius were known factors with regards to buildings and infrastructure. But more important to know was what effect they'd have on humans. Particularly those on the periphery. Specifically troops. Troops wearing a varied range of protective equipment, stationed at various distances from ground zero.

He was well aware that Marble Orchard had generated an incredible wealth of useful data: indices of blast destruction, radiation absorption, survival rates and post-radiation attrition rates. In the event of a nuclear war, the Ministry of Defence would need to know the likely initial casualty rates of their troops on the ground: how many in, say, a battalion, would survive; how many of them would still be able to function and for how long.

'The Americans used pigs in foil suits,' she said. 'We used men.'

Warner sighed. 'Ah, but then you can't ask a slowly dying pig to strip and reassemble an assault rifle. Or operate a field radio, or drive a supply truck, can you? What was done back then was done to save lives.'

∽

THE FIRST FAINT threads of grey were beginning to lighten the sky as they regrouped downstairs in the entrance hall once more. The front door had been left wide open, allowing a soft grey pall of light to push back against the gloom inside.

'Has anyone found anything?' asked Boyd.

'Nothing,' said Okeke.

Jay shook his head. 'It would help if I knew exactly what I was looking for.'

Charlotte wiped a loose tress of hair away from her face, leaving a smudge of soot across her forehead. 'Jay is quite right. We're fumbling around not knowing if we're looking for something the size of a floppy disc or a treasure chest.'

'And how long ago was this archive thing stashed here?' added Jay. 'I mean, we don't know if any kids have been in helping themselves, do we?'

Okeke shook her head. 'I don't know. It could have been yesterday, last week or even a decade ago.'

Boyd checked his watch. It was gone 6 a.m. They'd been searching the derelict building for over an hour now, and the longer they lingered, the more twitchy he was getting.

'She said it's here. Somewhere.' He glanced at the open doors. 'Are there any other buildings? Annexes?'

'She said it was in the *house*,' Okeke said. 'Not the barn or the summer guesthouse or –'

'Okay,' Boyd raised a hand to stop her. 'So then, have we missed a room? Was there any furniture pulled in front of a hidden fireplace? Did everyone check thoroughly?'

They all nodded.

'Shit,' he grumbled. 'We can't afford to leave empty-handed.'

'Yeah, we need it as leverage,' said Jay.

Boyd nodded. 'Without any... we're basically screwed.'

'What about Eleanora?' asked Charlotte. 'Is she screwed?'

Boyd could only hope that until *they* had what they wanted back in safe hands, they needed her alive.

The four of them stood together in silence for a moment,

listening to the hiss of mature trees stirring outside, the skitter of dry leaves across the hall's wooden floor and the soft scratching of pigeons somewhere far above.

'*The* house?' said Charlotte, breaking the silence.

Okeke nodded, then paused. 'Or it could have been *her* house.'

'I checked the bedrooms on the first floor,' said Charlotte. 'They were little girls' rooms, by the look of them.'

She looked at the grand stairs – which were not so grand-looking now.

'There's a doll's house in one of them.' Charlotte paused and repeated, '*Her* house?'

~

'WHAT I really don't understand is *why*?' said Warner. 'Why now, Ellie? After all this time?'

'Because of James Crowhurst,' Eleanora replied.

'Right, and... all we had to do was wait for that dear old boy to die. That would have been the end of it.'

'One less case,' she said, smiling. 'One less secret to guard.'

'Indeed. So, what the hell were you thinking? Sharing this with that –'

'Adam found out about it,' she replied. 'James wrote it all down. While he was still able to.'

'He did *what*?'

'I was a little... surprised to hear that... as well.' Gurgling breaths punctuated her words. 'It would have been... good... helpful... to have... his account.'

'Why, Ellie? To do what?'

'I thought... it was time. *Enough* time had passed...'

'To go public?'

She nodded. 'We muzzled... that man... and cruelly too.'

'He disobeyed orders,' Warner snapped, 'and was rightfully court-martialled.'

'He knew what was about to happen... to his troops.' Eleanora looked at her former deputy. Warner and Crowhurst were very different kinds of men.

'He refused his orders,' she continued, 'because they were *unacceptable*.'

Crowhurst had refused to deploy his men within the exclusion radius. And for that he'd been relieved of his command, and another officer had replaced him. Believing the men were being stationed at various safe distances, he had willingly followed orders.

And Crowhurst had been court-martialled. Kicked out of the army.

The sixties rolled on by and Britain's younger generation got a taste for campaigning against the bombs, against war and racism. The Boutique had checked in with James Crowhurst and reminded him that everything he knew about Marble Orchard was a sacred national secret.

'It was all in his journal, you know,' Eleanora continued. 'The orders he was given... How he was treated... How we came back to him later.... How we threatened him...'

Eleanora knew all about that, because she'd been the one tasked with having a quiet, friendly word in his ear. To tell him that one word and there'd be evidence discovered in his flat to show that he had an interest in young boys. Nasty photographs. The worst possible kind.

She remembered his face draining of colour. The threat made real by a sample image that she'd let him glimpse.

'What we did to him was wrong,' she said.

Warner's expression was impassive. 'Most of what we do

is wrong,' he said, 'but for the most part it's done for the right reasons.'

Eleanora sighed. 'He deserved better.'

∾

CHARLOTTE LED them into the second bedroom along the first-floor landing.

'It's over there,' she said, pointing at a dust-covered doll's house in the corner of the room. They hurried over, Jay's and Okeke's torch beams dancing across the miniature house's façade.

Charlotte went over to the bay window and pulled the threadbare curtain to one side. The grey light of predawn filled the room and caught a cloud of dust motes as they swirled slowly to the floor.

Boyd knelt down in front of the doll's house. It looked as though it was home-made, a labour of love, and he quickly realised it was a replica of the derelict building that they were standing inside.

'Does it open up?' he said, looking around for an obvious latch.

'Have you never played with a doll's house?' said Charlotte with a smile as she stepped over and squatted beside him. She reached around the side, flicked a catch and then gently eased open the front wall of the doll's house.

Okeke aimed the beam of her torch inside. Light glinted off a multitude of tiny surfaces: an oval vanity mirror on a dressing table; a miniature chandelier dangling above a staircase leading up from a miniature rendition of the entrance hall; a jade vase on a small round rosewood table. And there, among the furniture – for the most part mercifully spared a coating of dust from the real world – were porcelain figurines that presumably represented the Baxendale family. Mother, nanny and two little girls.

Boyd scanned the house. There was a drawing room, the entrance hall, then a dining toom and a kitchen and pantry on the ground floor, and two bedrooms each on the upper two floors.

Each room had a fireplace, topped by a mantelpiece and flanked by tiny Doric columns. The fireplaces themselves, though, were where the detailing ran dry. They were just archways of black-painted board without even an attempt at a recess.

Boyd reached in and tapped his index finger against the largest fireplace, downstairs in the drawing room. It didn't give, nor make an encouragingly hollow sound.

'Try the next one,' said Jay eagerly.

'That's the plan,' grunted Boyd. He tried the dining-room fireplace and got the same result.

'Now the kitchen,' said Okeke.

Boyd gave her a look.

'It's always the third one,' she said, grinning back at him.

He tapped it. Nothing.

'Okay, so maybe not always,' she said.

Charlotte reached into one of the girls' bedrooms, in which a miniature version of the doll house sat in the very same corner of the room: an Escher-esque illusion of scaling infinity.

'Surely not?' she whispered. She tapped the black facsimile of the fire alcove with her fingernail and it jiggered loosely. She tried to push it, but it wouldn't budge.

'Here. Let me.'

Boyd all but pushed her hand aside and jabbed it hard, as if he was poking someone's eye. The black hatch fell away and clattered down into the back of the doll's house. There seemed to be a gap between the back of the rooms and the back panel of the house. Boyd grabbed Okeke's torch and aimed it through the hole he'd created. Their heads all converged as they ducked down to investigate.

'Nothing,' he said flatly.

'Stick your finger in... Feel around the hole,' said Jay.

Boyd did as he said and immediately felt something.

'Shit. There's something taped to the back!'

Crooking his finger, he tugged at the object. It felt like a match box maybe, secured to the inner wall with tape. He had just about managed to free it – and it clunked to the bottom of the back gap.

'Oh, bollocks.'

Jay stood up, grabbed the doll's house in his large hands and shoved it roughly to one side, to the sound of several miniature items of furniture rattling, clunking and falling over. An alarming earthquake for the figurines inside.

Boyd aimed his torch at the bedroom floor. Thank god, the bottom of the doll's house wasn't sealed, because there in the stark beam was a box of Swan Vesta matches. He reached for it, fighting a fleeting instinct to find something forensically neutral to pick it up with.

The matchbox rattled as he picked it up. He pushed one end of the inner tray into the sleeve. The tray emerged from the other side, containing a single memory stick.

53

In the cool predawn light on a woody country lane, a chorus of birds brought the morning to life. That, and the crackle of gravel beneath tyres as a white transit van with 'JMS Plumbers' stencilled on the side drove along it. After a short while, it came to a halt and parked on the layby opposite an almost completely overgrown and easily missed driveway.

A few moments later a second identical van pulled up and parked behind it.

To the casual observer, it would appear that employees from the same plumbing company had pulled over for a pre-agreed fag break or a piss stop. Or even a driving break, given the ungodly hour. Except for two small things. No one climbed out of either van, and the windscreens of both were subtly tinted and reflective enough to obscure the faces behind the steering wheels and to avoid detection by the strobing flash of a speed camera.

Someone far more observant, trained to notice such things perhaps, might have noted from the laden suspension that both small vans were carrying a heavy load in the back.

And completely unobservable to anyone would have been the air around both vans, humming with the vibrating frequency of radio traffic.

'*This is Alpha. We've arrived at the entrance to an overgrown driveway. Iron gates are wide open. It looks like a vehicle has driven through recently.*'

'*This is Bravo. Copy that. Binoculars sight a white van parked a hundred yards down the track in front of the building...*'

∽

WARNER FELT HIS PHONE BUZZ. He pulled it out of his jacket pocket and answered it.

It was Moira. Both field teams had arrived at Barnham House. She informed him that they had the area figuratively taped off with a no-go area from any emergency response vehicles. Also, Gary had identified the nearest phone mast, five miles away, and had managed to take control of it.

They now had an operational dark zone.

'The field teams are now asking for instructions,' said Moira, ending her situation report.

'Just a moment,' Warner replied, then lowered his phone and looked at Eleanora. 'My people are there now, Ellie. Right outside Barnham House. They can see a van parked outside. They're asking me for instructions.'

She glared at him, but said nothing.

'That was Moira, by the way,' he said. 'You remember Moira?'

She nodded. 'My first choice to take over. Far better organised than you ever were.' She leant forward. 'Hear that, my dear?'

Warner's face flickered angrily as he covered the phone's mouthpiece. 'Now, this doesn't have to end up being an unpleasant mess. I presume those are your new friends and I'm going to hazard a guess you sent them there to collect whatever scraps of evidence you managed to squirrel out of the Boutique.' He took her silence as confirmation and nodded with grudging respect. 'Very sensible. Very prudent. Storing it somewhere other than home.'

'That's not my only stash,' she croaked. 'I took a lot more with me.'

'Well now, if we're talking about stacks of box files, then perhaps I could believe you'd spread them out over several locations. You're no amateur, are you?'

She hacked out a wheezy laugh. 'How very kind of you.'

Eleanora might be a fossil from the analogue era of spycraft, but she wasn't an idiot. All of the footage that she'd taken as a young woman with a bulky 8mm camera had long ago been digitised. The enormous amount of data Marble Orchard had generated – numerous filing cabinets full – could fit on a piece of silicon the size of a fingernail.

'I uploaded it,' she rasped.

Warner had to admire her tenacious bullshitting. 'Then you'd have given her a link to click, not a location to drive to, wouldn't you?'

'Jerry?' She pulled in a long deep breath. 'I'd very much... like something... to drink.'

'Of course.' He leaned over and patted her gently. 'When we're done, we can toast each other,' he said, producing a hip flask and setting it on the small shelf beside her. 'But a little sip now? Why not?'

She stared at it in silence for a moment. The hip flask meant what she thought it meant. 'So, it's this morning, then? For me?'

'Yes. I'm afraid so.'

'No debrief first?'

He shook his head. 'Just a tipple between old friends. No point dragging it out, Ellie. But first... we need to tidy this little mess up.' He inched forward, his face now close to hers. 'Let me present a couple of options to you. Option A: I send our people in and no one comes out alive... and what's left of your family home becomes another tragic heritage piece that ends up burned to the ground. Or B: you' speak to Okeke and tell her to come out and hand over whatever they have.'

'And you'll let them go?'

He tipped his head. '*They* will be interrogated and, if I think they can be reliably muzzled, then, of course, yes.' He smiled disarmingly. 'Less paperwork over all for me, right?'

She could tell he was lying.

'She sighed wearily. 'Right...'

∽

BOYD LED the way out of the derelict building, relieved that they could finally get on their way once again with something in hand that they might be able to use as a bargaining chip. The blue-grey sky had become a pale facsimile of daylight. He could see now that Barnham House was located in the middle of its own mature woodland, within grounds that he guessed had once been landscaped and well-tended. He caught a glimpse of a sagging tennis net amid a large patch of chest-high brambles, surrounded by a perimeter of rusting metal posts.

They approached the van and Emma wound down the driver-side window. 'Where is she?'

'Not here,' said Boyd. 'We got what she wanted us to get,

though.'

'What is it?' Emma asked.

'Evidence,' Boyd replied. 'I hope.'

Ozzie and Mia tumbled out as he pulled the side door open, eager to relieve themselves again. Charlotte quickly grabbed their leads before they were able to disappear into the undergrowth.

Okeke suddenly tapped her hip. 'Phone,' she whispered. It was buzzing: Eleanora's number again.

'Wait!' said Boyd. 'It could be her... or it could be *them*.'

Okeke stared at the screen. 'If it *is* them calling, then they've got her. Right?'

He nodded. That much was unavoidably obvious.

'So, I might as well answer?' She looked to Jay to back her up.

He shrugged. 'They may have a deal they want to make?'

'Or they're trying to pin our location?' Boyd added.

The phone's insistent buzzing continued, ridiculously loud amid the soft hiss of a breeze stirring the trees.

'It's just a dumb-phone,' said Jay. The best they could get from it would be the nearest cell mast. Out here in the middle of nowhere that could be several miles away. He had a point.

'Go on,' said Boyd.

Okeke accepted the call. 'Right. Who's this, then?'

∼

WARNER SMILED at the bristling and defiant tone of the detective's voice. 'I presume this is Samantha Okeke speaking?'

Her reply was non-committal. And somewhat brusque.

'Who the fuck am I speaking to?'

'You can call me Jeremy,' he replied. 'I have your friend right here with me.'

'Is she okay?'

He glanced at Eleanora. The old woman looked very far from okay. 'She's alive,' he replied.

'She needs a hospital,' said Okeke. 'Urgently.'

'She does,' Warner agreed. 'And we'll get her to one very soon. But, before we do that, I want you and your friends to hand over what you've got.'

'We've got nothing,' Okeke replied. 'We thought she was here. That's why –'

'Now we both know that's not true. Ellie sent you there to pick something up. I'm presuming you've found it. So, we can make this a very straightforward conversation. Hand it over, then Ellie gets to go to hospital, and you get to go home.'

No reply.

Warner mock sighed. 'I'm really not that keen to be responsible for the deaths of two police officers and their loved ones, Samantha. But I'm prepared to be. What you have in your possession are state secrets that aren't going to do anyone any good if they are let out into the open.'

'In your opinion,' Okeke replied.

'All that will happen, Samantha, is that some tabloid newspapers will sell a few more copies for a few days. But the damage to our country's reputation will be incalculable. It'll be the sort of reputational damage that will forever undermine this country's ability to make any kind of moral case –'

'Moral case for what?' Okeke asked.

'Well, for one, arguing against the proliferation of new WMDs, new nuclear powers, new weapons systems, nasty biochemical weapons systems. There's a Pandora's box of horror waiting to spill out, Samantha, and it's nations like ours that have some degree of influence on the world stage. But not, I'm afraid, if we're discredited.'

He took her silence as an encouraging sign.

'Do you even know what you have in your possession?' he asked.

'Marble Orchard,' she replied.

'All right. And do you know what that is?'

Warner looked up at Drummond. The man was waggling his phone in the air. Presumably Moira was on the line, waiting for instructions. The two field teams were in place nearby, still waiting to hear from her, waiting for the green light to go in.

Does she know? he wondered.

'Samantha?' Her silence continued. Perhaps not. Perhaps the code name Marble Orchard was *all* she and the others knew...

'I think this nonsense needs to stop now,' he said firmly. 'Ellie very much needs hospital treatment, and I'm sure you'd like to get back home. We have personnel on the ground nearby awaiting my orders. I'd really like to say to them that they can approach and that they'll encounter a fully cooperative target. Can I tell them that?'

He heard a loud rustling over the line as a hand, presumably, was clasped over the phone. Followed by a swift exchange between several muffled voices.

There was a further rustling and she was back. 'First, I want to hear Eleanora's voice,' Okeke said. 'I want to know she's alive. Let me speak to her.'

Warner looked at Eleanora. 'Samantha would like to say hello to you.' He held the phone out in front of her.

Eleanora lurched forward in her seat. 'Don't trust him. RUN!'

54

Two things happened in quick succession that made Boyd jump out of his skin. Okeke shrieked, 'THEY'RE COMING!' Then a heartbeat later he heard an engine snarling loudly in low gear and turned to see two white transit vans carving their way through the tall grass towards them.

Charlotte dragged the barking dogs back towards the van's open side door. Boyd ducked down to pick up Ozzie and hurl him in, wrenching his stitches in the process and howling with pain as he did so.

Charlotte tossed in Mia and then manhandled Boyd into the van, pulling the sliding door shut.

Meanwhile Emma had started the van up as Okeke clambered in the passenger side and Jay tried to enter from the driver's side.

'MOVE!' he bellowed.

'I CAN'T!' Emma screamed back. 'My belly's in the way!'

The two vans had diverged now, one bearing left, one right, with the clear intention of stopping in front and behind them to prevent them from moving off. As they drove off the overgrown driveway onto less even terrain, they began to bump and rock, their headlights casting flailing spears of light through the early morning mist.

'GO, GO, GO!' yelled Jay, hanging onto the open door, one buttock perched on the inch of seat that Emma had managed to wriggle over and cede to him.

Emma was still trying to manoeuvre herself from under the steering wheel and over the protruding gear stick. Jay planted one of his booted feet on the clutch, reached around her back and thrust the gear stick into first, slamming the accelerator down.

His van lurched forward, heading towards the old house.

'STEER!' he screamed in Emma's ear, as he manipulated the gear stick into second.

Emma gave up trying to extract herself from the seat, grabbed the steering wheel and wrenched it to the right. The van swerved at the last moment, clunking over something solid, and careered forward along the front of Barnham House.

Jay, was still half in, half out of his van, his left hand clinging to the door frame, his right to the wildly swinging open door. All the while, his dangling right leg was being whipped by heads of cow parsley and stung by spiked limbs of bramble. He looked back over his shoulder at their pursuers.

The left van was altering course to cut diagonally across the overgrown ground in an attempt to block them off at the far corner of the house, while the other was now following in their wake, taking the twin ruts in the grass that they left behind them as a guaranteed obstacle-free route to use.

His foot was hard down on the accelerator, the engine screaming at the unfair abuse being inflicted upon it.

'CHANGE GEAR!' he shouted at Emma.

She slammed her foot down on the clutch, then glanced down at his van's gear stick, an unfamiliar configuration of numbers worn down by years of use. 'Which way –'

'UP-RIGHT-UP!'

She jerked the stick straight up, then waggled it right and then took the first upwards nook that it seemed happy to accept. She pulled her foot off the clutch and the van suddenly ceased screaming and switched to a low and unhappy groan.

'TOO FAR!' snapped Jay. 'We're in FIFTH!'

They had slowed right down to a crawl and for a moment it seemed that they were in danger of stalling and lurching to a halt. Jay looked around, the van that had cut across was getting ahead of them. It was, in fact, going to beat them to the corner now. The van behind them was almost on top of them.

'Shit! Shit! Shit!'

Emma looked at him. Her eyes were practically screaming, *'WHAT DO I DO NOW?'*

The front white van, now just off to their right, jolted to an abrupt halt. The front windscreen shattered and its rear lifted a foot off the ground before dropping back down, its suspension rocking wildly. They'd run into something solid, hidden amid the swaying weeds.

'Keep going!' Jay shouted at Emma.

She held the steering wheel steady as they slowly picked up speed, the engine gradually rising in pitch as it bumped and rocked past the front of the ruin.

They reached the corner, and Emma blindly spun the wheel left, hoping they were turning into a gap rather than a dead end. Ahead of her – thank fuck – was a path between the side of the building and a number of derelict sheds and greenhouses. She carefully picked her way through, expecting at any second to hit something hidden and be thrown belly-first into the steering wheel.

Oh God, not that. Not that.

The path suddenly cleared and they drove into an open field topped with swirling skeins of morning mist. The field sloped gently uphill towards the treeline: a wall of mature oaks and horse chestnuts that were just beginning to shed their autumn-hued leaves.

'Where now?' yelled Emma.

Jay pointed to a dark patch on the right. 'There! Is that a track or something?'

Emma spun the wheel and they lurched towards the far corner of the field, bumping and rocking as they drove across a moonscape of unseen hummocks of grass.

∼

'Aghhh!' Boyd groaned as he and the dogs parted company with the van's floor for umpteenth time and bumped down heavily again.

Charlotte lifted his shirt to check his stitches. A couple of them had torn, revealing a small wet puckered opening of parted skin. A single track of watery blood had rolled down his side. 'You'll need to go back and have this loo–'

They all bumped into the air once more, both Ozzie and Mia scrabbling with panic.

'– looked at. It's coming open.'

'Is it bad?' he said, grimacing. 'Am I –' they bumped into the air and landed heavily again – 'spilling my guts?'

'No, not yet. But we keep this up –' the van lurched yet again – 'and the whole thing is going to –'

Boyd reached a hand to his side to have a feel. She smacked it away. 'No. You'll infect it. Leave it alone!'

'The fuckers knew where we were!' he groaned. 'How the –'

'Who knows?' Charlotte muttered as she looked around for something she could use to bandage him up. 'Maybe Emma's phone was hacked too?'

Boyd nodded. *Stupid, stupid.* He'd let that slip. He'd assumed, for some reason, that the net had been cast solely around Okeke and possibly himself. But no further. Why he'd assumed that, he had no bloody idea. Complacency? An arrogant presumption that he and Okeke had cleverly outwitted M–I-fucking-five?

He sat up, twisted painfully and rapped his knuckles on the front partition. A moment later, Okeke's face appeared.

'Sam!' he shouted as the van lurched over another hummock. 'Emma's phone. And our burners! Here's mine...' He held it up; her hand snaked through the hatch and grabbed it. 'Toss them out! Toss the whole lot. NOW!'

She nodded. Her face disappeared out of view. Boyd could hear Emma and Jay shouting instructions at each other as the van lurched, rattled and flung itself across what felt like a crater-strewn no man's land.

The jarring motion suddenly eased.

'What's going on?' Boyd shouted. 'How're we doing?'

There was no reply. Jay, Emma and Okeke sounded busy in the front.

'*Turn off! Turn off there!*'

'*NO! What if it's a dead end!?*'

'*Do it!*'

'*Watch the tree. WATCH THE FUCKING TREE!!!*'

The van swerved violently, throwing Boyd, Charlotte and the dogs from one side to the other into an untidy heap. Boyd yelped in agony, pressing a hand against his side once again.

'Bill, are you okay?' gasped Charlotte as she righted herself.

'It's bloody sore.' He winced. 'Shit. Take a look, will you?'

Charlotte lifted his shirt and moved his hand away.

'Oooh.' She frowned, pursing her lips. 'You've popped another stitch, I think.'

'Am I bleeding? Shit. It feels as if my guts are spewing out –'

'They're not,' she replied quickly. 'It's okay. The wound's weeping. That's all. I think it's going to need... No, I *know* it's going to need redoing but you're not going to –'

The van swerved in the other direction, rolling the four of them to the other side, back where they'd started.

∼

OKEKE POINTED AHEAD. 'CROSSROADS! TAKE IT!'

'Which way?' screamed Emma.

'Either!'

Emma swung the van right onto a single-lane road flanked on either side by open fields. Jay was still clinging to the door and frame, bum barely on the driver's seat.

'We need to stop!' he barked. 'I can't bloody hang on like this much longer!'

Okeke checked the wing mirror on her side. 'Wait! What if they're still –'

'Fucks' sake!' Jay bellowed. 'We need to stop! I'm gonna fall out!'

Emma reduced her speed. She shot a glance at Okeke. 'Can I?'

Okeke, eyes still on the wing mirror, finally nodded. 'Do it. but quickly!'

The van screeched to rapid halt, and Jay let go, dropping onto the road. 'Out! Ems! Let me drive.'

'We haven't got time, you muppet!' shouted Okeke. 'Come round to my side – let her drive!'

'But –' Jay started.

'DO IT!' Okeke snapped.

Jay made his way to Okeke's side, as Emma closed the door on her side.

'It would be better with me driving,' he wheezed as he shunted her along the seat and slammed the passenger side door shut.

'She's doing just fine,' replied Okeke. 'Okay, Em, NOW GO!'

55

Warner stared at the old woman. Her grey eyes were wide open, the whites bloodshot and riddled with a fine lace of burst veins. The eyelids were red and puckered, damp with tears.

Her mouth hung open, sagging on one side to show a denture plate that had detached itself, saliva dangling in a long string from her bottom lip.

Eleanora was dead.

And he'd been the one to do it.

He felt physically sick. He stood up, pushed his way past Drummond and stepped outside the beach hut into the cool grey morning. He crossed the promenade's decorative patchwork of paving and threw up on the shingled beach.

He could still feel her crushed mouth against his palm, her jaw scissoring, her pathetically weak tongue pushing, her nostrils flaring beneath his hand as he'd pressed down hard.

He could still feel her withered old body squirming, hear her feet drumming the floor as she slowly suffocated – a process that he wanted to think took mere seconds, but felt as though it lasted minutes. Even Drummond had looked horrified as Warner had finally lowered his damp and sticky hand from her face.

He couldn't believe he'd just done what he'd done. He'd intended to reach out to shut her up – to put a hand over her mouth before she said anything more. But then he'd just kept his hand there, leaning into the hold. Pressing harder and harder.

Drummond emerged from the hut holding up his phone. 'Sir, it's Moira for you.'

Warner dabbed at his own mouth with the cuff of his shirt, straightened his tie and then returned to the hut.

He took the phone. 'Moira, do we have them now?'

'I'm afraid not,' she replied. 'They managed to evade both teams.'

'They *what*?'

'I'm sorry, sir. They escaped.'

56

Emma pulled the van onto the forecourt of a petrol station. 'Park it around the back,' said Jay. 'Not on the forecourt. Just in case...'

She nodded and nursed the limping vehicle around the two pumps and over to the side of the petrol station itself, where she parked beside a rusty green Citroën with saggy, balding tyres. She switched off the engine, then let out a long sigh of relief.

'You did good,' said Okeke.

'I think I did a little wee at some point,' she said.

'I think we all did,' said Jay. He got out and dropped to his hands and knees. 'Yup... the suspension's completely screwed. The front left wheel's been rubbing the arch.' He got to his feet. 'Great.'

Okeke climbed out after him and pulled the sliding door aside. 'How're you lot doing?'

Charlotte emerged into the pale daylight first. 'I'm fine, but Bill really needs to see a doctor. His surgery wound's opened up.'

Boyd emerged slowly, bum-shuffling across the floor of the van until he got to the edge, dangled his legs out and stood up with a long and pronounced groan. 'Very, very bloody sore is how I am.'

Emma emerged from the driver's side and her eyes immediately rounded at the sight of Boyd.

'Dad!' cried Emma. 'Oh my God, you're bleeding!'

'Just a drop or two,' he replied. 'Charlotte's going to get some plasters if this place sells them.'

'Some of his stitches have popped, that's all,' Charlotte reassured Emma quickly.

'It's nothing that a staple gun won't fix, love,' added Boyd.

Okeke's attention was firmly locked on the road running past the petrol station. Parked around the side of the small building, the van was, hopefully, out of sight. All the same, she watched the road for any sign of their pursuer approaching.

'I think... I *hope*,' she corrected herself, 'that we got fucking lucky at that junction.'

Jay followed her gaze and pulled her back, behind the corner of the building. 'If they'd gone the same way as us, they'd be here already,' he said.

'If they took a wrong turn,' said Boyd, 'then that buys us a little time.'

Okeke took a deep breath. 'Would those bastards have got the clout to make use of the local force?'

'Probably,' Boyd replied. 'Which means there'll be a BOLO already out for this,' he said, slapping the side of Jay's mud-spattered van.

'BOLO?' enquired Charlotte.

'Be on the look-out,' said Okeke.

'We can't drive it anyway,' added Jay. 'The front left tyre's completely bald. I'm surprised we didn't have a blow-out.' He went to check the other tyres.

'We're literally in the middle of nowhere. We can't walk,' said Okeke, nodding at Boyd, then Emma.

'Oh, I can walk,' replied Emma. 'I just can't run.'

Okeke sighed. 'So, here we go... That question again. What now?'

'You've got the memory stick still?' asked Boyd

Okeke pulled it out of the back pocket of her jeans and held it up.

'Then the next step is to get it online. Get it out there,' said Emma.

'For which we'll need some Wi-Fi,' Okeke pointed out.

'And a computer, I believe,' said Charlotte.

'Great. Another internet café, then,' said Okeke. 'Only this time they'll be on their A-game when looking out for me.'

Boyd shook his head. 'No. No internet cafés. That's too obvious. No service stations. No Starbucks, Costa, McDonald's. Anyone with a computer and a Wi-Fi signal will do.'

Charlotte pulled a face; she still had a diagonal smear of soot sloping down across her forehead that looked like war paint. 'What? We just knock on random people's front doors? At this time in the morning?'

'Yup.' Boyd inspected their surroundings. They were in the middle of the countryside. There were plenty of trees, rolling fields and bemused-looking sheep, but not so many signs of civilization.

'Uh? Guys? There's this?' said Emma, patting the grubby plaster wall of the petrol station. Several brittle flakes of paint and plaster crumbled away onto a cluster of nettles below.

'Is it even in business?' asked Okeke.

Boyd peered round the corner, checking first for the faint sound of any approaching vehicle. Silence. He peered through the grimy front window for any signs of life inside. A fridge light glowed faintly, and he spotted a red dot of light from a fuse box on the back wall. He tried the door, but it rattled stubbornly in its frame.

Then he noticed a faded handwritten note taped on the glass door from the inside. *Opening hours: Monday to Friday 7 a.m. to 7 p.m.* He looked at his watch. It was 6.17 a.m. They could break in, but that would almost certainly trigger an alarm and a visit from the local constabulary, who would obviously be very happy to find a muddy white van and five grubby scrotes in the area.

We could wait? But the idea of lingering here that long made him uneasy. What was the alternative? Probably trooping along the side of that country road looking for a farmhouse to visit. If those spooks were combing the local back roads for any sign of them, they'd be screwed. He doubted he could jog, let alone run – and Emma certainly couldn't.

He headed back to the others.

Jay looked properly miserable. 'The suspension on another wheel's totally fucked as well,' he muttered.

'The petrol station opens at seven,' announced Boyd.

'All right,' said Okeke. 'I know it's the middle of nowhere, but I'm pretty sure they've learned about contactless here, which means this place must have internet. So we'll sit tight and wait till it opens.'

Boyd nodded. Okeke's confidence settled his unease. Whoever was due to come in and open up would surely have a phone. And this petrol station would surely have at least one creaking old computer inside. Just one spare USB socket and an internet connection was all that they needed.

'Okay, let's do that. In the meantime...' He settled down wearily on a small column of old tyres, wincing as the open wound in his side flexed. 'Arggh. Bollocking ouch,' he grumbled as he cradled his side.

'In the meantime?' Okeke prompted him.

'In the meantime, we need to discuss where the hell we upload what's on your memory stick.'

'WikiLeaks? Maybe Discord? *Telegraph*?'

He looked at her. 'And you know how to do that?'

She shook her head. 'Not really. How about we send it to Karl?'

57

Warner answered his phone. It was Moira.

'I have an update for you,' she said.

'Go ahead.'

'The Sussex police force have been given a category-one alert for the white van. Our Alpha team were immobilised at Barnham House.'

'What? Oh, for God's sake, what the bloody hell happened?'

'They ran their vehicle into a wall.'

Warner ground his teeth. 'I thought Dutton said these people were pros.'

'Apparently it was a low wall, hidden by tall weeds. Beta team are still mobile and combing the area.'

'Randomly or do they have a search pattern?' Warner asked without much hope.

'They said that they have a candidate route they're certain the target took. It ends at a village called Little Carbrooke, which has a speed camera at both ends of the road going through it. Gary says neither have flagged the number plate yet, which suggests they've gone to ground somewhere along the candidate route.'

'Right. And are there any small lanes or ways off it?'

'No,' replied Moira. 'But there are a number of properties, private and businesses along the way that they may have pulled into. Beta team are investigating those now.'

'Good. I'm on my way over from Seaford with Drummond. I've left Chapps to sit with the principle target's body –' He heard a sharp intake of breath.

'She's... she's dead?'

'She had a... stroke, Moira. There was little we could do for her. Chapps is going to call in an ambulance once he's tidied up there.'

'Right.'

'Is there anything Gary can do to black out the search area?'

'There's one phone mast in the area that he's identified and quarantined. But obviously there are still landlines and broadband to be mindful of – though that would require the targets to jump on any unsecured Wi-Fi, or knock on someone's door and ask politely.'

'All right,' Warner replied. 'Let Beta know I'm on the way. I should be with them in just over an hour's time.'

'Will do, sir.' And she ended the call.

Warner held onto his phone, toying with the idea of calling Dutton to update him, but then thought better of it. The director had been very specific: he didn't want to hear anything from Warner until a positive result had been achieved. He knew that, as far as Dutton was concerned, the road to damnation was littered with incriminating call records.

～

AT FIVE TO SEVEN, a whistling middle-aged man with a sandy-coloured Bobby Charlton comb-over and a set of jangling keys crossed the petrol station's small forecourt.

As he prepared to slot a key into the front door, Boyd appeared from round the corner. 'All right, mate?'

The man jolted with surprise and dropped his keys. He bent down to pick them up, eyes suspiciously on Boyd all the way down and all the way back up again. 'We're not open just yet, sir. Give me five minutes to –'

Boyd pulled out his police lanyard and flourished it brazenly.

'DCI Boyd, CID.' He neglected to mention he was from the Sussex Force. He took a step towards him. 'This is an emergency. I need to use your mobile –' se glanced at the plastic name tag on the man's chest – 'Steve. Please?'

'I don't have a mobile,' Steve replied.

Boyd narrowed his eyes suspiciously.

'Honestly, mate. No phone. Coverage is shit out here,' Steve assured him.

That Boyd could believe. 'All right, well, do you have a computer in the shop?' he asked.

Steve nodded. 'Yeah. To process the lottery cards.'

'And an internet connection?' For a moment, he was sure the old boy was going to proudly announce that he had the last functioning dial-up modem left in the country.

'Yeah, course.'

'Then I need to use it. Right now.'

It was Steve's turn to look wary. 'What's this about?'

Boyd jumped to the only answer that would unlock anyone's instant cooperation. 'Terrorism. I need to report a suspicious sighting.'

Steve nodded. 'Oh right.' Then he slot the key in calmly, as if this sort of thing happened to him every day. The door opened to the sound of a beeping alarm. He stepped inside, tapped in a number on the keypad by the door, and the beeping abruptly ceased. 'Better come on in, then, mate.'

'Just a sec,' Boyd replied. 'Sam!' Okeke appeared. 'She's a detective too.'

She pulled out her lanyard to display her ID.

'Christ. Any more of you hiding round there?' said Steve. 'It's like the Secret Policeman's Ball!'

Boyd decided honesty was probably best. 'There are three people, two dogs and a van.'

Steve shook his head, bemused. 'All right, you two can come in. The rest can stay outside unless they're buying something.'

He held the door open as they stepped in. 'So what kind of terrorists are they?' he asked.

'Dangerous ones,' said Okeke. 'Idiots with idiotic ideas.'

Steve shook his head solemnly. 'Bloody nutters are everywhere these days.' He sighed. 'Right, I've just got to switch everything on first. You stay there.'

He weaved past a revolving stand of bargain-bucket DVDs and pushed open a door that led to the back.

'So how're we doing this?' whispered Okeke.

'I'll upload to WeTransfer, then we can work out who gets a link to that later,' Boyd suggested.

Okeke shook her head. 'We may not have a later.' She paused. 'How about Karl?'

That was probably a good shout, he decided. As well as being handy with code, he was well travelled when it came to the less visited, darker corners of the internet, plus he was hardwired to buy into this kind of conspiracy and know what to do with it.

He nodded. 'Karl's good. You got his email address on you?'

'On my phone, yeah. But –' But that was lying among some nettles at the side of the road back in Sussex. 'His company's called Unit Seventeen.'

Boyd vaguely recalled that. They could look up a contact number via the website.

A couple of strip lights blinked on and Steve returned to the front of the store. 'All right, everything's waking up now. What can I do to help you two?'

'Just a computer with internet,' replied Boyd.

'Righty-o, that's here behind the counter.' Steve flipped up a counter hatch and beckoned for Boyd to step through. 'You might have to wait a few moments, though,' he added apologetically. 'It runs on that Windows thing.'

~

MOLLY WALCH RETIED the belt of her dressing gown, a little tighter, a little snugger, patted her wiry hair down and then finally cracked the front door open a sliver to find two young men and a young woman on the porch. All were smartly dressed. Which was a pleasant change.

But it was ten past seven in the morning, for lord's sake. She wasn't expecting any packages from DPD, any feed for her animals, and the lovely post lady, Sue, wasn't due to drop off her mail for another hour or so.

'Can I help you?' she asked timidly.

One of the men held out some sort of ID card, which, quite frankly, she couldn't read without going back up to the kitchen to get her glasses.

'MI5, counter-terrorism,' he announced crisply.

She thought that sounded intriguing. 'Oh, yes?'

'You're the owner of this house?' he asked. 'You live here?'

'Yes. For about thirty years now,' she replied. 'What's the problem?'

'We're tracking some people. We believe they may have come along this road within the last hour and gone to ground nearby.'

'What sort of people?' Molly asked. 'Terrorists?'

The man nodded, and her eyes rounded.

'It's an active terror cell,' said the other man. 'We believe they've been conducting reconnaissance.'

'Oh, my gosh! Am I in danger?' Molly asked.

'They *are* dangerous,' he replied. 'And we know they're nearby. Have you seen a white van pass by your farm in the last hour?'

'It's not really a farm,' she told him. 'It's an animal sanctuary, actually.'

'Right. Well, have you –'.

She shook her head. 'I don't think so.'

'It's a muddy van,' he added. 'It would probably have been travelling quite quickly. You might have *heard* it pass rather than seen it?'

'We know the vehicle was in a pretty bad way,' said the smartly dressed woman. 'It may have been clanking? Whirring?'

The other two nodded. They'd spotted slivers of tyre shavings on the road, like strings of liquorice.

Actually, Molly did recall hearing something that sounded unpleasant not so long ago, while she was in bed, still half asleep and mustering the energy to get up and start prepping breakfast for her menagerie of rescued animals.

'A bit like the whine of one of those old milk floats?' she asked.

All three nodded. 'Yes, it would probably have sounded a bit like that,' said the woman.

'I think I heard something like that about three quarters of an hour ago. Maybe it was about half six?' Molly pulled the front door open a little wider and stepped out onto the porch. 'It was going that way,' she said, pointing to the right.

'How do you know?' asked the woman. 'If you didn't see it?'

'There's a corner there,' she replied, pointing in the other direction, 'and a pothole. If there's someone coming from the junction towards Little Carbrooke, you hear the slow-down for the corner, then a clunk from the pothole. If it's the other way, it's clunk first, then it revving as it rounds the bend.'

The woman smiled at her detailed explanation. 'What's further along this road?'

Molly shrugged. 'Elm Nursery. That's just a small grocer's, really. Umm... then Big Tackle, the fishing supplier. And I think the last thing before Little Carbrooke is Steve's Pit Stop.'

'Which is?' the woman asked.

'A petrol station,' Molly replied.

58

Boyd looked at the landline phone tucked below the counter. 'Mind if I use that?' he asked.

Steve shrugged. 'Help yourself, mate. Calling in Special Branch, eh?'

Boyd wasn't sure if the old boy was joking or serious. All the same, he nodded. 'Sort of.'

He lifted the handset and dialled the number on the screen, half expecting no answer at this time of the morning. If he recalled correctly, Karl's team of coders were a bunch of scruffy young lads who didn't much look like the early-bird type.

But, incredibly, he got an answer, albeit a very sleepy one. 'Yeah?'

'I need Karl's number,' he said.

'Dunno his number,' Sleepy replied.

'Email, then,' Boyd tried.

'Uh, like, who is this?'

'The police,' replied Boyd. 'It's urgent. Very.'

'Um, like, how do I know you're the actual police, bro?'

'DCI Bill Boyd, Hastings CID. Look me up.'

He heard the clattering of a keyboard on the other end, followed by a snort of laughter. 'Wait, you're the police dude with the bra on his head who got bleeped on the news?'

Boyd rolled his eyes. That epitaph was going to end up etched on his gravestone, for sure. 'Yes, I'm that Boyd.'

'Ha ha... legend. Karl's mentioned you, man.'

'Can I have his email or phone, please?' Boyd repeated. 'It's v–'

'Yeah, yeah, yeah... no sweat,' Sleepy replied. 'Gimme a sec...'

A sec, Boyd was pretty sure, was something they didn't have. There was no way MI5 were going to give up on them this morning because they were flummoxed by a rural crossroad. They'd be close, combing the area, pulling in resources.

He looked back at the computer; Okeke had already made a start uploading the contents of the memory stick to WeTransfer. He'd also noticed the shop computer was running a creaky old copy of Windows 7. Nothing was going to happen fast, that much was guaranteed.

Sleepy was back on the line. 'Yeah, uh, okay. Like, here it is.... Oh, and you want his mobile?'

'Yeah – give me both,' replied Boyd.

∼

'*This is Bravo. Over.*'

Warner reached for Drummond's radio handset, in his car's grubby cup tray. 'Zulu, go ahead.'

'*We have eyes on the van. It's parked at the side of a petrol station. Over.*'

'Can you see the targets?'

He waited for the reply, listening to the hiss of white

noise and wondering if they'd abandoned the van and were now on foot.

The reply came a few moments later: '*Affirmative. Can confirm eyes on targets. Three outside beside the van. One male, two females. Two more inside the shop with a non-target. Over.*'

'Can you see what they're doing?'

'*Looks like they're buying something. They're at the counter... No, wait, one of them is behind the counter. Over.*'

Behind? Warner bit his bottom lip. Not just a pit stop, then. They had to be up to something. If he had to take a guess, using the shop's phone. But calling who? Their police station back in Hastings? A friend? Family? Some tabloid's hot-tips line? A news website?

'How far away are we?' he asked Drummond.

'Ten minutes. Maybe five minutes if I put my foot down, sir.'

Warner pinched his lip as he considered his options. He could give Bravo the green light to just go in, collateral damage and body count be damned. They were in a rural location; it was isolated. The pop of a few gunshots might be heard by a distant neighbour, but it probably wouldn't pull out any spectators – not in the middle of the countryside.

Or he could go for the more measured approach. If they were on the phone to someone already, then at this point it was just a conversation, and how many of those tip lines received crank calls from conspiracy wonks, or pranksters, or simply the lonely and deluded every day of the week?

There was also this... How much did they know yet? Given the one-sided calls they'd intercepted between Okeke and Eleanora, not very much at all. What they had in their possession was something important on a memory stick, presumably. There hadn't been enough time or any opportunity in the last hour for them to assess what they had. Surely?

Warner pressed the button on the side of the handset. 'Bravo, hold your position. I'm close.'

'Copy that. Hold position. Over.'

~

'SAM, SLOW DOWN,' said Karl. 'What exactly do you want me to take a look at?'

Okeke ground her teeth. She thought Boyd had been specific and clear enough already before handing her the phone. 'I've got a memory stick full of dirty secrets, Karl. Dirty *government* secrets and I'm going to send you a link.'

He huffed, mildly amused. 'Oka-a-ay. What sort of dirty secrets are we talking about? UFOs landing at –'

'There's no time for this. We've got a bunch of spooks on our arse,' she told him.

'Right.' She could hear a weary smile in his tone. 'Jesus. Jay put you up to this, did he?'

'For fuck's sake! This is legit. You want me to get Jay?'

'Not really, sis. Look, this is a shit time of the day to prank –'

Boyd had been leaning in, listening. He took the phone and cut in. 'Karl? This is Boyd again. Sam's not arsing about. This is real. We've got people looking for us right now. Okay? They want what we've got... And the sooner someone else knows what's on the memory stick, the sooner we'll start to feel a little safer.'

He let Karl digest that. 'Okay... so this *is* legit, yeah?'

'Yes. We're going to email you a link to what we've just uploaded. Look at it, work out what the hell it is, then make bloody sure someone else gets it.'

'Is this to do with that website Sam was on?' Karl asked.

'Yup. This is really dirty stuff, Karl. Dirty enough that our own intelligence agencies have already killed more than one person to keep it bottled up.'

'Serious?'

'I'm serious.'

'Where are you guys?' Karl asked.

'Doesn't matter. Just look at it. Figure out who's best to get hold of it.'

'Right. Okay. What's it about?' Karl asked.

Boyd wished he could say for sure. All they had was guesswork. 'You can tell *us* once you've had a chance to look it over,' he replied. 'Now give me your email!'

'Right, yeah. Okay. My email address is...'

Boyd jotted it down and read it back to him. Karl confirmed it. 'Karl, do you have a pen handy? The phone number I'm on now...' Boyd lowered the handset and turned to Steve for an answer. The old man enunciated the number slowly.

'You got that, Karl? Give me a call back on this number as soon as you've managed to download and check what's there.'

'Got it. Will do.'

Boyd ended the call and then looked at the cranky old PC. 'How're we doing?'

Okeke looked worriedly at the monitor. 'It's either a lot of stuff, or the broadband is really shit here. It's only on fourteen per cent.'

'It's not great out here,' said Steve. "Shit's a good description.'

∽

DRUMMOND ROUNDED a corner and immediately dropped his speed. A traffic cone had been placed in the middle of the country road, with flapping yellow police tape running from a tree branch on one side to a gatepost on the other.

'There they are!' he exclaimed.

Beyond the tape was a JMS Plumbers' van parked askance on the left, and several members of the team were already standing on the roadside wearing flak jackets over their civilian clothing.

Warner climbed out and left Drummond to park his car diagonally across the lane to assist the fluttering tape in ensuring any early-morning traffic coming this way wasn't going to get any closer. He ducked under the tape and hurried along the thirty yards of mud spattered crumbly tarmac to join them.

'Who's got eyes on?' he asked.

One of them pointed along the lane to where a pair of legs emerged from beneath a cluster of brambles onto the narrow road.

Warner quickened his pace, then ducked down low as he neared the man, crawling on hands and knees as he drew up beside him. Beyond the thick nest of brambles was the petrol station. It was the rural kind that doubled up as a general store for the few square miles of farms and homes dotted around the vicinity. A bedraggled and faded Union Jack dangled from a rusting flagpole; the two pumps outside looked as though they belonged in an old Norman Rockwell painting.

The agent was lying on his front – head, shoulders and chest hidden beneath the prickly foliage. He was studying the store through a pair of binoculars.

Warner tapped one of his legs. 'What do you see going on over there?'

'The three outside are taking their dogs for a pee,' he replied. 'The two inside are still behind the shop counter.'

'On the phone?'

'They were. I think... I think, it looks like they're now using a till screen.'

'You sure it's a till?'

'Wait. No... ' The agent adjusted his binoculars. 'Fuck. No, it's a computer.'

Warner felt his gut do a queasy somersault.

He was now down to one option.

∽

BOYD HAD BEEN WATCHING the upload bar for the last five minutes as it inched its way painfully slowly across the flickering screen. It was two thirds of the way across now. He was dimly aware that the station attendant had begun to hover. He was too interested and invading their space.

'So...' Steve began. He'd been silent since the call had ended. 'So, this *isn't* about bloody terrorists, then?' he said.

Boyd looked at him. His bushy eyebrows were locked together as though he was working out the final clues of a crossword puzzle.

'Not the bearded and brown-skinned kind,' replied Okeke.

'Government secrets?' Steve asked. 'That's what you said on the phone, right?'

Boyd ignored him.

Steve persisted. 'National secrets... and you're what? You're going to make 'em all public?'

'Not all. Just some,' replied Okeke.

The old man scowled and took a step forward. 'I'm not happy about this. Using my computer to spill –'

Boyd held out his arm to keep him back from Okeke. 'Just relax, mate. This is police business.'

Steve scowled at Boyd's arm blocking his way. In his own shop. 'Well, it clearly bloody isn't. Police don't do that!'

He glanced at Boyd again, and then at Okeke's ID, still dangling from her neck. 'Are those plastic cards even real?'

Boyd ignored him. The man could bluster and grumble all he wanted. Just as long as he stayed out of their way. The upload was at eighty-five per cent now. Another minute or two and they'd be done. They could thank him for his time, and leave him to try to work out what the hell he'd been a party too.

'What are you?' Steve persisted. 'Are you spies? Troublemakers?'

'We're CID,' Boyd assured him. 'We're definitely the police, mate.'

'Like bloody hell you are! I'm not having this!' He took another step towards Okeke and his computer, bumping against Boyd's blocking arm.

'Easy, there, mate,' Boyd told him.

Steve shoved Boyd's arm aside. 'I'm not having this!' he said again, and reached for the mouse but Okeke slapped her hand down on it first.

'Sorry. No.'

Steve's face reddened. 'Right. That's it! Get out!'

'In a minute,' she replied calmly. 'We're nearly done.'

The old man snorted angrily. Then, without warning, he reached for the memory stick.

'No!' yelled Okeke. She grabbed his hand before he could pull it out of the USB port.

Steve swung his other hand round and punched her. His fist glanced off her temple but it was enough to knock her.

She let go of his hand and staggered backwards into a rack of fruit gums, pastilles and Polos.

Steve jerked the memory stick out of the computer just as Boyd's fist connected with his chin. He dropped to the floor, unconscious, the memory stick falling out of his hand, skittering off into the dusty space beneath the counter.

Boyd dropped to all fours, doing his best to ignore the wrenching pain in his side, and probed the dark and grimy space to retrieve it.

Okeke had regained her balance and was rubbing the side of her head.

'Gimme a hand,' he grunted. 'We need to... Ahh!' His fingers found the memory stick. He grabbed it and stood up, and was about to plug it back into the computer when the front door crashed open.

59

The door swung inwards violently, the glass shattering in its frame.

'HAND ON YOUR HEADS!'

Three men filed in rapidly, guns at the ready, all aimed directly at him.

'HANDS ON YOUR HEAD!' the men repeatedly barked over each other. 'HANDS OVER YOUR HEAD!'

'Whoa! Whoa! Whoa!' Boyd shouted back. 'Jesus... lads!'

Okeke reacted likewise. 'Hey! Hey! Boys... No guns! We've got no guns here!'

The leading agent – who looked to Boyd more like Gareth from *The Office* than James Bond – advanced on them, eyes bulging with adrenaline as he stared down the barrel of his gun. 'HANDS. BEHIND. YOUR. FUCKING. HEAD!!!'

Boyd nodded. 'Okay, okay.' Behind his back, he discreetly fumbled at the computer's case, feeling the plastic fascia for the groove of the USB port. 'I'm going to move my hands, mate...' he said calmly. 'But I'm going to do it very, very slowly.' He offered the boggle-eyed young MI5 agent a friendly smile. 'Don't want any "*I thought he was reaching for a gun*" bollocks in your AAR later on. All right?'

'Just DO IT!' the agent snapped. 'Now!'

Boyd's fingertips had found the port and now he was angling the memory stick to insert it, hoping to God it would be the right way up, first time around.

Silently it clicked into place. Boyd made a theatrical slow-motion display of raising his hands up where the three agents could see them.

'On your head, I said! NOW!' one of them bellowed.

Boyd complied, then glanced right to make sure Okeke was doing the same. Boggle-Eyes looked as though he was one sneeze away from emptying his gun's magazine into both of them.

Just then, over their shoulders, he saw Emma's face as she emerged from outside to stand in the doorway. She was nudged forward inside by a woman, dressed like the others, flak jacket over civilian clothes and eyes bulging as though she'd been on Red Bull for the last twenty-four hours.

Entering the shop behind her was an old man in a creased grey suit, with pallid colourless skin and fine flossy silver hair. He looked like the world's most weary building-society branch manager. He picked his way down one cramped aisle that was stacked with life's basics – cans of Heinz beans, Fairy washing-up liquid and Pot Noodles – came to a halt beside Boggle-Eyes. At last, he cleared his throat and spoke.

'Good God. What a ruddy nightmare this has been. Samantha Okeke and William Boyd, I presume?' He made that sound like a question. It clearly wasn't.

'Right.' Boyd nodded. 'That's us.' He looked over the man's shoulder. 'And that's my *pregnant* daughter, you're pushing around back there.'

'Yes, Emma Boyd, with her very, *very* useful phone.' He smiled.

Boyd winced. 'Ahh...'

'It's easily done. It really is incredibly quick and convenient these days to enslave a smartphone.' He chuckled. 'It's those old *stupid* ones that are the problem, ironically.' He straightened his dishevelled jacket and adjusted the collar of his shirt. 'Let me introduce myself – I'm Jeremy Warner. Eleanora may have mentioned me.' He paused, as if waiting for a reaction, but none was forthcoming. 'Anyway... Now, look, I think we're all very tired. It's been a long night and I imagine no one's in the mood for any more silly games. So why don't you hand over what you retrieved from Barnham House earlier this morning?'

Boyd desperately wanted to turn round and look at the computer monitor directly behind him. He had no idea whether re-inserting the memory stick had automatically led to the upload resuming. Windows 7, he reminded himself, wasn't the sharpest tool in the shed.

'We weren't that clear on what Eleanora wanted us to find,' said Okeke. 'We assumed we were meeting her at the house.'

Warner glanced her way. 'Yes, I can well believe that. It was all a bit ad hoc and messy, wasn't it? I'm not even sure this was something she'd planned. I think she was perhaps caught off guard.'

'How is she?' asked Okeke. 'Is she okay? You know, she needs to be in a hospital. She –'

'I regret to say that she passed away,' replied Warner. 'It was all too much for her.'

'Fuck that!' snarled Okeke. 'You killed her!'

Warner shook his head. 'Quite honestly, no. She was in a dreadful state when we found her. I just wish she'd reached out to me earlier in the week.' He turned his eyes back to Boyd. 'Anyway, I need you to hand over the goods.'

'We found nothing, mate,' replied Boyd. 'We were looking for her. We were extremely concerned for her –'

'DON'T!' snapped Warner. His face flickered with a vicious scowl before settling back to an expression of profound weariness. His voice softened. 'Don't waste my time, please. I'm really not in the mood. I'm expecting you to hand over a hard drive. Or perhaps a memory stick. Despite her advanced years, Ellie, was certainly compos mentis enough to know how to use either of those.'

Boyd really, *really* wanted to glance back over his shoulder to see if Steve's PC had finished the job.

'Mate,' said Boyd, ' she sent us on a wild goose chase. I'm not sure what she was hoping to achieve. In fact, I'm beginning to wonder if she wasn't losing it.'

Warner suddenly snatched the gun from Boggle-Eyes and aimed it right at Boyd's face.

'ENOUGH!' His bark was shrill. 'Just hand over the fucking thing! NOW!'

Boyd blinked hard and focused on the wavering gun barrel a mere two feet away from his nose. Stalling was beginning to feel like a foolish tactic. If Boggle-Eyes' twitchy trigger finger had been unsettling, this idiot's was even more so.

Sod stalling. Bluff it, he told himself.

'All right,' Boyd relented. 'All right. You're right. Enough pissing around. A memory stick is what she wanted us to pick up. And, yeah, we managed to find it.'

Warner sighed, though the gun didn't waver. 'Good. So hand it over, please.'

'I would do,' said Boyd. 'But we stashed it on the way here.'

Warner smiled. 'If I wasn't so tired, I'd probably enjoy sparring with you, detective. But I am rather tired. I'm exhausted, in fact. So I'm just going to shoot your colleague and we'll start again.' His aim swung towards Okeke.

'Stop!' shouted Boyd. 'You're too late!'

Warner's eyes narrowed. 'Meaning?'

'It's uploaded. We just did it. It's on the internet. It's pointless shooting any of us. It'll just be more mess you're going to have to explain away.'

Warner's trigger finger seemed to be trembling – and the gun was still pointed at Okeke.

'Hand it to me or I will shoot your colleague,' he said calmly. 'In precisely five seconds. One...'

Fuck-shit-bollocks.

'Two...'

Boyd stepped to one side and turned to pull the memory stick out, only to see in the middle of the monitor a grey dialogue box awaiting a Yes/No click.

Resume Upload? 97%: Yes/No

Boyd quickly reached for the mouse –

– and the small, rural shop rang with the deafening crack of a single gunshot.

60

A glass cabinet full of colourful vape liquids shattered, and several small boxes tumbled out and onto Boyd's ducked head.

'FUCK!' screamed Okeke. She threw a display box of Trebor Softmints at Warner, but it bounced off his shoulder, and tubes of mints scattered everywhere.

Okeke dropped down behind the counter as more shots rang out. Grimy glass cases behind the counter exploded, sending shards of glass and Rizla papers into the air. Boyd was down too. Their eyes met briefly as glass and cupboard debris rained down on them. Boyd still had his hand up, in view at counter level. Holding the mouse.

'ENOUGH!' he shouted when the gunfire paused. He stood up slowly, his other hand raised.

'Take a look!' he barked. 'Look at the bloody screen!'

Warner frowned, then his eyes settled on the monitor. There was a cursor hovering above the YES button. And Boyd's hand was holding the mouse steady.

'You're going to need to kill me with one shot,' said Boyd, quickly lifting up the old-fashioned rubber-ball mouse in both hands. He was holding it tightly like a suicide bomber holding a detonator – with a finger resting oh-so lightly on the left button. 'And even then, if you shoot me in the head, I'm likely to flinch, right?'

Warner gritted his tidy little teeth. 'Put that bloody thing down, detective, and just step away.'

Boyd shook his head. 'Nah. I'll tell you what we'll do. You're going to let Sam go. And let Emma go. Let them step out of the shop –'

'I'll do nothing of the sort.'

'And you'll let them and the others borrow your car.' He dearly wished he could feel the weight of that Russian gun tucked securely in the waistband of his trousers. But he couldn't. It must have fallen out in the back of Jay's van. He'd spent the last two days carrying the bloody thing around with him and, finally, when he needed it, it was in a van full of scattered carpentry tools.

On the other hand, maybe the mouse clenched in his sweating fists was the better weapon to be holding. An exchange of gunfire he would undoubtedly lose within seconds. And if he was shot dead, then almost certainly the others would be too.

But the mouse? He might as well have been holding a nuke.

'You let them go,' continued Boyd. 'And when they're gone, I'll put this down.'

He could see movement. Emma was shaking her head frantically at the back of the shop, mouthing, 'No, no, no, no!'

He nodded briefly at her, then quickly directed his gaze back to Warner. The tired agent in his crumpled suit.

'I think that's how we can resolve this, eh?' said Boyd.

'They leave. You get this memory stick. You keep all your dirty secrets. Mission complete, right?'

Warner narrowed his eyes. 'And what then? I just let you walk away?'

Boyd cracked a smile. 'Well, that would be awfully nice, but I suspect I'm going to get the hood-over-the-head treatment. Or am I wrong?'

61

Two Weeks Later

'Are you nervous?' asked Charlotte.

She looked down at Boyd's bouncing left leg, his shoe heel tapping Morse-code gibberish against the linoleum floor.

'A bit,' he replied.

She squeezed his hand. 'Not good with needles, hmm?'

He shrugged. 'Not good with having a litre of highly toxic chemicals pumped into me.'

The waiting room had been almost completely full an hour ago, full of older patients, calmly solving Sudoku puzzles or reading Kindles. It only seemed to be himself and Charlotte in the room without a pensioner's bus pass and something to do. The chemo ward had been running late today, and gradually the backlog had cleared to the point where it was Boyd, Charlotte and a couple of other relaxed-looking geriatrics.

It was ridiculous, really. As his oncologist had reminded him in their pre-treatment appointment yesterday, cancer wasn't a death sentence any more. It was eminently treatable. And the drugs they were about to carpet-bomb him with for the next six months would leave no rogue cells standing.

It was ridiculous to be so nervous about a treatment that the sweet old lady sitting opposite him without a hair on her head seemed not to have a single concern about.

And also ridiculous given that he and everyone he cared about had nearly wound up being executed in a crusty old petrol station in the middle of the countryside. Two weeks on, and he was still certain that was no exaggeration. They'd come *that* close to a swift execution.

If he'd handed over the mouse.

If he'd clicked 'Yes'. If he'd clicked 'No'.

If he'd had that gun tucked in his belt…

He wouldn't be sitting here with Charlotte now.

His crazed eye-swivelling, I-will-fucking-click-this-button stunt had done the trick. It had created a pause – a gap in time long enough for common sense to prevail. For the situation to step down from a Quentin Tarantino Mexican stand-off to a very English exchange of passive aggression, followed by an arrest and a twenty-four-hour debriefing for all involved at an anonymous, disused RAF base. Then the signing of an Official Secrets Act form that assured them that they would all end their days in somewhere not too dissimilar to Guantanamo Bay if they breathed a single word of what had occurred in the last ten days to anyone.

How close, they'd come.

A rather well-spoken gentleman who'd introduced himself as Aubrey had rounded off the MI5 debrief by assuring Boyd that the UK was not some tinpot dictatorship where loose mouths were dealt with by firing squads. He'd assured Boyd that here in Great Britain a person's life could be destroyed in far less noisy, less messy ways. That police careers could be ended abruptly with the surprise discovery of wads of dirty, blood-spattered money. He's assured Emma that babies could be whisked away and disappear into the care system if evidence of physical abuse should somehow manifest in a post-natal midwife's report.

'There are many, many wonderful and imaginative ways we can devise to fuck up your life forever, old boy – so be a good chap. Mum's the word, eh?'

It was not the way it should have gone. Not what poor old Eleanora Baxendale would have wanted. There'd been no justice for a poor young care worker who'd grown too close to a frail old man and stumbled upon something he shouldn't have. And certainly no justice for James Crowhurst – a valiant army captain, who should have earned a medal for disobeying the orders he was given on a remote Pacific island in 1962.

But what had remained secret for sixty-one years was now going to remain secret for evermore. And Marble Orchard? Those were merely two ghostly words whose true significance would one day soon expire and vanish.

If that hadn't already happened.

'William Boyd?'

He looked up from his lap to see a young nurse with a broad smile and a clipboard in her hands looking around the nearly empty waiting room, her eyes eventually settling on him.

'Yup.' He stood up. 'That's me.'

Charlotte squeezed his hand. 'It won't be as bad as you think, Bill.'

'Right. Well... we'll see. Better get started on it, then, eh?'

Charlotte folded the corner of the page she was reading and tucked the thick hardback of Truman Capote short stories under one arm as she stood up with him. One day, she'd finish it.

She kissed his cheek. 'I'll be right out here. Waiting for you.'

EPILOGUE

Many Years Later

Michael Crews tried another key on the jangling ring of rusty keys. *This* one – thank Christ – finally seemed to be right one. The old door lock *clacked* loudly, echoing down the hallway. He reached for the handle, pushed the door inwards and switched on the torch in his other hand.

He panned the beam of light around inside.

'Annnd... another one,' he muttered to himself.

Another store cupboard. This abandoned residential home seemed to have an endless supply of them along its winding labyrinthine corridors, each one crammed full of an accumulation of dusty old tat that was going to need to be recycled or processed. Then the crumbling, waterlogged building could be stripped of hazardous materials and valuable copper and nickel wiring before being surrendered to the advancing flood-risk markers.

The Archive

His torch picked out shelves laden with faded, dog-eared jigsaw-puzzle and board-game boxes. He hadn't played with any of those since he was a tiny little boy; he vaguely recalled some bizarre game that had involved a little metal boot, a racing car and a top hat running round the outside of a colourful board.

He panned his torch up and down the stacks of games and puzzles, his eyes scanning the vaguely familiar names until he came across Monopoly.

He smiled. That was it. That was the game he used to play with his grandfather.

Michael reached for the box and was pleasantly surprised that it wasn't damp. Even though most of the corridors of this place exhibited waterlines a few feet up as a result of repeated surge flooding, the shelves in here had preserved these wonderful little treasures. Carefully, he eased the Monopoly box out from the unsteady stack, eager to lift its lid to check whether those little metal playing pieces were still inside. He'd love to hold one of them once again, to be transported back to his childhood, to better times – if only just for a brief moment.

As he moved the box, something that had been sitting just below it clunked heavily onto the floor. He stopped what he was doing and aimed his torch downwards to find what appeared to be a leather-bound notebook resting on the toe of one of his wellies, and thankfully, not on the sodden floor.

A notebook.

He squatted down and picked it up. His torchlight lit up the front cover to reveal the faded scrawl of someone's handwriting: *Volume Three*.

Curious, Michael gently opened the cover. The notebook was filled with endless pages of relentlessly tidy handwriting.

Quite incredible. Last time he'd held something as charmingly old-fashioned as a pen, he'd managed to scrawl no more than a dozen scruffy words with it before his hand had begun to cramp at the task.

He scanned some of the passages, the curling loops and swirls of faded ink strangely pleasing to his eyes. Then a number caught his attention.

A year.

1961.

He shook his head as he marvelled at that. Almost a century ago someone had written that. He smiled. He was actually holding in his hands what appeared to be the memoir of someone long since gone and forgotten. Their life story.

He stood up slowly with the notebook carefully cradled in his hands, as if it was some ancient papyrus scroll, debating whether he should slide it back under the Monopoly box and leave it to be converted into reusable paper pulp.

Or he could just pocket it?

And why not?

A charming little piece of personal history. It might even be worth something to a dealer in twentieth-century curios.

Michael Crews opened his shoulder bag and slid the notebook in. Then, on impulse, he pulled the Monopoly box out, lifted its flimsy lid and pocketed all the little metal playing tokens that were scattered amid faded cards and plastic houses. He grinned at the little metal dog, the racing car, the top hat… and the battleship sitting in the palm of his hand.

Those he wasn't going to sell to anyone, though. No sir.

Michael smiled. There were some incredible finds one could recover from the waterlogged remnants of these condemned southern coastal towns.

He closed the door on the storage cupboard and carried on with the task of surveying the doomed building for useful salvage. The sea would be coming for it all too soon.

THE END

DCI BOYD RETURNS IN

A MONSTER AMONG US available to pre-order
HERE

ALSO BY ALEX SCARROW

DCI Boyd

SILENT TIDE

OLD BONES NEW BONES

BURNING TRUTH

THE LAST TRAIN

THE SAFE PLACE

GONE TO GROUND

ARGYLE HOUSE

THE LOCK UP

Thrillers

LAST LIGHT

AFTERLIGHT

OCTOBER SKIES

THE CANDLEMAN

A THOUSAND SUNS

The TimeRiders series (in reading order)

TIMERIDERS

TIMERIDERS: DAY OF THE PREDATOR

TIMERIDERS: THE DOOMSDAY CODE

TIMERIDERS: THE ETERNAL WAR

TIMERIDERS: THE CITY OF SHADOWS

TIMERIDERS: THE PIRATE KINGS

TIMERIDERS: THE MAYAN PROPHECY
TIMERIDERS: THE INFINITY CAGE

The Plague Land series
PLAGUE LAND
PLAGUE NATION
PLAGUE WORLD

The Ellie Quin series
THE LEGEND OF ELLIE QUIN
THE WORLD ACCORDING TO ELLIE QUIN
ELLIE QUIN BENEATH A NEON SKY
ELLIE QUIN THROUGH THE GATEWAY
ELLIE QUIN: A GIRL REBORN

ABOUT THE AUTHOR

Over the last sixteen years, award-winning author Alex Scarrow has published seventeen novels with Penguin Random House, Orion and Pan Macmillan. A number of these have been optioned for film/TV development, including his bestselling *Last Light*.

When he is not busy writing and painting, Alex spends most of his time trying to keep Ozzie away from the food bin. He lives in the wilds of East Anglia with his wife Deborah and five, permanently muddy, dogs.

Ozzie came to live with him in January 2017. He was adopted from Spaniel Aid UK and was believed to be seven at the time. Ozzie loves food, his mum, food, his ball, food, walks and more food...

He dreams of unrestricted access to the food bin.

For up-to-date information on the DCI BOYD series, visit: www.alexscarrow.com

To see what Ozzie is up to, click on the instagram link below...

ACKNOWLEDGMENTS

I'd like to thank Debbie Scarrow for her editing and second draft contributions to this one. This book turned out to be a little longer than normal and a little harder to write than usual. If you've been following the series you'll know that Boyd and I picked up bowel cancer in the last year. I decided to share with you (and Boyd) as much as possible about the experience, as accurately as possible. Obviously, where our experiences diverge, is being on the run from the British Secret Services. Luckily I haven't invoked their ire... yet.

As always the wonderful Wendy Shakespeare, my copyeditor, has saved my bacon again, ensuring character's names and hair colours don't change and masking my general incompetence from the wider world.

I also owe a debt of gratitude to my team of beta readers collectively known as 'Team Boyd' who act as the final Quality Assurance net, scooping up the errors that remain in the mix.

And finally, you, reader... for staying with the series, and my good friend Bill Boyd for this long. Book nine already!

Printed in Great Britain
by Amazon